CAMP
LOST AND FOUND

Praise for Georgia Beers

On the Rocks

"This book made me so happy! And kept me awake way too late."
—*Jude in the Stars*

The Secret Poet

"[O]ne of the author's best works and one of the best romances I've read recently…I was so invested in [Morgan and Zoe] I read the book in one sitting."—*Melina Bickard, Librarian, Waterloo Library (UK)*

Hopeless Romantic

"Thank you, Georgia Beers, for this unabashed paean to the pleasure of escaping into romantic comedies…If you want to have a big smile plastered on your face as you read a romance novel, do not hesitate to pick up this one!"—*The Rainbow Bookworm*

Flavor of the Month

"Beers whips up a sweet lesbian romance…brimming with mouth-watering descriptions of foodie indulgences…Both women are well-intentioned and endearing, and it's easy to root for their inevitable reconciliation. But once the couple rediscover their natural ease with one another, Beers throws a challenging emotional hurdle in their path, forcing them to fight through tragedy to earn their happy ending."
—*Publishers Weekly*

One Walk in Winter

"A sweet story to pair with the holidays. There are plenty of 'moment's in this book that make the heart soar. Just what I like in a romance. Situations where sparks fly, hearts fill, and tears fall. This book shined with cute fairy trails and swoon-worthy Christmas gifts…REALLY nice and cozy if read in between Thanksgiving and Christmas. Covered in blankets. By a fire."—*Bookvark*

Fear of Falling

"Enough tension and drama for us to wonder if this can work out—and enough heat to keep the pages turning. I will definitely recommend this to others—Georgia Beers continues to go from strength to strength."
—*Evan Blood, Bookseller (Angus & Robertson, Australia)*

The Do-Over

"You can count on Beers to give you a quality well-paced book each and every time."—*The Romantic Reader Blog*

"*The Do-Over* is a shining example of the brilliance of Georgia Beers as a contemporary romance author."—*Rainbow Reflections*

The Shape of You

"I know I always say this about Georgia Beers's books, but there is no one that writes first kisses like her. They are hot, steamy and all too much!"—*Les Rêveur*

The Shape of You "catches you right in the feels and does not let go. It is a must for every person out there who has struggled with self-esteem, questioned their judgment, and settled for a less than perfect but safe lover. If you've ever been convinced you have to trade passion for emotional safety, this book is for you."—*Writing While Distracted*

Calendar Girl

"A sweet, sweet romcom of a story…*Calendar Girl* is a nice read, which you may find yourself returning to when you want a hot-chocolate-and-warm-comfort-hug in your life."—*Best Lesbian Erotica*

Blend

"You know a book is good, first, when you don't want to put it down. Second, you know it's damn good when you're reading it and thinking, I'm totally going to read this one again. Great read and absolutely a 5-star romance."—*The Romantic Reader Blog*

"This is a lovely romantic story with relatable characters that have depth and chemistry. A charming easy story that kept me reading until the end. Very enjoyable."—*Kat Adams, Bookseller, QBD (Australia)*

Right Here, Right Now

"[A] successful and entertaining queer romance novel. The main characters are appealing, and the situations they deal with are realistic and well-managed. I would recommend this book to anyone who enjoys a good queer romance novel, and particularly one grounded in real world situations."—*Books at the End of the Alphabet*

"[A]n engaging odd-couple romance. Beers creates a romance of gentle humor that allows no-nonsense Lacey to relax and easygoing Alicia to find a trusting heart."—*RT Book Reviews*

Lambda Literary Award Winner *Fresh Tracks*

"Georgia Beers pens romances with sparks."—*Just About Write*

"[T]he focus switches each chapter to a different character, allowing for a measured pace and deep, sincere exploration of each protagonist's thoughts. Beers gives a welcome expansion to the romance genre with her clear, sympathetic writing."—*Curve magazine*

Lambda Literary Award Finalist *Finding Home*

"Georgia Beers has proven in her popular novels such as *Too Close to Touch* and *Fresh Tracks* that she has a special way of building romance with suspense that puts the reader on the edge of their seat. *Finding Home*, though more character driven than suspense, will equally keep the reader engaged at each page turn with its sweet romance."—*Lambda Literary Review*

Mine

"Beers does a fine job of capturing the essence of grief in an authentic way. *Mine* is touching, life-affirming, and sweet."—*Lesbian News Book Review*

Too Close to Touch

"This is such a well-written book. The pacing is perfect, the romance is great, the character work strong, and damn, but is the sex writing ever fantastic."—*The Lesbian Review*

"In her third novel, Georgia Beers delivers an immensely satisfying story. Beers knows how to generate sexual tension so taut it could be cut with a knife…Beers weaves a tale of yearning, love, lust, and conflict resolution. She has constructed a believable plot, with strong characters in a charming setting."—*Just About Write*

By the Author

Romances

Turning the Page

Thy Neighbor's Wife

Too Close to Touch

Fresh Tracks

Mine

Finding Home

Starting from Scratch

96 Hours

Slices of Life

Snow Globe

Olive Oil & White Bread

Zero Visibility

A Little Bit of Spice

What Matters Most

Right Here, Right Now

Blend

The Shape of You

Calendar Girl

The Do-Over

Fear of Falling

One Walk in Winter

Flavor of the Month

Hopeless Romantic

16 Steps to Forever

The Secret Poet

Cherry on Top

Camp Lost and Found

The Puppy Love Romances

Rescued Heart

Run to You

Dare to Stay

The Swizzle Stick Romances

Shaken or Stirred

On the Rocks

With a Twist

Visit us at www.boldstrokesbooks.com

CAMP
LOST AND FOUND

by

Georgia Beers

2022

ISBN 13: 978-1-63679-263-7

This Trade Paperback Original Is Published By
Bold Strokes Books, Inc.
P.O. Box 249
Valley Falls, NY 12185

First Edition: December 2022

Credits

Editor: Ruth Sternglantz
Production Design: Stacia Seaman
Cover Design by Jeanine Henning

Acknowledgments

I went to summer camp for two consecutive summers when I was a teenager. I was an awkward kid whose formative teenage years were marred by my parents' bitter divorce and my struggle to keep everything as calm as I could, resulting in my growing up way too fast and with some behaviors I've carried into adulthood. My dad left my mother with me and my younger sister, and I took it upon myself to become the "man of the house," so to speak, keeping an eye on my sister, trying to make my devastated mother laugh whenever I could, and just generally being a kid who never rocked the boat, never got into trouble, flew under the radar. From the time I was thirteen to the time I graduated, I went to three different schools, so making and keeping friends was hard. But at camp? It was a clean slate. I made new friends, strong bonds, and wanted desperately to be a counselor when I turned sixteen. I didn't get the job—my first professional disappointment—and it crushed me. But I still remember those two summers at camp in great detail, from the mud wars to the cabin I stayed in with five other girls to the skits we put on for the whole camp. (I did a mean John Travolta when Kristin and I lip-synced to "You're the One That I Want," and it took me two days and a full jar of peanut butter to get the Vaseline out of my hair!) I also had a crush on our camp nurse, as well as one of my counselors, though at the time, I had no idea why I wanted to be around them so much. Camp definitely left a lasting impression.

I decided I wanted to write a story about somebody who'd been just as touched by her time at summer camp as I was, and I came up with Cassidy Clarke, a woman who has suffered a loss, compounded by guilt, and needs to be alone. She decides her old summer camp, which is now fairly abandoned, is the best choice. Little does she know that Frankie Sisto is already there, also trying to be alone. I really loved these two women. I related to them. I wanted to hug them both and tell them to hang in there, that everything was going to be okay. I hope they resonate with you the way they did with me.

As always, my gratitude to Radclyffe and Sandy Lowe and Ruth Sternglantz and Cindy Cresap and Stacia Seaman and everybody at

Bold Strokes Books who makes my career run smoothly. I'm so lucky to work with such a professional group of people.

Thank you to my writer friends and my not writer friends for all the support. I say it all the time, but writing is very solitary. And even this introvert needs to have people I can reach out to, I can ask for advice or guidance, who make me laugh, and who bolster me when I'm feeling undervalued, irrelevant, or uncreative. I'm lucky to have the people in my corner that I do, and I know it.

Special thanks to Anne Shade, Patrice James, Toni Whitaker, Pam Stewart, and Virginia Black for their invaluable guidance.

To all of us who have struggled to find ourselves.
Don't stop looking.

CHAPTER ONE

A hammock chair hanging in the middle of a living room was ridiculous, right?

All white canvas and weirdly knotted—what was the stuff her grandma used to do? Something French...*macramé*, that was it. Ropes knotted into different designs to make plant hangers or wall hangings or, yeah, hammock chairs that hung in the middle of living rooms, apparently. Who knew?

Frankie loved the thing. She hated to admit it—it was such an eyesore. But it was comfortable, and it hung in front of the giant picture window in the main house at Camp Lustenfeld where she'd been living and working for the past month and a half. She sat in it way more often than she'd ever admit to anybody, sipping her coffee—or something stronger—and watching as the nature that surrounded her went by.

She sat there now, alone, sipping her second cup of coffee and losing herself in the quiet. If Francesca Sisto was familiar with anything at this point in her life, it was isolation and quiet. She needed them. She craved them.

She deserved them.

It had to be fate that caused her to stumble across this job. Camp Lustenfeld, in its heyday, was a thriving summer camp for kids of all ages. But it had long since been defunct and empty. The main house, where she was living now, was actually in pretty decent shape, and it was her job to keep it that way, functional and lived-in. The six smaller cabins on the property were all empty and fairly run-down, magnets for kids and vagrants and whatever kinds of riffraff populated the small town of Shelton, New York. Frankie wasn't from there, so she had no idea, but she'd had to clean up empty beer cans and liquor bottles and the occasional used condom (so gross). She was basically being paid by the Lustenfeld family, who lived in Massachusetts, to make sure the camp didn't look abandoned.

And so, she lived there.

Her coffee was hot and strong, and she took a sip as she watched a doe and her two fawns amble across the front yard. The fawns were growing quickly, their spots almost gone now, and soon they'd be on their own to fend for themselves. Frankie had put out salt licks and carrots and such for them when she'd arrived, and they knew exactly where to find them. She was grateful the Lustenfelds owned so many acres and there was no hunting allowed, as it was mid-November, deer-hunting season. She'd never be able to bear seeing a deer gunned down by some bearded macho man in camouflage and an orange vest, carrying a gun or a bow and beating his chest. Yes, she understood the reasoning behind deer season. No, she didn't have to like it.

Her coffee mug had one last sip, and she swallowed it down, then headed to the kitchen for a refill.

The main building was large, meant to house the counselors and staff when the camp was in business. The ground floor consisted of a main living space with a huge stone fireplace, a dining room where the staff ate, a kitchen that wasn't quite industrial but came close, a large suite in the back where the camp director had lived year-round, and three smaller bedrooms, though one had been converted to an office.

As Frankie poured herself another cup from the ancient Mr. Coffee pot, her cell phone pinged an incoming text. Cell coverage was surprisingly good for the Adirondack Mountains, though it could be temperamental and spotty once in a while, depending on the weather.

She doctored her coffee with Coffee mate—she preferred actual milk but tried to limit her trips into town, and milk spoiled pretty quickly—and picked her phone up off the counter where she'd left it. It was early, so probably her mother checking on her. Or her sister. She'd become a pro at dodging their calls, so they texted pretty often.

Nope.

Ethan Lustenfeld had sent a text: *Hey, listen, guest arriving tomorrow for an undisclosed amount of time. Put upstairs. Keep room and bathroom clean. I'll put a bonus in your next check. Thanks.*

"What the fuck?" she said in disbelief to the empty room. A guest?

Here? Now? Why? First of all, that wasn't part of the deal. Wasn't part of her job. She wasn't managing a hotel. Dealing with *people* had never been part of the package. Second, who in their right mind wanted to be a guest here? At a camp that was no longer functional or open to the public? Up in the mountains in the middle of nowhere? Third, *keep room and bathroom clean*? She was a maid now? And was she supposed to feed this person?

Poking the inside of her cheek with her tongue, Frankie let it sit for a moment. Stared at her phone. Read the text over and over. Ethan Lustenfeld had done her a favor by hiring her. It was clear he'd expected to have a man up here in the middle of the woods looking after his camp, but she'd begged and pleaded and promised she was capable. And she was. But she'd wanted to be up here *alone*. That was the whole point. She needed solitude, and she'd told him that, sort of. She deserved to be away from the rest of the world, and now this mystery guest was going to be here…and for an undisclosed amount of time. Seriously?

"What the fuck?" she said again, but this time, it was more of a whisper. She couldn't argue. She had to accept it. And she needed to respond. Her thumbs flew over the keyboard.

Will make up room. What about food? There was a ton more she wanted to say, but she left it at that, not trusting herself, not wanting her tone in text to be misunderstood or, worse, understood completely.

The gray dots bounced along. *No worries. Just keep the room clean. Sheets and towels and such. Thx.*

She snorted. She *was* a maid now, clearly. Had to make somebody else's bed. Perfect. She groaned and texted back, *Arrival time?*

Ethan's response came immediately. *Tomorrow afternoon. No specifics. Thx for this. Appreciated.*

She sighed. No, groaned. Loudly. She would let herself be annoyed for fifteen minutes, and then she'd need to let it go. It was a new method she'd employed recently when she realized that she was either mad, annoyed, or irritated—or all three—about three-quarters of the time she was awake. Negative emotions were wreaking havoc on her mind and her body, and she'd realized she needed to make a change in that department. Thus, she'd instituted time limits for each.

She picked up her coffee and took it back into the living room to see that the doe and her babies had moved off into the trees, taking their time and nibbling what was left on the cold November ground.

Snow would be coming soon, she thought as she reclaimed her seat in the hammock chair. On the small, round end table next to it lay a stack of books and an open notebook with a list of things she needed to do today. She picked up the notebook, along with the pen next to it, and added, *Prepare room upstairs for intruder.* And then she began to wonder about them. The intruder. Okay, fine, the *guest*. Who would be *intruding* on her peace and quiet. Was it a man or a woman? How long would *an undisclosed amount of time* actually be? Were they loud? Would they be blasting music? Constantly on their phone?

Oh God, would they want to chat with her incessantly?

Also, what kind of person booked an indefinite stay at a camp that was no longer functional? Yeah, lotta questions about them.

She closed her eyes and shook her head slowly. It didn't matter. None of it mattered. There was nothing she could do but take care of things.

With a loud sigh, she wiggled herself out of the hammock chair, took her coffee, and headed up the wide staircase in the middle of the first floor that split the living space from the dining area. The second floor boasted four bedrooms and two full bathrooms. This was presumably where camp counselors lived during the times the camp was full. She chose the room closest to the top of the staircase because it would get the most heat from the fireplace. The furnace was dodgy, to say the very least, and Frankie had taken to leaving the thermostat set at sixty degrees and building a roaring fire, as midfall turned to late fall. If she tucked the guest into a room in a far corner, they'd likely be too cold.

In the hallway was a large closet, and Frankie knew it was filled with shelves of linens and towels and blankets because she'd washed them all when she'd arrived. She pulled a set of sheets out, along with a blanket and a comforter. She'd wash them all again today, get them smelling fresh and clean instead of musty from being in a closet for weeks. Then she'd dust and vacuum the room, make it presentable for somebody to stay in. Hopefully, the undisclosed amount of time wouldn't be more than a few days. After all, what was there to do out here but think and be alone?

Exactly the things that drew Frankie to it in the first place.

❖

If there was a tinier airport than Saranac Lake, Cassidy Clarke would have been surprised. It consisted of one café…and that was about it. She'd come from Boston's Logan International on a disturbingly small plane, and it took everything she had not to drop to her knees and kiss the tarmac when she'd deplaned.

But tiny didn't mean incompetent, something Cassidy had learned in life and also in Saranac Lake, as the SUV she'd rented was ready and waiting for her. She stopped at the restroom first to get herself together after many, many hours of travel, with a couple more still to go. She traveled a lot in her line of work, so she knew the things to keep handy. Fresh makeup and brushing her teeth always made her feel like a new woman, so she took care of those things. Then she stopped at the smallest café known to man and got herself a large coffee and a homemade chocolate chip cookie that looked too good to pass up from the smiling woman behind the counter, who looked like every mom in every Hallmark Christmas movie ever made. Bags tossed into the back of the SUV, she hopped in and began the two-plus-hour trek to the even tinier town of Shelton.

Blasting her music was the only way to combat her swirling thoughts. At least while she'd been on planes, she'd been able to do work, communicate with her staff, give orders, sign documents, return emails—all the day-to-day things a CEO of a successful company did—and that had kept her mind off the actual reason she was flying across the damn country in the first place.

Mason was dead.

She still had trouble wrapping her brain around that. She'd basically sleepwalked through his funeral, didn't want to think about the things his ex had said to her. Tears pooled in her eyes as she drove, and she clenched her jaw to will them away.

She hadn't spoken to him in many, many months. Too many months. She'd been too submerged in her work, in her life, in herself to make the effort to reach out. And now she knew that he'd probably needed her. And it was too late.

She cleared her throat and turned the volume up, let Halsey take up all the space in her brain with her music. At least for now.

Driving through the Adirondacks was gorgeous, even now, in November, when most of the Northeast was brown or on its way to brown. She'd missed the colors of fall, knew from experience, from growing up in this part of New York, how gorgeous it could be in October. But once the oranges and yellows and reds of autumn faded and fell off the trees, it was brown and gray until the snow came and gave everything a fresh, clean start.

Mason loved the snow.

Cassidy did not. No, that wasn't true. She thought the snow was pretty, but she hated the cold. It was a big part of why she'd moved to San Diego in the first place. Sunny and seventy-two almost year-round was exactly perfect as far as she was concerned. The first few years there, she'd missed the change of seasons, but after a while, that didn't really compare to being pleasantly comfortable one hundred percent of the time. Southern California was perfect for that.

The road was winding, and the SUV was top-of-the-line, so Cassidy made herself focus on the drive, enjoying the twists and turns, yawning several times to clear her ears as the altitude increased by small increments. It was early afternoon in mid-November, too late for leaf-peeping and a little early for ski season, though many slopes had man-made snow and were likely already spraying it all over the hillsides. Skiers didn't like to wait for Mother Nature.

Two hours and sixteen minutes after leaving the airport parking lot, Cassidy cruised into the tiny hamlet of Shelton, New York, population thirteen hundred and twelve. Or so the very old sign said. She absently wondered if it had been updated since she'd been here as a teen.

The town *had* been updated, at least a little. She noticed that immediately as she decreased her speed to thirty and rolled down the main street that ran through the center. A couple of things were the same. The diner. The library. The town hall. The post office. The general store had changed hands and was now called Dobbs's. It was bigger than she remembered and looked to be part grocery, part bakery, part liquor store? Was that right? She squinted at it, then slowed and turned into the diagonal parking on the street. She was going to need food. And wine. Lots and lots of wine.

A cute, old-fashioned bell hung over the door and tinkled sweetly as she opened it and headed inside, and holy cow, the sign was exactly right. The left half of the store held shelves of food. Canned goods. Boxed items like pasta and cereal. A cooler against the wall with milk, eggs, yogurt. A freezer toward the back. And a deli counter along the back wall. On her right was a glass display case filled with baked goods that had Cassidy's mouth watering at the sight. Cookies and Danishes and pies, oh my. At the end of that case, several shelves of wine and liquor finished off the stock, complete with their own cash register because, if she remembered correctly, you couldn't buy alcohol other than beer or cider in a grocery store in New York. Why, she had no idea. Laws were weird sometimes.

"Afternoon," said the woman behind the bakery counter. She was pretty—early forties maybe? Her light brown skin was creamy smooth, her head topped with a mass of ringlet curls that Cassidy instantly envied. When she smiled, deep dimples were on full display. "What can I help you with?"

Cassidy stood still for a moment as she looked around. "This place is quite the mix."

The woman gave a gentle laugh. "I think my parents were aiming for a one-stop shop and ended up with an amalgamation of necessities." She shrugged. "It works, though."

"It really does." Cassidy liked this woman—whose name tag said she was Eden—immediately.

"You visiting or passing through?"

"I'm visiting for a bit," Cassidy said as she stepped closer to the bakery case. "I need to grab some basics." Her eyes fell on the triple-berry pie on the top shelf of the display, and she tapped her finger on the glass in front of it. "And some not so basics."

"Grocery essentials are all behind you," Eden said as she slid the pie off the shelf. "Pies are made by Baked Expectations down the street, homemade every day." She gestured toward the wine with her chin. "Any wine or liquor?"

"I said basics, didn't I?" Cassidy winked.

Eden laughed again, a sweet, musical sound, and pointed to the corner near the door where carts were. "Help yourself. We'll ring the alcohol up separately over there. If you need anything you don't see, I've got a delivery coming tomorrow. Just leave me the address where you're staying, and I'll have it brought to you." She lifted the pie in both hands. "I'll box this up for you."

It took Cassidy about an hour, but she loaded everything she needed into the back of the SUV. There were a few things she wanted that Eden didn't have in stock but was promised would be delivered to her by tomorrow afternoon. Eden seemed slightly surprised when Cassidy gave her the address, but she assured Cassidy that Frankie would take care of everything, no worries. Back in the car, she pulled up her GPS again and pointed herself in the right direction. She hadn't been there in—she squinted as she did the math in her head—twenty-two years. Would it look the same? Would there be a deluge of memories that washed over her like a tidal wave?

She snorted at that. "Of course there will," she said aloud to nobody. "How could there not be?"

And then, there it was. The sign that indicated her turn. It was old and faded and rotting in places, but it was still legible. Camp Lustenfeld.

With a deep breath, she hit her turn signal and indicated the left-hand turn, onto the cracked and uneven pavement that morphed into just gravel and pointed up, up, up. A beat passed. Another. She stared, knowing she needed to brace herself for what was coming, for everything that lay ahead. Laying a hand on the large duffel in the passenger seat, she cleared her throat and asked quietly, "Ready for this, Mason? It's too late to turn back now."

This was it. After twenty-two years, the time had finally come, and somehow, she'd always known it would. She made the turn and headed up the long, narrow, two-mile driveway.

She was going back.

Back to Camp Lost and Found.

CHAPTER TWO

Wow. It was a damn good thing Cassidy had rented an SUV because a regular, sits-closer-to-the-ground car would never have made it up the camp driveway without completely bottoming out.

"This must be what popcorn feels like," she muttered as she bounced along, woods on either side of the rattling SUV. Adele stopped singing abruptly when her phone cut in, and it took her several tries to hit the correct button on the touch screen because of the shimmying and shaking.

"You there yet?" Jenna's voice was a welcome distraction.

"Heading up the driveway now," Cassidy told her. "Though two and a half miles is gonna take a really long time at seven miles an hour." A breathy *oof* was released from her lips when she hit a particularly deep pothole.

"Well, drive faster. Duh."

"Not if I want to keep all four of my tires. This driveway is a wreck." She steered around another deep hole. "Things okay?"

"Absolutely. I wasn't calling about work." Jenna's voice softened. "I just wanted to check on you. You left before I had a chance to really see how you were. So...how are you?"

She *had* kind of fled. She'd gotten the news about Mason, called Jenna to see if she could handle things at work for a while, then flew across the country without so much as a see you later. Which wasn't really fair, but Jenna was made of steel and barbed wire. She'd handle things without issue. Cassidy knew that. It was the only reason she'd been able to drop everything and go.

"I'm okay."

"Well, thank you for that very detailed answer."

Cassidy grimaced, tipped her head from side to side. "I know. I'm sorry. I've gotten my food and my wine, and I'm exhausted and starving, and I'm just trying to focus on this road."

"Okay, okay, we'll talk about your state of mind later." There was a pause, and then she added, "I wonder what the state of the camp is like if the driveway is that bad."

"I guess we'll find out. From what I could ascertain from my call, there's some guy on the property named Frank that's supposed to get me settled."

"Are there other people staying there? Or just you and...Frank?"

"I have no idea. I didn't ask."

"Yeah." Jenna let go of a small snort. "That's part of what's got me worried. The not asking. You just went." It was clear how she felt about that, and Cassidy couldn't really blame her. But she was too tired to try to explain it all now.

"I know." She sighed quietly. "I'm sorry. Listen, let me get myself all situated, and I'll check in with you later. Okay? I'm basically wiped."

"Yeah, okay, go ahead to the camp in the middle of East Jesus where there's a dude named Frank, who could be a serial killer, and nobody else. No worries." Jenna's tone made it clear that she was most certainly not okay with this direction but would take it anyway because she was Jenna, and that's what she did when it came to Cassidy. "But if I don't hear from you, *you* will be hearing from *me*. Got it?"

"Yes, ma'am," Cassidy said with a soft laugh. They said their good-byes, and she hung up and tried not to wonder if her internal organs would be completely rearranged after this ride.

And then her brain let the memories begin to sift in as the cabins came into view on either side of the car.

Camp Lost and Found—as the foster kids had dubbed it—was made up of several buildings. There were six small cabins, three on each side of the property, fanned off from the main building. Girls on one side, boys on the other. The main building housed the kitchen, common area, dining hall, and counselors' quarters. There was a large building behind that where the toilets and showers were, and then several other small buildings for indoor activities when the weather was bad. Art, reading, movies. But the camp was mostly about the outdoors.

The pond was large enough for canoeing, swimming, fishing—they'd actually called it a lake back then because they were young and from the city, and most of them had never seen a body of water larger than a swimming pool. There was hiking and volleyball and soccer. While it was true that many—okay, most—of the kids that attended Camp Lost and Found's foster weeks came from less-than-ideal backgrounds, the three weeks each summer they spent there were some of their happiest. At least for Cassidy. And for Mason.

The cabins on either side looked much more run-down than she'd expected, but she decided to reserve judgment. The guy she'd spoken to on the phone, Ethan Lustenfeld, had told her it wasn't really up to snuff as far as housing guests. She assured him she didn't require much, and then she proceeded to tell him what the place had meant to her as a kid. He had sighed and been hesitant, but the money she offered, plus the sizable donation to his family's foundation for foster kids, convinced him. But she'd have to stay in the main house, he'd told her.

Fine. Whatever. It didn't matter. She wasn't there for a vacation.

The woods finally emptied her into the open in front of the main house.

Holy shit.

She barely recognized it.

The white paint was faded and cracking, dirty in some places, split in others. The wraparound porch railing was missing spindles here and there. It didn't look damaged so much as simply old. Run-down. Not at all the way she remembered it.

"I mean, it *has* been a couple of decades," she said quietly as she sat in the idling car and looked out the windshield. "But wow."

Sudden rapping on her window scared the living hell out of her, and she was pretty sure she hit her head on the sunroof, she jumped so high. She caught her breath and pressed a hand to her chest, calming her heart rate enough to finally notice a woman standing next to her car. A steadying deep breath, and she powered down the window.

"You scared the crap out of me," she said, a bit snippier than she'd intended, but Jesus Christmas in St. Louis, she was pretty sure she'd had a mild heart attack.

"Sorry," the woman said, her dark eyes flicking away and then back.

"I'm Cassidy Clarke. I'll be staying here for a while. I'm looking for Frank?" She realized too late that she'd said it as a question instead of a statement, and she hated to sound uncertain in general, but she didn't know anything more about this Frank than his name. Which was on her for not asking for more detail. God, she wasn't herself lately.

"Frankie."

She blinked at the woman. "Okay. Frankie, then. Is he here?"

"Yes. I'm her."

Squint. "You're her. Oh, you're Frank? Er, Frankie?"

"I am. Yeah. Mr. Lustenfeld said you'd be here for a while, and I should get you settled." She stepped back to allow Cassidy to open the car door.

"Oh. Well, okay then." Cassidy got out, grateful to stretch her legs after spending so many hours in a sitting position, on planes and then in a car. She held out her hand. "Cassidy Clarke."

The woman looked at her hand for a beat before taking it. "Frankie Sisto." Her grip was firm, but she didn't hold on one second longer than necessary, and again, her gaze darted away. She was pretty—Cassidy would have to be oblivious not to see that—but almost seemed to be hiding it. She had dark curls that were pulled back in a ponytail, and thick, dark brows that were perfectly arched. No makeup. She was tall and solid and dressed in jeans, a red hoodie, and a black puffy vest. Worn Timberland work boots were on her feet. Her face was dead serious, and she looked like somebody who didn't smile often. At all. "Follow me," she said, then turned and headed toward the house.

Realizing with a start that she'd clearly be carrying her own bags, she left them in the car and scampered after Frankie to get the lay of the land first.

"Watch your step," Frankie said as she pointed at a hole in one of the front steps on her way up. Cassidy dodged it, then followed her through the front door.

Okay, so the inside wasn't quite as run-down. Still, older and it definitely felt kind of empty. Despite the faint scent of must in the air, it was fairly clean and seemed somewhat functional.

"Interesting choice," she said before she could stop herself as her gaze landed on what looked to be some kind of hammock-like chair dangling from the ceiling in the living room.

Frankie Sisto actually almost smiled. Almost. "Yeah." She headed for the stairs, which Cassidy remembered as a grand staircase of sorts, but now seemed like just regular stairs. She followed Frankie up and, when she found herself watching the jeans-clad ass in front of her, tore her gaze away and focused on her own feet. Clearing her throat seemed super loud. God, it was quiet here.

At the top of the stairs, Frankie opened a door and led her into a large room that was clearly freshly cleaned, the scent of furniture polish grabbing her nostrils immediately. Two twin beds with a nightstand between them were both made up neatly with plain, functional navy-blue bedspreads, a folded quilt at the foot of each one. There was also a dresser, and a wardrobe filled out the remainder of the space. The Ritz, it was not.

"The bathroom down there will be yours," Frankie said, pointing to the left out the door, and Cassidy blinked at her.

"I remember these rooms being bigger," Cassidy said as she looked around, took in the space. "The counselors lived here, and I was only up here once, but when you're fifteen, things seem big. You know?"

Frankie looked at her in surprise. "You've been here before?"

Cassidy continued to look around, taking it all in as she said, feeling almost dreamy, "A lifetime ago, yeah."

Frankie nodded once but said nothing.

"I guess I always assumed the counselors had their own bathrooms in each room."

Frankie shrugged, then said, "I'm downstairs in the back, so let me know if you have questions or anything." She turned to leave.

"Um..." Cassidy said, wanting to stop her because hello? That was it? "What about the kitchen? Meals? I have some groceries in the car, and the store is delivering more when they restock."

"Yeah, help yourself. Whatever you need should be in there. Pots and pans and dishes and such."

"You don't cook?" Frankie stared at her for a second or two, and Cassidy felt the need to fix whatever she'd said. "I mean, Ethan said I should bring food, I just..." She felt stupid and could feel her face heat up with the embarrassment. "I just assumed..."

Frankie took a deep breath and looked off into the middle distance. "Look, I'm not the concierge. This isn't a hotel. Taking care of guests wasn't really on my radar when I took the maintenance job here."

"Oh. Okay." Cassidy's embarrassment was starting to get on

her nerves, and she stood straighter, irritated that this woman was so standoffish. "I apologize then. I'll take care of myself. No worries."

"Good. That's good." Frankie shifted her weight from one foot to the other but still didn't look at her. It was clear she was itching to leave the room. "If you have questions, you can find me. I know pretty much where everything is."

"How long have you lived here?"

A shrug. "A month and a half or so?"

"I see." She really didn't see a thing, but whatever. This woman clearly didn't want anything to do with her, and Cassidy decided she'd best adopt the same attitude. She waved a hand absently. "Okay, thanks for your help." She'd had plenty of practice expelling people from her office with just the right tone, and she felt the tiniest glimmer of satisfaction when it registered on Frankie's face that she'd been dismissed.

That'll teach you to be short with me, she thought.

And then Frankie turned and left, and Cassidy stood there in the middle of the small room, realizing she had to go haul all her own stuff in and up the stairs.

"Son of a bitch," she said softly.

❖

Frankie tried not to clomp loudly down the stairs. Oh, she wanted to, but she didn't want to give Ms. Cassidy Clarke the satisfaction of knowing she'd annoyed her. She held the railing and made the effort to walk softly and managed to make it down the stairs quietly, but she felt the anger welling up inside, so she grabbed her coat and gloves and hurried through the kitchen and out the back door, needing to blow off some steam.

You'd think she'd be used to the feeling by now. The way the anger started in her gut like a small fire, the flames licking and growing until things turned orange-red and became hot embers of emotion. It had certainly happened often enough, had become a regular thing. At least, up here in the middle of fucking nowhere, she could ride it out, find ways to channel it, use the outlets she'd discovered in the past few weeks.

The air was brisk today. Snow had been forecast and had yet

to arrive, but the sky was the color of dull steel, like an old nickel, and Frankie grabbed the ax from where she'd left it leaning against the house near the back steps. She carried it about twenty-five yards into the backyard where there was a huge, flat stump. Next to that lay many pieces of an old fallen tree she'd chainsawed up on Monday and dragged to the yard. Now, she picked a piece up, set it upright on the stump, and grasped the ax handle in both hands. Then she lifted it over her head and behind, the way her father had taught her when she was younger, planted her feet, and let loose.

The ax head hit the log, splitting it neatly in two, as if she'd cut butter with a hot knife.

So. Fucking. Satisfying.

Splitting wood had been one of the best ways she'd found to alleviate her stress. Her anger. Her frustration. Whenever she felt herself about to be swamped by emotion, she came out here and swung the ax until she was either out of wood or couldn't lift it anymore because her arms felt like spaghetti. And she always felt better.

Who the hell was Cassidy Clarke?

She hadn't asked Ethan because, simply, she didn't really know him. His dad knew her dad from the Army, way back. They hadn't spoken in many years and met up on a fluke. One thing led to another, her father knew she was looking to retreat for a while, and after some reassurance that she could handle things here on her own, the rest was history. She had no idea how long she planned on staying, and Ethan had no idea how long he wanted her to stay, but she did know this was where she needed to be right now.

But Cassidy Clarke? Who was she and why was she here, at a deserted camp in the Adirondacks with winter tiptoeing in? She clearly came from money. Her SUV and pricey clothing made that clear. Her short dark hairstyle was modern. Her leather boots were designer—and would absolutely not keep her warm out here, by the way, hope she had some that were more appropriate. Same went for her coat, though it was wool and probably warmer than the boots. Frankie had taken a quick peek in the window of the SUV and, much to her dismay, saw a large suitcase, a smaller one, and about four bags from Dobbs's. The evidence said Cassidy Clarke planned on staying awhile. Hopefully, she had some heavier clothing with her.

She blew out a breath and whacked another log in two. She hated the idea of another person in what she'd come to think of as her space, even if that person was rich or stunning or—

"Nope. No, no." She cleaved another log and did her best to rid herself of any and all thoughts about Cassidy Clarke.

Of course, that left things wide open for other thoughts. Sounds of screeching brakes and shattering glass and screams of pain.

Swallowing down the lump that pretty much came and went in her throat on its own damn schedule, she continued to chop until a voice interrupted her.

"Hey! *Hey!*" Cassidy Clarke had clearly called her name more than once by the time Frankie heard her. When she looked up, Cassidy was crossing the yard without a coat, her arms crossed over her chest, presumably to keep warm. She had rich brown eyes, Frankie noticed, the color of a good bourbon. "Hi." Cassidy looked around at the split pieces of wood that littered the area, then brought her gaze back up. "Um, I was just going to make myself a grilled cheese sandwich. Are you hungry? I'm happy to make two."

Don't be rude. Don't be rude. Don't be rude.

"No, I'm good. But thank you."

Cassidy held her gaze for a moment, like she was waiting for her to say more. When she didn't, there was a nod. "Okay, then. Chop away." And she turned and headed back to the house, and yeah, Frankie was watching her go. Because the jeans and the boots and the probably cashmere sweater and the sharp hairstyle and the figure inside all of it? Made for a really nice picture walking away.

She wasn't oblivious after all.

It had been a while since…well…that. Since she'd looked. At anybody. She let herself watch until Cassidy reached the back stairs, and then she shook herself back into action. Picked up a log. Set it on the stump. Lifted the ax.

Whack!

❖

What was Frankie Sisto's deal?

At least she was somewhat polite this time. Cassidy's thoughts were plentiful as she headed back to the house. Most prominent was this one: What was a young, very attractive woman doing out in the middle of nowhere, taking care of an empty old summer camp in the winter? Her first thought was that maybe Frankie was part of the Lustenfeld family and this was somehow partly her property. But she'd referred to Ethan as *Mr. Lustenfeld*, so she was likely off base on that.

"Whatever," she said softly and stopped at the stainless-steel counter in the kitchen. She'd unloaded her groceries, put the perishables in the large refrigerator, and carefully pushed to the side some of Frankie's things to make room for her own on the counter and in the cupboards. She might hear about that later, but she was paying a pretty penny to stay here, and she was reasonably sure that money should cover cupboard space in the kitchen.

A chef, Cassidy was not. She was a very regular customer of both DoorDash and Grubhub, but she was pretty sure she could manage a grilled cheese and some soup. She pulled out the bread, the American cheese slices, and a can of Campbell's tomato soup and got to work. The last thing she'd eaten—besides the cookie at the teeny-tiny airport— had been breakfast on the first leg of her journey from San Diego to Boston, and that was hours ago. Her stomach had made its empty status loudly known the whole time she'd hauled her bags up to her room and her grocery bags into the kitchen. She hadn't unpacked any clothes, but she was afraid she'd faint from hunger if she didn't eat, like, *now*.

Twenty minutes later, standing at the counter, she took a bite of a not-quite-black-but-almost sandwich as the back door opened, and Frankie walked in carrying an armload of wood. She smelled like the outdoors, fresh and clean and woodsy.

"All chopped out?" Cassidy asked.

Frankie nodded, and was that a grunt? Woman of few words, clearly. But then she surprised Cassidy by using her chin to indicate the burnt sandwich. "Use mayo next time. Instead of butter. Browns the bread better." And she walked through the kitchen and disappeared into the house.

"Noted," Cassidy said to the empty kitchen.

She was so hungry that she barely noticed the burnt taste of the sandwich. Maybe that was because the first spoonful of soup was way too hot and scorched the inside of her mouth. Her taste buds were probably useless now, sizzled right off her tongue, so she could eat charcoal—her sandwich wasn't far from that—and not notice.

From the back pocket of her jeans, she felt her phone buzz just before the ding sounded, and she knew immediately who it was. "Damn," she muttered as she slid the phone out to see Jenna's message. *HAVE YOU BEEN KILLED AND DISMEMBERED AND BURIED IN THE WOODS ALREADY?*

She chuckled. She couldn't help it. Before she could respond, another text popped through.

Seriously. Answer me. And a couple of wide-eyed emoji.

She wiped the black crumbs off her hands onto her jeans and typed back. *All limbs intact. Had to eat before I fainted. Sorry.*

And Frank? How is he? came the next text.

A quiet snort. *He is a she. Frankie. And she's…a woman of few words.* She added an eye roll emoji in the hopes of expressing how she felt about that.

Well, it's not like ur there to chat, right?

That was true. While she wasn't a hundred percent sure exactly what had driven her here, it wasn't to chat with some stranger who grunted responses and pretty clearly didn't love Cassidy's presence.

No. True. Needing a subject change, she went with her usual. *How are things there? Anything come up I need to know about?* She didn't love being away from her business, even though she knew perfectly well that Jenna could handle things. She hadn't built Scentsibilities into the hugely successful company it was by pawning off the responsibility of running things to others.

All is fine. Meetings are covered. I've got everything under control.

She knew it was the truth but couldn't keep herself from asking for details. *Target? That meeting's set? I'll call you before…*

Jenna's dots began bouncing before Cassidy had even hit send. *Stop worrying. I got this.*

She knew if she pushed any harder, she'd be crossing the line between worrying because she was away and simply not trusting her business partner. Yes, she hated not playing an active role, but Jenna knew what she was doing. She'd been with Cassidy from the very beginning.

Okay. Thanks.

They chatted a bit more, then signed off, and Cassidy slipped the phone back into her pocket. She could hear Frankie in the front room making a fire, the sounds of wood hitting wood and paper being crumpled making it clear, and she turned to head that way. A moment later, she could smell it. The smell of the woodsmoke and the crackling of the flames brought her instantly right back to her childhood here, and suddenly, she could see kids in her mind's eye. Yellow Camp Lustenfeld T-shirts, kids playing board games at the dining room table as she walked past it, the sound of a video game coming from the corner where the TV used to be. They didn't have fires often, as they were here during summer, but on rainy days when it got chilly, the counselors would stoke it up, and the place would be toasty and inviting.

When she turned into the living room, there was only Frankie, squatting in front of the large stone fireplace, and the sounds of kids faded into her subconscious.

"Hi," she said, taking a seat on the couch. "Good fire."

"Thanks," Frankie said. A moment of silence went by as Frankie watched the flames, used an iron poker to adjust different pieces of wood, added a log here, another there, until it was roaring. Finally, she turned to Cassidy. "The furnace is old and not terribly reliable, so it's set low, and I mostly use the fire for heat." She pointed up the stairs. "You're right at the top where it's open, so the heat should rise and keep you warm enough, but if you're cold, let me know and we'll figure something out."

Cassidy blinked at her, wanted to make a comment about how Frankie clearly could speak more than monosyllabically, but her face was still serious. Not an expression for joshing. Instead, she just nodded and said, "Okay, got it. Thanks."

And then Frankie looked around, her eyes falling on the hammock chair, and that's when Cassidy saw the stack of books for the first time. Oh, this must've been where Frankie spent her evenings. And here Cassidy was, hanging out in her space. Quickly, she got to her feet. "Well," she said, holding her arms out and dropping them to her sides. "Okay if I take a bath?"

"Knock yourself out," Frankie said, and the relief on her face was evident.

Okay, so not the type to visit. Got it. Cassidy headed up to her room, deciding that a glass of wine and a bubble bath sounded divine right about then.

CHAPTER THREE

Up in her room, Cassidy sat heavily on the bed. The one on the right, and seriously, when was the last time she'd slept in anything smaller than a queen? She hadn't expected a bunch of other people to be here, but she also hadn't expected to be lacking even the most basic of conversation. Again, the questions floated into her head: What the hell was Frankie's deal, anyway? What was a young, attractive woman doing out here in the middle of nowhere, chopping wood and building fires and reading books all alone?

It was weird, right?

And, also, none of her business. Frankie could very easily be asking the same questions about her. She had her own reasons for being out here.

On the other bed was her duffel, and she went to it, zipped it open, and pulled out the sealed wooden box. She'd held it in her hands a total of four times now, and every time, her eyes had welled up with the magnitude of emotions that punched her in the stomach. This time was no different. She marveled at the fact that it weighed about five pounds. How was that even possible? All that talent. All that charisma. All that heart. Reduced to five measly pounds sealed in a wooden box.

She sniffled and set the box on the dresser, then returned to her seat on the bed and stared at it.

"Tomorrow, I'll take a walk and see if I can find the perfect spot, okay, handsome?" Her voice was soft, barely a whisper. "I promise." Then she undressed, tied her robe around her waist, and headed for the bathroom.

Pleasantly surprised was a good way to describe Cassidy's reaction to the bathroom. While it still had that slight smell of must, it was also a bit more modern than the bedrooms, making her think it must've been remodeled at some point. Or at least updated. The walls were wood. Not shiplap exactly—a word she'd learned from a couple of meetings she'd had with Joanna Gains about getting her Scentsibilities products into her Magnolia line—but something similar, in a brown that bordered on rust colored, both walls and floor. There was a shower stall tucked into a corner, but the huge clawfoot tub standing along the back wall practically called to her.

"Now we're talkin'," she said happily and crossed to turn on the water. She unscrewed the cap on the Toasted Marshmallow and Cocoa shower gel, which also doubled as a bubble bath—part of the beauty of the product—and dumped in a generous amount. Then she left it running while she headed down to the kitchen to get herself a glass of Argentinian Malbec to keep her company while she soaked.

Frankie was in the hammock chair, a book open in her hands, and while Cassidy was careful not to disturb her, she was pretty sure she saw her do a double take as she hit the bottom step and made a left to the kitchen where she'd lined up her wine bottles in a row in the corner of the counter. She thanked the wine gods above that it was a screw top, because she didn't want to have to ask Frankie for a corkscrew. She found a glass tumbler, filled it halfway, and made her way back to the stairs.

Frankie's eyes watched her over the top of the book. She was sure of it this time, which was pretty amusing, she wasn't gonna lie.

Back in the bathroom, she set her wine down after taking a delicious sip of it and feeling it instantly start to warm her body. The tub was about two-thirds full, bubbles galore, and the whole room smelled like a cup of hot cocoa, perfect for a chilly November evening. She slipped off her robe and reached in to gauge the temperature and spread the bubbles around.

And pulled her hand back in shock.

The water was ice-cold.

❖

Seriously? With the silky robe? The sexy legs? The sexy legs that went on for days? Was that necessary, Universe?

Frankie closed her eyes and shook her head as Cassidy went back upstairs. From her spot in the hammock chair, she probably could've seen right up that robe when Cassidy was at the high end of the staircase, and she'd managed to pull her gaze away, thank freaking God, so she couldn't confirm her suspicions.

She did her best to refocus her attention on the book in her hands. On the words on the page. There were words on the page, right? Weird how she couldn't seem to make them out because of all the sexy bare legs now walking around in her brain.

"Goddamn it," she muttered, just as Cassidy reappeared at the top of the steps.

"Um, Frankie?" she called down, and her tone was an odd combination of hesitation and irritation.

"Yeah?"

"Can you come up here? I think the hot water's not working."

"Oh. Sure." She set down her closed book and headed up the stairs, carefully not looking at Cassidy as she passed her.

The bathroom smelled like warm sugar and chocolate, but it definitely lacked the steamy warmth it should've had when a bath's been run. She felt the water in the tub. Not even a little warm. She turned on the hot water faucet for the sink and let it run and stared at it, feeling Cassidy standing in the doorway.

"I didn't think to check it until it was almost full," Cassidy said. "Which was silly, I know." With a sigh, she added, "I haven't really been thinking all that clearly," but it sounded like she was almost saying it to herself, rather than to Frankie.

"I think I know what the problem is. Let me check the hot water heater." She headed back down the stairs, stopped by the hammock chair to grab her boots, which she'd kicked off a while ago, shoved her feet into them, and headed for the basement without lacing them up.

With a loud sigh, she noticed the pilot light had gone out on the hot water heater. Again. She'd told Mr. Lustenfeld last week that the hot water had been iffy. The same thing had happened to her when she was doing dishes. No hot water. An examination had revealed the same thing as right now—the pilot light had gone out. Frankie was no expert on such things, but she knew that hot water heaters didn't last longer than ten years or so nowadays. If the dates on the maintenance sticker were correct, this one was nearly fifteen.

She relit the pilot light, heard the whoosh as the hot water heater started to do its job once again, and made a note in her phone to contact Mr. Lustenfeld in the morning.

Back upstairs, Cassidy had pulled the drain plug and drained all the cold water out.

"Give it some time to warm up, and then you can fill the tub again," she said to Cassidy, who was still clad in her robe. Absently, Frankie wondered if it was as silky as it looked, all baby blue and shimmery, but she was careful to look at Cassidy's face as she spoke. And only at Cassidy's face.

Cassidy sighed. "I'm too tired to try again." She waved a hand in the air and picked up her glass of wine. "I think I'll just turn in."

"Suit yourself," Frankie said and turned toward the stairs.

"Thank you, though. For fixing it."

"No problem."

"I'm sorry."

"For what?" She turned back to face Cassidy again.

"For hauling you away from your book."

With a shrug, she said, "No worries. Not your fault." And then she headed back down the stairs, calling, "Sleep well," over her shoulder. The scent of sugar and chocolate was still hanging out in her nose when she repositioned herself in the hammock chair and picked her book back up. Focusing on the words, however, proved to be difficult, her subconscious filled with silky robes and creamy legs and melted chocolate.

She sighed and closed the book, and when she heard the door to Cassidy's room click closed, she spun herself with her feet so she was facing the big picture window. The forecast called for snow this week, and she was ready for it. She needed that clean slate feeling that came with a fresh layer of crisp, white snow.

No, she couldn't focus on her book right now, but she was far from sleepy, so she headed to the kitchen and made herself a cup of decaf Earl Grey tea. When it was ready, hot and steamy in a big ivory mug, doctored with a little honey the way she liked it, she headed back into the living room, stoked up the fire, turned off the light, and sat back in the hammock chair again.

It was her nightly routine and had been ever since she'd realized that sleep was not her friend, that it didn't come looking for her at night anymore, that it in fact seemed to avoid her at all costs. And she became okay with that when she realized that less sleep meant less nightmares. Rather than toss and turn in her bed, she preferred to sit and watch out the window. She'd seen any number of animals during those times, and tonight was no different. In less than an hour, the deer came through, walking slowly, scanning the ground for nourishment, eventually finding the salt lick and the carrot tops she'd tossed out there earlier. Raccoons almost always showed up. A fox. Rabbits. Possums. There was a whole slew of nature visible from that window at night, and Frankie watched them all from her swinging chair, slowly sipping her tea.

❖

You'd think with all the traveling Cassidy did for her job, she'd be used to the different beds and would have learned to drop off to sleep no matter where she was. And she didn't always have trouble. But it was so damn *quiet* here. Not only were there no sounds of traffic, no sirens, no middle-of-the-night car alarms, there wasn't even a slamming door or a barking dog. There was nothing. The occasional hoot of an owl, maybe. The snap of a twig that told her something was moving outside. But for the first time in her life, Cassidy understood what the phrase *the silence was deafening* meant. The quiet was almost loud. How that was possible, she had no idea, but it was almost a roar in her ears. Which made no sense, she knew, but there it was.

She drifted a little bit here and there. Pulled the quilt up over her comforter as the temperature dropped. She missed her Tempur-Pedic. And again, she wondered—when was the last time she'd slept in anything smaller than a queen? Anytime she moved, she pictured herself rolling right off the bed onto the floor with a loud thump.

She even pulled out her laptop and did a little work until her eyes were too scratchy to focus on the screen, and she gave up, closed the computer, and flopped back onto the pillow. She lay there at one point and just stared at the box on her dresser. Stared as if it would morph into something else. As if the lid would open and drop backward and a tiny little Mason would step out, take a seat on the edge of the dresser, and talk to her.

"Ever think we'd be back here, Mase?" she whispered into the dark. "I sure as hell didn't." And she knew if she didn't yank her mind away from that and focus on something else, she'd get lost in regret. Guilt. Sadness. Three emotions that had become far too prevalent in her head lately.

With an annoyed sigh, she glanced at her phone: 3:12 a.m. She'd been mostly awake. And had to pee. Damn it. She threw off the covers and crossed to her door, opened it quietly, and padded down the hall to the bathroom, the hardwood floor icy on her bare feet. On her way back to her room, she glanced over the balcony and was stopped in her tracks.

The fire had burned down to just some glowing orange embers. The floor lamp was off. And Frankie was *still* in the hammock chair, her back to the stairs. Her stack of books was on the table and a mug sat next to it. Cassidy assumed she'd fallen asleep in the hammock chair—until she moved, sat forward, and leaned toward the window like she was watching something.

It crossed her mind to say something. Hell, it crossed her mind to pad down the stairs and join her, see what she was looking at. They didn't have to talk, but it sure would be nice to have an I-can't-sleep-either buddy. But something stopped her. Maybe it was remembering the day, the slight standoffishness she'd felt from Frankie since her arrival. The very clear message that said she, Cassidy, was a bother. An annoyance. Maybe she could change that opinion. She hoped she could. If there was one thing Cassidy excelled at, it was winning people over. She'd never have been as successful as she was now if she didn't possess that talent. She could definitely use it on Frankie.

But maybe not tonight.

CHAPTER FOUR

The hot water was all charged up and back to normal in the morning, and Cassidy's shower was blessedly steamy. She wanted to take her time, to linger under the hot spray, but she was also nervous the hot water heater would crap out again, so she did a quick wash and shave of everything and was out in less than six minutes.

She'd managed to drift off a little in the early morning hours, and she touched base with Jenna, via text, the second she'd opened her eyes. Jenna, of course, was already in the office. God, she was lucky to have her as her business partner.

The weather app on her phone told her the high today was going to be in the upper thirties, but sunny, so she put on jeans, a white T-shirt, a blue V-neck sweater, and thick socks, and then decided her mission in life in that moment was coffee. Finding. Brewing. Consuming. She'd gotten a total of maybe two and a half hours of sleep, and she needed caffeine if she was going to stay upright today. Lots of it.

There was a definite chill in the hallway when she left the bedroom, and she wondered if the fireplace was the only thing actually heating the house. The fire was crackling again, the logs fresh, so it was clear Frankie had got it going it again recently.

Speaking of Frankie, she was in the kitchen, pouring coffee into a mug, her back to Cassidy.

"Good morning," Cassidy said. "Chilly this morning. Is there more of that?"

Frankie didn't say anything, just pulled a mug from an overhead cabinet and set it on the counter, then stepped aside so Cassidy could see the old Mr. Coffee, its pot filled with that liquid gold that she needed to survive.

"Great. Thanks." She poured herself a cup, then added sugar from the bowl sitting next to the pot.

"Sleep okay?" Frankie asked as she gazed out the back door.

It speaks. Cassidy tamped down the inner thought. "I did okay. Not used to the quiet." Frankie nodded. In agreement? Cassidy had no way of knowing because that's all she said. "I think I'm gonna take a hike this morning." Why she was telling Frankie this, she had no idea. She wouldn't care. To her surprise, though, Frankie turned to look at her. God, her eyes were dark, her lashes long, her brows defined and thick and gorgeous.

"You know where you're going? The woods can get pretty confusing." She sipped from her mug, her eyes on Cassidy the entire time, and Cassidy realized it was the first time since her arrival that she felt Frankie actually see her, actually *look* at her. Inexplicably, it made her heart rate pick up speed.

When she tried to speak, her voice caught, and she had to clear her throat. "I think so," she said with a nod. "I remember the basic layout."

"Still. Take your phone." Frankie turned and rinsed her cup out in the sink. "Reception can get spotty, but just find a clearing, and you should be all right." She stood there for a moment, her back to Cassidy and her hands braced on the edge of the metal counter as if she was contemplating something. Finally, she turned around, and with an obvious sigh, she held out her hand and wiggled her fingers. "Here. I'll give you my number in case you get lost."

Cassidy wasn't sure which was more annoying, Frankie's clear irritation and hesitancy over sharing her number or her obvious assumption that she'd likely get lost and need help. And for a split second, she considered telling Frankie to fuck off, that she'd find her way around just fine. Luckily, her good sense kicked in at the thought of wandering aimlessly in the woods and the knowledge that it was a distinct possibility out here, and she pulled her phone out, unlocked it, and handed it to Frankie. Watched her as she entered her number. Stared at her long fingers, her dark curls as they fell in a curtain alongside her face. She was very attractive, and Cassidy found herself wondering what she'd look like if she smiled once in a while. She could smell the coconut scent of her shampoo so figured she must have showered and therefore knew the hot water worked. Maybe that was why she hadn't asked.

"There." Frankie handed the phone back. "Be careful out there."

And with that, she left the kitchen.

Man, she was interesting. Rude and standoffish, but interesting. *And sexy and smells good*, her brain added, which made her chuckle softly and shake her head. "It has clearly been too long since I've gotten any action," she said quietly to the empty kitchen.

She stood at the back door, looking out and sipping her coffee. The sun had made its appearance, the sky a soft blue. The leaves were mostly gone, a few red, orange, or yellow stragglers still clinging desperately to branches. The overwhelming color was brown, but she'd expected that.

Things were weird.

It was about the only thing she was sure of right then. She felt lost. Out of sorts. Confused by her place in the world. Normally, she'd be freaking out about not being at work, but she wasn't, and *that* was freaking her out, and she didn't know what to do about it.

That's why she was here. It was the only place she could think of to go. The only place she could think of to bring Mason.

I wasn't you.

That's what Mason's ex-wife had said to her at the cemetery. She wasn't mean about it, hadn't been sarcastic or even angry. More… resigned. Exhausted about it. She'd handed him over, said those three words, and turned away. Walked away. Cassidy was reasonably sure they'd never talk to or see each other again.

She shook her head. Hard. No, she wasn't quite ready to deal with this yet. She just wanted to walk. Wanted to breathe fresh air and look at trees and rocks and not talk to anybody.

With a sigh, she rinsed out her mug, then went upstairs to get dressed for the outdoors.

❖

Frankie was on her hands and knees, using a drill to drive screws into the new tread on the front step. It was a task that had been bumped to the top of the to-do list now that somebody else was there. That was the last thing she needed: to have Cassidy—the guest—hit that hole and break an ankle. Ethan Lustenfeld would have things to say about that, she was pretty sure, so she'd gotten to work prying it up and replacing it as soon as Cassidy had left for her walk.

One of the things she liked most about being at Camp Lustenfeld was that she could hear somebody coming long before they were ever in view. No sneaking up on her here. She kept working on the step for several minutes as she listened to the crunching sound of tires on the gravel—or what gravel that was left, which was not much—of the driveway as a vehicle approached. It was a good five or six minutes before a truck finally came into view, and Frankie wasn't surprised when she saw the red pickup.

Eden Dobbs pulled up next to Cassidy's SUV—a freaking Infiniti QX80 of all things—and cut the engine. Her driver's side window was down, and she sat there until Frankie glanced up at her.

"You don't get that window fixed, you're gonna freeze to death, you know." She stood up and brushed her hands on the thighs of her jeans. "It's almost winter."

Eden sighed as she pulled the door open and slid to the ground. She was small in stature, but large in personality, Frankie had learned early on. She already counted Eden as a good friend, one of the few who knew some of her details. Reaching into the bed of the truck, Eden pulled out a green canvas grocery bag and passed it to Frankie, then hauled out two more and headed inside.

"Watch your step," Frankie warned as Eden stepped over the new tread. "What am I carrying?"

"Groceries for your houseguest," Eden said, then grimaced and lowered her voice to a whisper. "Is she here?"

"Nope. Out walking." Frankie glanced at her watch, realized Cassidy had been gone for more than two hours now, and was annoyed by the slight jolt of concern that whooshed through her.

"She seems really nice," Eden said, unprovoked.

Frankie grunted.

Eden laughed. "You are so predictable—you know that, don't you?"

She shook her head. Eden was alarmingly astute. She picked

things up—intuited them, as she liked to call it—and it was a little unnerving, to be honest.

"Where is she from?" Eden asked as they set the bags on the counter in the kitchen and began pulling items out.

"No idea."

"What does she do for a living?"

Frankie shrugged, set down a plastic can of chocolate frosting. Then a second one of vanilla.

"Why is she here? Vacation? Seems like a weird choice."

"Not a clue."

Eden stopped what she was doing and stared at Frankie, hands parked on her hips. "You get a big fat *F* in detective work, you know that? Veronica Mars, you are not."

Another shrug. Seemed to be her go-to move lately. She glanced around at the groceries they'd unpacked as well as the ones Cassidy had grouped in a corner of the counter, likely trying to stay out of Frankie's way, which gave her a quick spark of guilt. Mostly processed, prepackaged foods. Velveeta Mac and Cheese. Several Lean Cuisines in the freezer. Three bags of salt and vinegar potato chips. Lots of wine.

"She's definitely not a health nut," Frankie said, and Eden barked a laugh.

"There ya go. Good detecting." Then her voice went quiet, and she added, "It's not a bad thing that you have another human being up here with you, Franks-n-Beans. So much alone time isn't good for you." She reached up and tapped a finger softly against Frankie's temple. "No matter what you think you might deserve."

She swallowed hard, the lump in her throat appearing out of nowhere. She cleared it, gave herself a shake, and took a small, subtle step away from Eden. "Yeah. Well." She went back to unloading the bags so Eden could have them back, and she could feel the eyes on her, feel the sympathy in the air as if it was something she could reach out and touch. But she didn't want it. Because if they were going to talk about what she did and didn't deserve, she knew she didn't deserve anybody's sympathy.

❖

It was interesting to Cassidy how walking around the campground and through the woods could feel so familiar and so foreign at the same time.

It was cold. Not in the general sense of being in the Adirondack Mountains in mid-November. Thirty-seven degrees was actually pretty typical. But to a person who'd been living in San Diego for about ten years now, it was downright frigid.

She'd planned well. After all, she'd grown up here. You didn't just forget the weather or how to handle it when it was in your blood. She'd made sure to buy herself some decent warm hiking boots, a couple sweaters, and things for layering. Gloves. A hat. A warm coat. Things she never needed in Southern California, but that were essential here. Now, would she survive a blizzard in these items? Absolutely not. But she'd be fine for a few weeks.

What struck her the most wasn't the weather, though. What took her back, what conjured up the memories of her time here wasn't the cold or even the trees. It was the smells. The scent of the evergreens, crushed leaves, rich earth. And cold. Yes, she could smell the cold in the air. Crisp and fresh. She'd stopped walking more than once simply to inhale, take a big, deep breath of nature.

Her first order of business had been to visit the cabins. Camp Lustenfeld was set up with the main house in the center and the smaller cabins fanned off to its sides, three in a row for the girls to the left and three for the boys to the right. Each cabin held six kids. The three summers she'd attended, all the cabins had been full, so her summers had included thirty-six foster kids and anywhere from six to eight counselors, plus other staff, for a full three weeks. Being a foster kid could suck in a lot of ways, but summer camp was a definite highlight. She'd been lucky like that, and she knew it. The horror stories people associated with foster kids weren't made up. But Cassidy had managed to survive.

Each of the cabins was named for an animal, and she peeked through the windows of Bluebird, the cabin she'd stayed in, then swallowed a gasp at the sight of it. Cobwebs hung from the corners. The mattresses on the three sets of bunk beds spilled their stuffing out, which was then trailed all along the floor, likely by mice or squirrels or chipmunks using it for their nests. She pushed on the door and was surprised to find it unlocked, so she stepped inside, making the floorboards creak loudly. The smell was dank. Must and mold and rotting wood. But her memories were bright. Colorful. She could see the other girls in the room, different every year. She crossed the length of the cabin to the far wall and looked high up on the side of one of the support beams, and her face broke into a smile.

Cassidy Clarke was here, bitches!

She'd used the Swiss Army knife Mason had given her to carve it from her top bunk, working on it each night after her cabinmates had fallen asleep. She'd had to hide the knife in her pillow—contraband. It had taken her an entire week to carve it—the knife was a gift, but it wasn't new, it was actually kind of dull, and she found out later that Mason had stolen it from somebody. She smiled at the carving and couldn't believe it was still there twenty years later.

After visiting the cabins, she wandered into the woods, her brain surprising her by remembering the paths despite the time that had passed and the growth of the forest. Paths tended to disappear when they were no longer followed, but she recalled them instantly, could still make them out the slightest bit.

The reason for this hike wasn't simply to reminisce, though. It was to find the perfect spot. She had a few ideas, but she needed to wander and look and figure it out before she made a decision.

And so she wandered.

The sun was lovely, high in the sky at this point, and she checked her watch, surprised to see she'd been away from the main house for nearly three hours. Lost in the past. She tromped over dead leaves and fallen branches and stopped dead to stand quietly when she saw a deer a few trees away, something she rarely saw in San Diego. White-tailed deer would always remind her of upstate New York. She loved them. They were so regal and graceful and peaceful. She stood for a long time, not moving, breathing as quietly as possible, and just watched as the buck nibbled at tree branches, gave a snort here and there, and slowly meandered away.

"So beautiful," she whispered as she began to move again, walking in the opposite direction.

It was a little while later and she was lost in thought when the barking began and scared the bejesus out of her. She gasped loudly, stopped in her tracks, and pressed a hand to her chest as a dog came bounding toward her. As it got closer, she could see it was some kind of Lab-shepherd mix, its tail wagging like crazy, eliminating any threat she might've felt. As did the bright orange vest it was wearing.

"Okay, so not a vicious wolf coming to tear me limb from limb then," she said as she squatted down. "Hi," she said as she petted the dog, but before she could say anything else, a piercing whistle punctured the air.

"Duke!" came a rough male voice. "Get back here, boy!"

And then there was a man, tromping through the woods heading her way. He was big, with long silvery hair and a beard to match. Imposing, that's what he was, and Cassidy suddenly realized just how vulnerable she actually was, alone in the woods. She stood up, slipped her phone out of her back pocket, and glanced down to see she had one bar.

"He won't hurtcha," the man said, his voice softening considerably. "He's a lover, not a fighter." He got closer, and she could see he was older, maybe in his late sixties or early seventies. He seemed to sense her concern and stopped several feet away from her with a shrug. "I wanted a hunting dog. I got a cuddler instead." His blue eyes were watery, his clothes worn, his boots dirty, and there was something vaguely familiar about his face.

Meanwhile, Duke continued to push against her leg, clearly looking for attention from her, his tail wagging so hard that it took his rear end with it so that the entire back half of him seemed to wag. It was hard to be on her guard when she had this goofy four-legged guy in front of her, begging for attention.

The man kept his distance and also kept his hands where she could see them, and she appreciated that he seemed to get how scary a strange man was to a lone woman in the woods.

She cleared her throat. "Well, he's a good guard dog just the same. He scared the crap out of me."

The man smiled, a few teeth missing. "He's definitely a barker. But just 'cause he wants to get loved on."

"He has great fashion sense," she said, giving his orange vest a little tug.

"It's deer season, and he's kinda deer color. Don't want him gettin' shot." A beat passed, and the man finally asked, "What are you doing out here all by yourself? You lost?"

She squatted back down to pet the dog some more but kept an eye on him. "No, no, not at all. I'm staying over at Camp Lustenfeld and was just taking a walk."

The man's bushy gray eyebrows furrowed. "You're staying at the camp? With Frankie?"

Relief flooded through her. "Yes! Well, not with Frankie, but yes, in the main house."

"Why in the hell would you wanna do that?"

And for some reason, that was the funniest thing she'd heard in a long time. Laughter burst out of her, surely aided by the relief she felt that this guy was likely *not* a horror movie serial killer who was going to chop her up and use her as food for the winter. "That is an excellent question, sir." She got her laughter under control, then asked, "How do you know Frankie?"

He shrugged and looked off into the distance. "I don't know her well, but I know the camp. I worked there for a lot of years."

"You did?" Cassidy couldn't hide her surprise. "When? I was a camper there in the late nineties and early two thousands."

"I worked there for about twenty years. Grounds and maintenance."

Recognition hit her like a bolt of lightning. "Jack, right?"

His blue eyes went wide. "Yeah, that's me."

"I remember you! I was there with the foster kids' sessions. My name's Cass—"

"Cassidy Clarke?" he said, shocked recognition on his face as he pointed at her.

"Yes! How could you possibly remember that?"

There wasn't a lot of his face visible under the beard, but she was pretty sure she saw his cheeks redden. "I remember most of you kids, but the foster kids especially, since I was once one, too." He paused, then added with a matter-of-fact shrug, "Plus, you carved your name in Bluebird."

That made her laugh again.

Duke had been swinging his head from one of them to the other and back as they spoke, as if he was watching a tennis match. Cassidy pet him absently, feeling a weird sense of being exactly where she was supposed to be.

"So, what are you still doing here in the woods?" She was sure he didn't live at Camp Lustenfeld.

He gestured over his shoulder. "I've got a cabin a little ways back that way. When the camp closed, the Lustenfelds gave me a chunk of land as a thank-you, knowing how much I love it up here."

"Wow." Cassidy shook her head, still kind of stunned that Jack recognized her. "Very cool. So you're out here all alone?"

"I'm not alone. I have Duke."

"You do. That's a good point."

"And you're out here all alone...why?"

She sighed quietly and felt completely at ease with Jack. Which was weird and inexplicable. "I'm trying to...find some answers, I guess." She grimaced at the vagueness of her response, but Jack seemed to accept it, and he nodded slowly as he looked off into the forest.

"It's a good place for doing that." They were silent for a beat, and then he spoke again. "Well, listen, I'll leave you to it. But if you ever want to shoot the shit, my cabin's about a quarter of a mile that way. Be nice to have a visitor." He smiled again, then patted his thigh with a hand to call Duke to him, and they headed off back the way they'd come.

Cassidy watched them go, replaying the entire conversation in her head. How weird that Jack—she had no idea of his last name—how weird that he was still here. And how weirder that he remembered her. But it made sense if he'd also been in foster care that he'd be more apt to be affected by other foster kids. She'd heard of teachers who'd taught for years and remembered the majority of their students' names. Cassidy could barely remember what she had for breakfast yesterday.

"A croissant," she said quietly to the crisp air, suddenly proud of herself.

She smiled and kept walking.

CHAPTER FIVE

Once Eden had left, Frankie made herself a turkey and avocado sandwich, grabbed a Diet Coke, and settled herself into the hammock chair. There was some puttering still to do, things she could busy herself with, but she was tired. She'd fallen asleep in this stupid thing again last night—it was great for sitting and relaxing, but not so great for sleeping, as her neck muscles made clear today—and her lack of good rest was catching up with her.

She'd texted Ethan Lustenfeld, letting him know that a new hot water heater was likely in his future, and while she wished she could put it in on her own, she didn't really know much about plumbing, so she'd need help. Ethan never texted back right away, so she set her phone aside and took a bite of her lunch.

Cassidy had left for her hike hours ago, and Frankie wondered how long she should wait before she started to be concerned. If she was being honest, there was already a sliver of worry, which irritated the crap out her. She wasn't here to look out for somebody else. She shook her head and took another bite, then nodded in approval at the sharp tang of the Dijon she'd decided to spread on the bread at the last minute. *Good call, Chef.*

The kitchen door opened, and when she heard it, a wave of relief hit—both because Cassidy was alive and also because she didn't have to be bothered to go looking for her. But it wasn't Cassidy.

"Hey, Franklin," came the familiar voice of Reiko Dobbs. She clomped through the living room in her untied Doc Martens, then kicked them off by the front door, and flopped down onto the couch like a rag doll who'd had way too much to do today.

Only a twelve-year-old could act so exhausted from doing nothing.

"Hey, Rakes," Frankie replied, then held up the other half of her sandwich, which Reiko happily took, as Frankie knew she would. "Your mom know you're here?"

Reiko sighed the put-upon sigh of preteens everywhere. That meant no.

"Text her," she said, then turned the hammock chair with her feet so she faced the window. She listened to Reiko typing on her phone. When she finished, Frankie asked, "No school today?" without looking at her.

"Half day. Superintendent's day or something."

They were quiet for a while. Frankie didn't mind Reiko popping in because Reiko didn't talk a lot. Well, sometimes she did, but most of the time, she just hung out. She'd help Frankie with tasks. Chopping or stacking wood. Hauling downed trees into the yard for sawing. Reiko liked to fill the bird feeders and replenish the salt licks and toss old veggies out for the deer. Then she'd pull the old ottoman next to the hammock chair, and they'd sit and watch the animals through the window.

It was nice to have company that didn't want anything from her.

"Whose Infiniti's out there?" Reiko asked after several minutes of silence. Her dad had been a mechanic, and she knew cars.

"Woman staying here."

She could hear Reiko sit up. "Your girlfriend?" she said, partly teasing and partly curious, both clear in her voice, and not for the first time, Frankie was annoyed both by how much detail Eden gave her daughter and also how astute Reiko actually was.

Frankie's head snapped around. "What? No. Somebody who knows Mr. Lustenfeld, I guess."

"That's weird. Who'd want to stay here?" She caught herself and quickly added, "No offense."

Frankie shrugged. "None taken. I have no idea why she's here."

"You didn't ask her?"

"Nope."

"Of course you didn't."

Frankie turned to look at her. "And why are you here?"

It was impossible to offend Reiko. Truly. Frankie had tried.

Reiko always just grinned at her, and there was something about that toughness, that hardheadedness that Frankie grudgingly admired. "I was craving some hot cocoa?" And then Reiko blinked her eyes rapidly, feigning innocence, and the move never failed to lighten Frankie up.

She sighed loudly and with tons of mock irritation as she pushed herself to her feet. "*Fine*. Come on."

They headed into the kitchen and fell into a routine that they'd come to do in tandem, almost as if they were choreographed.

Reiko got out what she had dubbed the hot cocoa pot and set it on the burner. Frankie grabbed both milk and half-and-half out of the refrigerator and poured milk into the pot. Reiko found the chocolate syrup and the marshmallows. She held up the bag. "Getting low on these."

"Doesn't your mom own a grocery store?" Frankie took a long-handled spoon from a drawer.

Reiko snorted a laugh as she pulled two mugs from a cabinet. "Good point." Then she put her elbows on the counter next to the stove, propped her chin in her hands, and watched Frankie work.

Setting the burner to low, she slowly warmed up the milk, stirring constantly. This was when they were quiet. All the supplies were out. Now, it was just patience. Frankie stirred for several minutes, and when the milk had started to warm, she nodded once. Reiko squirted in the chocolate syrup. As Frankie continued to stir, Reiko found the vanilla, and at a second nod from Frankie, she tipped the bottle and let a few quick droplets drip into the pot. They'd done this enough times that she knew the exact right amount. She put the vanilla away and added another squirt of chocolate.

The milk was beginning to steam now, the only sound that of the spoon scraping softly along the bottom of the pot.

Frankie actually enjoyed the time she spent with Reiko. She was a good kid. Troubled, a little, but a good kid. She showed up often, usually when she'd had a fight with Eden, who said Reiko liked that Frankie was quiet and didn't try to force her to talk.

A few more minutes of stirring, and then Frankie turned the burner off, and Reiko slid the mugs closer to her. She filled each one, leaving enough cocoa in the pot for maybe one more mugful. Then she added a small splash of half-and-half to each mug, just to up the creaminess, and Reiko tossed five mini marshmallows in Frankie's mug and about thirty-seven in hers. When Frankie arched a brow and shook her head, Reiko just grinned at her.

Without a word, they carried their mugs back into the living room. Reiko pulled the ottoman over next to the hammock chair, and they sat together, sipping their hot cocoa like mirror images of one another.

That's when the back door opened again.

❖

The kitchen was warm and smelled like chocolate. Cassidy hadn't quite realized how cold or how hungry she was until those two facts hit her square in the stomach.

There was a small pot on the stove that she peeked into and saw what looked like hot cocoa. A bottle of chocolate syrup and an open bag of marshmallows sat on the counter, and in that moment, she wanted nothing more in the world than a mug of hot chocolate.

She kicked off her shoes and was unzipping her jacket as she walked into the living room, but she stopped when she saw a second person, sitting next to Frankie at the front window.

"Oh. Hey." She stood there for a moment when two sets of eyes turned to look at her. And it wasn't just a person next to Frankie, it was a kid. Maybe eleven or twelve. Corkscrew curls tucked under one of those ski caps with the danglers on either side for tying under your chin—even though nobody ever tied them, just left them hanging. Jeans, socked feet, a gray hoodie, and a quick smile that revealed two deep dimples.

"Hi," the kid said.

Frankie gave her a nod. "Good hike?"

"Yeah," she said, walking farther into the room, not sure if she was invited to, but doing it anyway. "It's cold, but gorgeous out. I ran into a guy out there…"

"Jack," Frankie said matter-of-factly.

"Yeah."

"Oh, did you get to see Duke?" the kid asked, clearly envious.

"I did. He scared the shi—er—heck out of me."

The kid laughed and paired it with a slight eye roll. "You can say *shit*. I've heard it before. And that dog is the best."

Cassidy let one more beat go by before deciding Frankie wasn't making introductions. She crossed the room, hand outstretched. "I don't believe we've met. I'm Cassidy Clarke."

The kid looked surprised for a split second, and she glanced at Frankie—who had the good sense to look slightly embarrassed—before grasping her hand and shaking it. "Hi, I'm Reiko Dobbs."

"Oh, that's a very cool name."

"You think so?" Reiko scrunched up her nose. "I've never liked it."

"You will when you get older," she said. "Take it from somebody with a last name for a first name. Unique names are pretty cool."

Reiko barked a laugh, then looked to Frankie and said, "I like her."

"Dobbs," Cassidy said. "From the store?"

Reiko nodded. "Eden's my mom."

That's when Frankie decided to speak and jerked a thumb over her shoulder. "She dropped off the rest of your groceries. I put them away for you."

"Oh, that's great. Thank you."

Reiko held up her mug. "Hey, you want some hot chocolate? There's some left."

"I would *love* some," Cassidy said, and without a word, Frankie stood, and she and Reiko headed toward the kitchen. "If it's not too much trouble," she added as Frankie passed her.

"No worries," Frankie said.

"It's already made," Reiko told her as they entered the kitchen and Frankie turned on a burner. "Just needs to be warmed up. Franklin here makes the best hot cocoa on the planet. Just wait."

"Don't overhype me," Frankie said, but Cassidy could tell by the shadow of a smile that she appreciated the kid's words.

"So, you were hiking?" Reiko asked as Frankie stirred the hot cocoa. It was clear she was going to do the talking. "Did you have fun?"

Cassidy nodded, happy to have somebody to talk to for the moment. "I did. A lot has changed—and also, not much has changed."

"What do you mean? Have you been here before?" Reiko had her elbows on the island countertop and was bent at the waist, shifting her weight from one foot to the other, sort of fidgety as kids her age often were.

"I went to camp here many, many years ago."

Frankie turned to regard her. "Really?"

Cassidy blinked at her before saying, "Why do you think I said I'd only been upstairs once and thought the rooms were bigger?"

Frankie was still for a second or two before nodding. "Oh. Right. Yeah." She went back to stirring, and it was clear she hadn't really been listening when Cassidy was talking yesterday. Which was irritating, for sure.

Returning her attention to Reiko, she said, "When I was a teenager, every summer, there was a three-week session for foster kids. A bunch of us came here and had a blast. Campfires and crafts and canoeing on the lake. Hikes. It was a lot of fun."

Reiko's dark eyes lit up, and when she smiled and revealed her dimples, her resemblance to Eden was shocking. "Did you sleep in one of those spooky cabins?"

Cassidy laughed. "Yes. Bluebird. They weren't spooky then like they are now, though."

Frankie flipped the burner off, and Reiko grabbed a mug from the cabinet. The hot cocoa was poured, and Reiko held up a near-empty bag of mini marshmallows, her eyebrows raised in question.

"Duh," Cassidy said with a nod, and Reiko grinned and poured a bunch into the mug. Then she handed it over with a flourish.

"There you go. Best hot cocoa you'll ever have."

"Putting the pressure on Frankie here," she said with a smirk.

"I'm not worried," Frankie said back, giving her head a tilt, and Cassidy felt a surge of heat shoot through her body to settle low in her hips. She blew on the cocoa for a minute before finally taking a sip, getting some melty marshmallow in with it.

And holy heavenly drinkable things, Reiko was not even close to kidding. "Wow," she said after her first sip. She took another. More marshmallow. There was something beyond the creaminess of it, an extra sweetness.

"It's the vanilla," Reiko said, as if reading her mind. "Gives it that little extra *bam*, amirite?"

She nodded and her eyes met Frankie's. Held them. "This is fabulous," she said and hoped her sincerity was clear.

Frankie glanced down at her feet, then back up, and was that a bit of a blush on her cheeks? "Thank you. I'm glad you like it."

"Did you know Frankie's a chef?" Reiko asked, and Frankie's eyes widened for a second before she shook her head and began cleaning.

"I did not know that." Cassidy watched with interest as Frankie seemed to be trying to ignore this tidbit about herself. She was clearly uncomfortable, so she decided to steer things in a different direction. "So, Jack said he has a cabin out there somewhere, that the Lustenfelds gave him some land as a thank-you for his service?"

Frankie glanced at her over her shoulder, and Cassidy was pretty sure she saw a flash of gratitude. "Yeah. He lives off the land. Gets a few staples from Eden. He comes by every so often to check on things."

"Must be lonely out there by himself," Cassidy said softly.

"He's got Duke," Reiko reminded her with enthusiasm. Then she sighed. "I wish I had a dog."

"Me, too," Cassidy said.

"Why don't you have one?" Reiko asked.

"I'm away from home too much. I travel a lot for work."

"What's your work?" Reiko asked, and Cassidy decided she liked this kid. She was friendly, naturally curious and conversational.

"I own a company, Scentsibilities. We make lotions and bath gels and bubble baths and stuff."

"Oh my God, I love that stuff! The cucumber cantaloupe is my very favorite in the whole world!" Reiko spoke in exclamation points, her excitement clear, and it wormed its way into Cassidy and made her smile genuinely for the first time since she'd heard about Mason's death.

"Yeah? Well, how about I get you some on the house?"

"Seriously?" Reiko's dark eyes were wide, astonished.

"What good is being the boss if I can't do what I want, right?"

"Definitely. I wanna be a boss, too, one day."

"Not gonna lie, being in charge is pretty cool. Stressful sometimes, but pretty cool." She glanced at Frankie, who was watching the conversation with what looked like it might qualify as amusement. "By the way," she said, holding eye contact, "I might need you to make that hot cocoa again at some point because the smell alone is amazing. I noticed it as soon as I walked in and felt an instant"—her gaze went to the ceiling as she tried to find the right words—"like, a sense of warmth and safety and home."

"You wanna put that in a lotion?" Reiko asked, clearly fascinated.

"I do. What do you think?"

"I think it sounds amazing." Reiko turned to Frankie. "Doesn't it?"

And for the first time since her arrival, Cassidy witnessed what a large, genuine smile from Frankie Sisto actually looked like.

And it was fucking beautiful.

CHAPTER SIX

It was probably too cold to stain, but Frankie wanted to get the new tread on the front steps covered before the snow came, and since that was forecast for the upcoming weekend, it was now or never.

She'd applied the first coat an hour and a half ago and was putting on the second coat when she heard that telltale crunch of gravel telling her a vehicle was coming up the driveway. The red pickup came into view, and for a split second, Frankie had a flash of déjà vu. Except this time, it wasn't Eden driving.

"Hello there, neighbor." Luthor Dobbs slid out of the driver's seat dressed in his usual jeans, work boots, Carhartt coat, and Dobbs Grocers trucker hat that had seen way better days. His dark skin was weathered like leather, and his deep brown eyes were filled with stories, though you really had to know him before he said more than a few words.

"Hey, Luthor. What's new?"

"What's new is the hot water heater I've got in the back of my truck. Sadly, I can't get it off the truck on my own, or you know I would."

That was Frankie's cue, and she set the stain aside to help. Together, they slid the box off the truck bed and onto a handcart, which Luthor then wheeled around to the back of the house and, with Frankie's help, guided it down the basement stairs.

"Smart to change this out before the old one actually shits the bed and floods things down here," he said as they unboxed the thing.

"Well, there's a guest, believe it or not, and she likes to take baths, so…" Frankie let the sentence dangle as if it was common knowledge.

"Nothing like a good soak," Luthor said as he pulled the cardboard away and flattened it into a neat pile.

"Didn't peg you for a bubble bath kinda guy, Luthor," Frankie said with a grin.

"Hey, I've got layers. I'm a complicated man, you know."

"I see that," Frankie affirmed, and they got to work.

She loved working with Luthor. He didn't talk a lot, but when he did, he was funny and kind. If she didn't know what she was doing, he didn't get annoyed with her. Instead, he taught her. He reminded her so much of her own grandfather, whom she'd lost a couple years before, that it almost brought tears to her eyes when they had a job to do together.

"Who's this guest?" he asked after they'd worked quietly for ten or fifteen minutes. "I didn't talk to Ethan. His secretary called to put in the order."

Frankie shrugged. "I really don't know much. Apparently, she camped here when she was a kid, part of the foster kids' camp they used to have. That's about all I know."

"Reiko said she's a CEO of some perfume company?"

Frankie sighed internally. So much for being alone up here and keeping to herself. Yes, she'd heard everything Reiko and Cassidy had discussed. She'd been standing right there. And she'd filed it all away, yeah. And she might have googled the company Scentsibilities last night after Reiko had left and Cassidy was closed in her room. And it was possible she'd learned from that Google search that Scentsibilities was a two-million-dollar company and that Cassidy was one of two owners. Which would confirm she was probably very wealthy and successful.

So why the hell was she hanging out at a run-down camp from her childhood?

"That's what she said," Frankie answered. "No idea why she's here."

"Crazy idea for you, but…" Luthor began, and Frankie knew exactly what was coming. "Maybe you could ask her."

"Fantastic idea," she said with an eye roll.

Luthor kept on working, never looked at her once as he asked, "How long you gonna stay here and beat yourself up, anyway?"

"Why, you got something to do after that?"

"I'd just like to put it in my calendar, you know? So I don't plan anything that day."

She let herself smile. She couldn't help it. Luthor had a way of shining a light while keeping things casual. "I'm not beating myself up."

He snorted a laugh as he grabbed the right wrench out of his portable tool box. "If you say so."

And that was the end of that conversation, which was par for the course. He didn't poke at her all the time, just once in a while. But he knew everything. She had visions of both Eden and Reiko spilling anything and everything she mentioned to either of them directly to Luthor. Probably at the dinner table. There were only the three of them. Luthor's wife had died long ago. Ten or fifteen years, if Frankie remembered correctly. Eden's husband was his only child, and he'd died of cancer less than two years ago. Reiko was their only child and, therefore, Luthor's only grandchild. Frankie was pretty sure that Luthor understood her a lot better than most people, but that didn't mean either of them liked to talk it to death.

The next two hours were pretty quiet. They got things fixed and hauled the old hot water heater out of the basement and into the bed of Luthor's truck, and he was on his way not long after, refusing Frankie's offer to make him lunch.

She checked the newly stained step, happy to see that, thanks to the fall breeze, it had dried more quickly and better than she'd expected, so she put her supplies away and went inside to make herself something to eat. In the kitchen, she saw a note on the counter and picked it up:

Took a hike. Back in a bit. Cassidy

"I don't care what you're doing," she muttered. "You don't have to leave me a note. I'm not your mom."

And then a weird thing happened. Two weird things. First, she realized she *was* happy Cassidy left a note because she would've wondered when she didn't see her. And second, she *wanted* to know where she was going when she walked. Why? No idea. But the feeling was compelling, and without allowing herself to analyze it, she grabbed her coat, pulled on a knit hat, and stuck some gloves into her pocket.

All of a sudden, a hike sounded good.

❖

The day wasn't gray, but it wasn't sunny. There was a slight wind that the trees mostly absorbed, but on the outcropping where Cassidy sat, it was much more apparent. And it was freaking cold.

Yet she sat.

This spot. Yeah, this spot was familiar. She'd found it about half an hour into her hike. She had a vague recollection of where it was, and she remembered that she and Mason had always entered the woods from behind the cabin called Wolf, where the boys—including Mason—slept. Today, she'd done that, entered from there. She did her best to call up memories that were literally from twenty years ago, and obviously the forest looked way different after that much time. New trees had sprung up. Old trees had come down. Paths that were well-worn when the camp was functional were now overgrown and hard to find. But she stopped and squinted and spun and racked her brains to try to remember. And she'd found it.

She and Mason had spent so much time sitting on this outcropping, looking out over the Adirondacks. It was high and, Cassidy guessed, not part of camp land. It was far too dangerous a spot for campers to frequent. Accidents would be far too easy.

But she and Mason had gone walking one day when he was upset, and they'd found this spot. And often during the day—and sometimes at night, which Cassidy realized now had been astonishingly dangerous—they'd meet there and sit. Sometimes, they'd talk. Sometimes, they wouldn't. But they were there for each other on that cliff for three weeks of three consecutive summers. Cassidy didn't have a ton of fond memories from her teenage years, but she remembered those times with Mason, and they were precious to her. She could remember almost every talk they'd had on that rock.

"I hate therapy," Mason said quietly and casually as if he'd told her he hated peas. "I hate that I have to go."

"Why do you hate it?" she asked, curious, because she didn't hate it. "I kind of like it."

"Of course you do—your parents didn't dump you off as a toddler. Your mom has a drug problem. Doesn't mean she doesn't want you."

It was an issue that came up for Mason often. Sometimes, he could tamp it down. Other times, he got so mad, and Cassidy was the only one he talked to about it. She knew there wasn't much she could say to make it better, so she did her best to listen.

"I mean, how many times can we talk about it? My mom didn't want me. End of story."

There were so many things Cassidy wanted to say to that. She wanted to tell him to stick with therapy because it would help. To be honest with his therapist like he was with her. That maybe his mom did the best she could, and letting him go was the best thing. But she knew when it was okay to say those things and when they would send him into an angry tirade. Today was a tirade day, so she kept quiet and let him vent, nodding here and there to let him know she understood.

"How am I supposed to go through life? If my own parents didn't want me, who ever will?"

Cassidy sighed deeply, letting her breath out into the open air where it was cold enough to see it, the vapor rolling away from her and dissipating over the treetops below. They'd had that same conversation several times over the years at camp. Between stays, they'd email each other. Sometimes as often as once a week. Sometimes months would go by before they connected again. But they always did connect. Nobody got her like Mason had. And she was pretty sure she was the only one who truly understood him.

"God, I miss you," she whispered and hoped the wind would carry her words off to wherever Mason was now. So he'd know. So he'd be certain.

A twig snapped not far away from her. She turned her head at the shuffling of leaves, expecting to see a squirrel or a deer. What she did not expect to see was Frankie.

"Hey," she said, the surprise clear in her voice.

Frankie stopped several feet back, her hand on the trunk of the tree next to her. "Hi. What, um, what are you doing? You're not about to jump, are you?"

Cassidy felt her eyes go wide and she almost let herself be insulted until she realized that Frankie could have no idea about Mason. "No! God, no. No, I was just…sitting here. Thinking."

Frankie nodded and wet her lips, and that's when Cassidy realized she was nervous.

"You okay?" she asked.

Frankie blinked rapidly. "Yeah. Yeah. Do you...do you think you could just come away from the edge"—she rolled her hand in a come-here gesture—"a little?"

"Afraid of heights, are you?" Cassidy said, recognizing the signs.

"Yup. Now come away from the edge. Please."

"So you're saying, if I were to slip and slide over, you wouldn't save me?" She was teasing her now, and she was pretty sure Frankie knew it—she thought she saw a quick flash of a grin zip by before Frankie caught it and put it away.

"Nope. You'd plunge to your horrific death, I'm sorry to say. I mean, I'd *want* to save you, but my feet won't let me move any closer, so..." She shrugged.

"I'd be a goner."

"'Fraid so."

"Well. Can't have that." Cassidy slid herself back from the edge until there was room to stand. She did so and was surprised when Frankie grasped her by the arm and pulled her farther from the cliff. Her sigh of relief was apparent. "Wow. You really were scared."

"I hate heights."

"Yet you choose to live in the mountains." Cassidy squinted at her. "Interesting."

"I don't live here," Frankie said as she turned on her heel and headed back into the woods. "I'm only here temporarily."

"Oh? How come?"

As if the Fates orchestrated things so she wouldn't get an answer to her question, Duke came bounding through the trees in his neon orange vest, not stopping at all until he was on his hind legs, his front paws up on Frankie as if he was trying to hug her.

"There's my boy," Frankie said as she dropped to her knees on the cold ground and loved on the dog. Cassidy watched in surprise as Frankie became more animated than she'd seen her. Baby talk, playful shoves, scratches, and hugs ensued. It was adorable, and Cassidy couldn't help but stand there and smile until Jack came through the trees to join them.

"Had a feeling it was you, the way he broke into a spring," Jack said, his eyes on his dog and Frankie, practically rolling in the leaves together. Then he raised his eyes, and his gaze met Cassidy's. "Hi again."

"Hey, Jack. How are you today?"

"Can't complain," he said. "Can't complain." The three of them were quiet for a moment before Jack glanced up at the sky, which had turned gray like dull steel. "Gonna snow tonight, I think."

Frankie agreed from her spot on the ground. "Calling for it."

"You got enough firewood?" Jack asked.

"I'm in pretty good shape," Frankie told him. "Gonna chop some more this afternoon."

Cassidy almost laughed out loud as she watched them converse. Neither of them made eye contact. Frankie's focus was on Duke. Jack was looking at trees and leaves and the ground. It was like they were purposely avoiding eye contact, though she was pretty sure this was just normal for them. Loners.

Finally, Jack looked her way, then over her shoulder. With his chin, he gestured behind her. "You sittin' over there?"

She nodded.

"You spent a lot of time there as a camper." He said it matter-of-factly, and Cassidy felt her eyes widen.

"How could you possibly remember that?" she asked, slightly unnerved.

"You and that skinny boy came here late at night." His voice went kind of soft, like he was watching a memory. As if talking to himself he whispered, "What was his name? Tall. Kind of intense, but internally. Rarely outward..."

"Mason." Cassidy's regular voice seemed loud compared to his whispers. And now Frankie was watching her.

"Mason!" Jack snapped his fingers. "That's it. Seemed like a nice kid with a lot on his mind."

"He was."

Frankie stood, and Cassidy got the impression she felt a need to break up this party. With a glance toward Cassidy, she said, "I'm headed back. You?"

"Sure," Cassidy said with a nod, and she gave Duke a pat on his big head as she passed him.

"Take care, Jack," Frankie said as they headed in the opposite direction. "Stay warm, okay?"

"Back atcha," was Jack's reply, and then he and Duke forged ahead farther into the woods.

They walked in silence for a few moments before Frankie spoke. "Listen, I know he can come across as kind of creepy, but Jack has a memory like a steel trap. It may seem weird and suspicious when he names names or says he remembers you, but he really does. And he remembers everybody, not just you and your friend. I've heard him tell stories of the camp at so many different times, and he always has names, descriptions, very detailed conversations from the campers." She held a branch aside so it didn't hit Cassidy in the face. "I don't think he realizes how very stalkery he sounds sometimes, but in reality, I think he's got some kind of gift." She tapped her temple and Cassidy took it to mean mentally.

Relief washed through her. She had to admit it. "Okay, whew. I feel better. You're right, I was starting to get kind of weirded out by the things he recalled."

"I could tell by the look on your face."

They walked for a few more minutes before the woods ended and they found themselves behind the cabins.

"So, you came here when you were a kid?" Frankie asked.

"Three years in a row." Cassidy let go of a sigh. "I loved it here. It was the only thing I could count on. And as a foster kid, when you found something you could count on, you grabbed it with both hands and held on tight."

"A foster kid, huh? That must've been hard."

In the past fifteen minutes, Frankie had said more words than the entire time Cassidy had been there. And for some reason, she wanted to keep her talking. Her voice was a little deep. Kind of husky. A little smokey. "Wasn't easy, that's for sure. But I managed. I didn't have a great childhood, but I had it better than some."

"Better than Mason?" Frankie asked.

Cassidy didn't usually talk about Mason. It seemed somehow disloyal. Even now that he was gone, she hesitated. But Frankie seemed to carry pain of her own, and somehow, Cassidy knew if she could trust anybody with Mason, it was her. "Mason had a rough time. I think it's harder on boys. Especially Black ones. He was written off so many times, and I think that just…makes you angry, you know?" They crossed the expanse of lawn, the lush green of summer grass having shifted to the dull green-gray of fall grass, and she was sure Frankie and Jack were right about the snow—she could smell it in the air, like a frozen sweetness. Even after living in California for years, she still knew what impending snow smelled like.

"I imagine it would," Frankie said as they reached the back door of the main house. She held the door open for Cassidy. "I need to grab some more firewood. I want to be ready for the snow."

"Let me help," Cassidy said, and Frankie half shrugged, then led her around to a small lean-to that she hadn't noticed before. Stacks of logs were piled under the slanted roof. Cassidy held out her arms and Frankie put three logs into them. She tipped her head to the side. "Three? That's it?"

"You want more?"

"Yes, I want more. I'm stronger than I look."

Was that a smile that zipped across Frankie's face? "Yes, ma'am." Three more logs were added to her armload.

"One more."

Frankie picked up a piece that was no more than a twig and set it on top, and Cassidy burst out laughing.

Did Frankie Sisto have a sense of humor after all?

"I was going to throw a Lean Cuisine in the microwave," Cassidy said later that night when it had gotten dark. "Want one?"

Frankie wasn't used to eating on a regular schedule. But that was mostly because she wasn't used to having somebody else in the house with her. And also, she didn't eat much. It had been almost two months of flying solo, so having Cassidy there threw a wrench into everything. Also, a Lean Cuisine? No, thank you. She was getting the fire going and had her back to the kitchen, so Cassidy couldn't see her grimace.

"I'm good, thanks." She could hear Cassidy rattling around in there, and then her own stomach grumbled, the traitor. She *was* hungry, but she wasn't going to eat that processed crap, and she couldn't very well make herself something in front of Cassidy. "Damn it," she muttered as she pushed to her feet and headed for the kitchen.

Cassidy had a box in her hand—chicken Alfredo, by the looks of the front—and was studying the microwave. She looked up as Frankie entered the room. "I think this microwave is older than I am."

"I wouldn't be surprised." Frankie crossed to the fridge and took out a carton of eggs. "Listen, I'm gonna make an omelet. I can just as easily make two." Her gaze moved to the box in Cassidy's hand. "Then you don't have to eat…that."

Was Cassidy blushing? She looked away and moved to the freezer. "I've never learned to cook," she said quietly, and it clearly embarrassed her.

"No?"

Cassidy shook her head, and Frankie wanted to smack herself. Cassidy probably hadn't had somebody to teach her. *Jesus, Frankie, why don't you shine a freaking spotlight on that.*

"Well." Frankie cleared her throat. "Lucky for you, I know how. And eggs are easy." Frankie grabbed the large frying pan from a lower cupboard, and the words were out of her mouth before she could even think about them. "I'll teach you."

And Cassidy's face lit right up. Just lit up, like a kid. They were just eggs, but she seemed thrilled. And something about that warmed Frankie from the inside. She directed her to grab the mushrooms and mozzarella from the fridge as she gathered cherry tomatoes from the bowl on the counter, and the water glass on the windowsill that contained the remains of a bunch of fresh basil.

"Okay. The key to a good omelet is you have to cook up the veggies first. If you throw them in with the eggs, they won't cook enough."

"Got it."

On a cutting board, she showed Cassidy how to chop up the mushrooms and then sliced the tomatoes in half.

"And I don't care what anybody says, butter is the way to go here." She tossed a pat of butter into the pan, and they stood side by side, watching it melt. "Repeat after me—butter makes everything better."

Cassidy grinned and said the words back to her.

"Good. Now, throw the veggies in."

"All of them?"

"All of them."

Into the pan went the mushrooms and tomatoes, the satisfying sizzle filling the air.

"I'm out of garlic, or we'd have used some of that." Frankie made a mental note to get more.

It had been so long since she'd cooked for somebody—longer than she cared to think about—and it felt good. She didn't want to think about *that* either. Cassidy was a good student, watching, listening, doing as instructed, asking questions.

Also, she smelled wonderful. Like sandalwood and something else Frankie couldn't quite pinpoint.

"This is easy," Cassidy said, once the eggs were stiffening up. Her eyes were big, her smile wide.

"Told you." And for the first time in longer than she could remember, Frankie was actually enjoying spending time with another person. Cassidy's excitement was contagious, and Frankie felt it, let it wash over her. They dumped the veggies onto the cooked egg, sprinkled cheese and basil, and then Frankie carefully folded it over. Cassidy held a plate, and Frankie slid the omelet onto it like the pro she was.

"This is amazing," Cassidy said, the pleasure clear in her voice. "If it tastes half as good as it looks…"

"It will. I promise. The fresh basil makes it." She cut the omelet down the center and transferred the second half to another plate, added a couple basil leaves on top to complete the presentation, then held up two forks. Cassidy took one and they sat down.

Then Cassidy jumped right back up. "Wait. I don't know about you, but I could use a glass of wine. You shared your eggs, so I'll share my wine. Yeah?"

"Great."

Cassidy scanned the several bottles she'd amassed in the corner, then glanced back. "Since you seem to know about cooking, do you have a pairing preference?"

Frankie didn't even need to stop and think about it. She loved wine and food pairing. "Well, the ideal complement would be a sparkling wine because of the acidity." She pointed her fork. "But that sauv blanc you've got there will do nicely."

Five minutes later, they were seated at the old dining room table and eating their eggs in happy silence. Well, silent except for the humming sounds of approval Cassidy made with pretty much every bite.

"This is, hands down, the best omelet I have ever had," she said happily. "And I've eaten in some pretty fabulous restaurants."

The praise wrapped around Frankie like a warm blanket. It was unexpected, that feeling. "I'm glad," she said.

"How'd you learn to cook?"

"I went to culinary school."

Cassidy's brows rose. "You did?" At Frankie's nod, she seemed to put the pieces together. "Reiko said you're a chef."

Another nod.

"So…" And then the next logical question. "What are you doing up here in the middle of nowhere all alone?"

"I needed a break. Some time." That was as detailed as she was ready to be, and something in her face must've broadcast that because Cassidy studied her for a moment, nodded, and didn't ask anything more about it. Thank God.

A few more moments of silence went by. They finished eating, and Cassidy gave a slight shiver as she sipped her wine.

"Chilly in here, isn't it?" Frankie asked. "Like I said, the furnace is old, so I tend to stoke up the fire so it doesn't have to work so hard."

"Why don't you get that going, and I'll clean up the kitchen?" Cassidy stood without waiting for a response and grabbed the plates. Frankie headed into the living room.

Building a fire was something she'd come to enjoy. The precision of it. The stacking of kindling, the placement of the first flames, watching it catch and grow, and adding more logs, one at a time. It had become one of her favorite things to do here, and she did it nightly. There was a peace to it.

By the time Cassidy returned with both wineglasses topped off, Frankie had the fire roaring.

"It's snowing," Cassidy said quietly as she handed Frankie her glass.

She was right. Big, fat flakes had begun to fall, just as the forecast said. They sat quietly, sipping their wine and watching out the big window.

"It's beautiful," Cassidy said, her voice barely a whisper, as if she was afraid of disturbing the scene before them.

Frankie turned to look at her, and her breath caught in her lungs. The moon was full, and it cast a blueish light through the window. Combined with the light from the fire, Cassidy looked warm. Inviting. Beautiful. Her profile was soft—straight nose, small chin, full lips—and something stirred in Frankie. Something that had lain dormant for a long time now.

The moment was broken when Cassidy turned to look at her, and

Frankie felt caught. Quickly, she smiled and said, "Forgot to tell you—I replaced the water heater today, so you're good to go if you want that bath."

"Oh, that sounds like heaven right about now." Cassidy smiled back at her and pushed herself to her feet. She'd walked only a couple steps toward the stairs when she turned back to look at her. Very softly, she said, "Thanks for dinner, Frankie."

"You're welcome."

Their gazes held across the room for what was likely a second or two, but felt like an hour to Frankie. She had to force herself to turn away, to return to looking out the window. She sipped her wine as she listened to Cassidy's steps go up and then retreat. A few moments later, the sound of the water running, filling the tub upstairs, could be heard. She continued to sit. To sip. To watch as her brain tossed her images of a very nude Cassidy stepping into the tub. Gingerly, because it was probably super hot judging from the little bit of steam that had filtered out into the upstairs hall. She could smell vanilla. Brown sugar. Something like that, and she wondered if it was a scent Cassidy had come up with, the way she had wanted to bottle the hot cocoa smell.

Right then, the deer and her grown babies wandered across the lawn, looking for food, their hooves leaving tracks in the new-fallen snow. Frankie relaxed into the hammock chair and sipped her wine and watched the deer and smelled Cassidy's bath, and for the first time in weeks, she felt almost content.

CHAPTER SEVEN

Cassidy jerked awake, the same fucking dream robbing her of any semblance of restful sleep. She blinked rapidly, and when she rolled over and almost dropped off the tiny bed, it took her several moments to remember where the hell she was. Then her memory cleared, and her ragged breathing evened out and she lay there, staring at the water-stained ceiling. A twin bed. She snorted in derision.

She'd promised herself when she'd aged out of the foster system and enrolled in community college, taking as many business courses as she could handle while working three jobs, that she would never sleep in a twin bed again. It was double or nothing. At least. And then she'd met Jenna in Economics. Jenna, who hadn't been in the system, but had had just as rough a childhood and had made the same promises Cassidy had made to herself. They'd recognized that they were kindred spirits, had become BFFs and business partners, and Scentsibilities was born. Thank God for Jenna or Cassidy wouldn't be able to be here, doing what she was doing.

What *was* she doing, anyway?

She'd accomplished nothing. She'd been here for three days now but still felt lost and confused and alone. Mason was still dead, and she still hadn't been there for him, just like she hadn't been there for him for the past five years. Okay, more than five, if she was honest. Seven. At least. Probably ten was more accurate.

They lived across the country from each other but talked on the phone pretty regularly. Or FaceTimed. Whichever worked. But then Mason married Emily, and she wasn't a huge fan of their friendship—

something Cassidy never really understood for many years—and they sort of drifted.

The dream was the same every time—Mason calling out to her from every single direction and Cassidy never able to find him. The foggy vapor of a dreamscape made visibility nearly impossible, and she'd spent what felt like hours running around, trying to find the source of a voice she knew so well and hardly knew at all, and she'd wake up fucking exhausted, as if she'd gotten a total of zero sleep.

This morning was no different. So much for the relaxation of the wine and fire and hot bath from the previous night. She might as well have stayed up and run around in the cold for all the pleasure she felt right now. A glance at her phone told her it was barely five a.m., but she already knew she wasn't going back to sleep. Might as well get up and get some coffee. She threw off the covers with a resigned sigh.

She was surprised to see the kitchen light on and smell the wonderful scent of coffee as she reached the bottom of the stairs. It was still fully dark out, and the fire looked like it had burned down to embers and had then been rekindled, the flames licking at some new wood almost cheerfully.

Frankie stood in the kitchen, pouring herself a cup of coffee from the ancient Mr. Coffee, and if she was surprised to see Cassidy so early, she didn't show it. She simply held up the pot and, when Cassidy nodded, pulled down another mug and filled it as well.

"You're up early," Frankie said.

"Couldn't sleep."

"I hear that."

As if by unspoken agreement, they both headed into the living room. The lights were off, the fireplace the only source of illumination, and they took their spots from the previous night in front of the window.

It must have snowed all night because there was a good six inches or more on the ground. Cassidy had always loved the snow, the way it gave everything a clean, fresh look, like the world was helping you start over. Clean-slating things. It was the one thing she missed, living in Southern California.

"Are you warm enough up there?" Frankie asked, and even though her voice was low and quiet, it seemed loud in the silence of the morning. "I tried to build up the fire last night before I went to bed, and the heat should rise…" She didn't finish, just lifted one shoulder.

"I'm fine. Though I almost fell out of my bed a little while ago. Been a long time since I slept in a twin." She chuckled, realizing that, annoyance aside, it actually was kind of amusing.

"Does anybody sleep in a twin bed once they're an adult?" Frankie's dark brows furrowed. "I don't think I know of any."

"Now that I think of it, neither do I."

They grinned at each other for a moment, then sipped in tandem.

"You know," Frankie said, "you could move to a different room. There are a couple in the back near mine. Double beds. One might even be a queen." She gestured with her head in the direction of the bedrooms on that floor.

"Maybe I'll take a look in a bit."

Frankie nodded, and they got quiet again.

That was the thing with Frankie—Cassidy was beginning to understand. She was quiet, and that was okay. She didn't pry. And Cassidy returned that favor. She suspected they were both there for their own reasons, sort of kindred that way. Oh, she wanted to ask Frankie all kinds of questions. Wanted to dig, to probe, to learn all about her. Where was she from? Why was a culinary-school-taught chef out here in the woods of the Adirondack mountains in a run-down summer camp all by herself? She was young—Cassidy put her in her thirties, maybe. She was gorgeous. Not for the first time, Cassidy wondered what it would feel like to dig her fingers into all that dark hair. She had people. Besides Reiko and Eden, Cassidy had seen Frankie's phone buzz with texts. Somebody was in contact with her.

So what was her story?

Before she could even think about broaching anything close to the subject, she heard Frankie's breath catch, and she pointed out the window.

"The fox," she said softly.

Sure enough, a fox was slinking across the front of the house. If it weren't for the snow, they probably wouldn't see her so clearly, her rust-colored body with the black legs, her big eyes carefully watching for any kind of predator.

"She's so small," Cassidy breathed. "I don't think I realized." Frankie nodded in seeming agreement.

There was something indescribably peaceful about that early morning, sitting in the quiet, watching nature and sipping coffee as the world woke up, and they stayed that way for a long time. She got up to refill their mugs once, and Frankie stoked up the fire, and then they reclaimed their seats like they'd lived that way for years. No words. Just presence. Cassidy had no idea how long they sat like that until things started to become light outside, the sun eventually peeking over the horizon in a big ball of crimson pink, the trees gradually going from one mass of dark to individual trunks and branches. The birds came alive, flocking to the feeders Frankie had around the property, squirrels helping to clean the seed off the snow.

"I need to fill those feeders," Frankie said finally, and Cassidy wasn't sure if she was speaking to her or just in general.

"I should probably check my phone." She only just then realized she'd left it upstairs. Jenna had likely sent several messages by now and would send a search party if Cassidy didn't respond soon. How strange that it never occurred to her to even check in. That wasn't like her at all.

She was reluctant to let the peace of the morning end, but when Frankie finally pushed herself to her feet and reached out a hand for Cassidy's empty coffee mug, she had no choice. She smiled up at Frankie, who took the mug and headed into the kitchen.

Upstairs, she was right—there were four texts and two missed calls from Jenna, the last one saying Jenna trusted her if she needed time and space, but she wasn't allowed to just go MIA without some kind of a heads-up. That was beyond reasonable, and Cassidy felt instantly guilty—both for not calling and for not caring about her own business right now.

With a sigh, she sent off a text, and Jenna immediately responded with, *You're alive. Thank fucking God.*

And then the phone rang in her hand. She sighed again, did her best to put on her CEO hat, and then pressed the green button.

❖

Frankie's grandmother would be so amused by how much she loved birds now. How well she took care of them, out nearly every day filling feeders, spending too much money on birdseed and suet. Hell, she had a bird book sitting on the end table next to the hammock chair, so she could look up what kinds of birds landed out her window.

Binoculars, too! She shook her head and smiled to herself. She was clearly an eighty-year-old woman in a thirty-three-year-old body.

The chickadees were her favorites.

They were small and chubby and black and white and tough. They stuck around through the winter. No wimpy flying south for them, no sir. They weathered snowstorms and wind and frigid temperatures to sit high among the bare branches and sing their little hearts out. The least Frankie could do was keep them well fed.

She unhooked a feeder from a branch and set it on the ground so she could pour fresh sunflower seeds into it, and as she did, she thought about the last two and a half hours of her life. Sitting there quietly with Cassidy, sipping coffee, watching nature and, eventually, the sunrise. It had been weirdly not weird, and she had no idea what she was supposed to do with that. Her opinion hadn't changed—she still preferred to be there alone, at least until she could figure how to live with her past. That's why she'd taken this job, to be alone. Cassidy Clarke was still infringing on her peace, her quiet, her penance. And she'd had the damn nightmare again last night, which was why she'd been up so early. But there was something comforting about Cassidy's presence, and Frankie didn't want to admit that, to herself or anybody else.

And yet...

Her train of thought was broken by the sound of tires slowly crunching through the snow up the driveway, and as expected, the red pickup soon came into view, though slower than usual, the tires on it old and spinning in the fresh snow. It finally pulled to a stop, and Frankie approached it, Eden in the cab.

"Morning," Eden said, then handed a box through the open window. "Margaret made you some doughnuts." Margaret Brookstone owned Baked Expectations, a local bakery. Frankie met her the first day she'd arrived in Shelton and had been buying supplies to stock up. The second Margaret heard that Frankie was staying at the camp by herself, she'd leapt into something like mother mode, popping up to check on her, bring her baked goods, and subtly remind her that she was uncomfortable with Frankie up there alone. "She says the extra calories will keep you warm."

Frankie rolled her eyes, but it was good-natured, and she added a smile because Margaret meant well, always. The truth was, Frankie's parents would be thrilled to know so many folks in Shelton were looking out for her. It was clear that Frankie had no say in the matter, so she just accepted it. What else could she do? She opened the box to see what today's three flavors were, as Margaret only made three flavors a day. Boston cream, crullers, and powdered jelly.

"How's it going with your houseguest?" Eden asked.

Frankie shrugged. "S'okay."

"She driving you crazy?" Eden clearly expected the answer to be yes. In the two months she'd been at the camp, Eden had gotten to know her pretty well, much to Frankie's surprise. Eden was what Frankie's sister Ashley would call an intuitive, meaning she could sense things, feel things, pick up on the emotions and feelings of others, and be disturbingly accurate.

"Nah." Frankie glanced toward the house, wanting to look away because the way Eden intuited was to look in your eyes. But it was too late, damn it.

"Interesting," was all Eden said, but she drew the word out like she was rolling it around, examining it. And then she let it go, maybe sensing that Frankie was in a precarious spot. "Luthor says to plan on coming down for Thanksgiving."

That got her attention, and she turned back to face Eden, astounded. "Thanksgiving?"

Eden blinked at her for a moment before giving a snorted laugh. "Um, yeah, it's next week. In six days, to be exact."

To say Frankie wasn't keeping track of time was a gross understatement. She hardly remembered what month it was, let alone the exact date. "Wow."

"Yeah." Eden gestured toward the house. "Think she'll still be here?"

It was a valid question, and one Frankie hadn't considered yet. She shrugged again. "No idea. I mean, I don't know why she would."

"What's she doing here, anyway?"

"No idea," she said again, and it was a surprising truth. She didn't know a whole lot about Cassidy Clarke, and that's because she simply hadn't asked.

"Reiko said she's the head of a big lotion company?"

Frankie nodded. "Seems so."

A quiet growl escaped Eden. "You understand that you are the worst at information, right?" Like, you legit suck at it." But her eyes were bright, and there was a ghost of a grin on her face, so Frankie knew she was teasing.

"I know that, yeah." She grinned back.

"All right." Eden waved her away. "I've had enough of you." She shifted the truck into gear but stopped and met Frankie's gaze, her face suddenly serious. "You're okay, though?"

A wave of gratitude for this person, who had known her for a mere tiny fraction of her life but was always concerned for her, hit Frankie hard right then, and she smiled. "I'm okay. Promise."

Eden took a beat to study her face, something that always made Frankie want to squirm, but she forced herself to stay still. Finally, Eden gave one nod, apparently satisfied, and was on her way, leaving Frankie standing in the snow with a box of doughnuts in her hand.

Cassidy had been on the phone with Jenna for almost a half hour, and it was freaking her out a little bit. Not because of the time, but because of the clear role reversal they were suddenly playing at. Normally, it was Cassidy who was demanding and hyperfocused and driven. Today, it was Jenna, and Cassidy felt like she almost couldn't care less.

What was happening to her?

"Cass? Cassidy, are you listening to me?" Jenna's voice held an unfamiliar edge.

"Yeah. I'm here, I'm here. I hear you." She wasn't being fair. She knew it. She'd dropped so much in Jenna's lap. Yes, they were business partners, and Jenna could handle it. She could make major decisions without Cassidy's input, but she didn't like to, and Cassidy knew it. Lately, Jenna liked to emphasize the word *partners*, and Cassidy couldn't blame her. She was pretty much absent.

Jenna sighed. "Look." Her voice went soft, as if she'd made a conscious effort to take that edge away. "I know you're struggling. Grief is hard. It can suck you dry or shove you into a corner you never want to leave. And I want you to take whatever time you need." A pause. "But I don't want to run this company without you. I need you to at least check in, okay? I don't want to have to chase you down."

She wasn't asking a lot, Cassidy knew. It was fair. More than fair. But in that moment, all she felt was irritation. She knew it was unreasonable. She knew it wasn't a good balance. But she couldn't seem to tamp it down. "*Fine*," she said, and it was one bitten-off syllable.

Jenna paused, so Cassidy knew she'd felt it. Jenna knew her better than anybody at this point. She didn't sigh, but Cassidy heard her let out a breath, as if she was resigned to making no more progress on this call. "I'll email you a couple things I need your input on. *Please* look at them. Today."

Cassidy forced herself to take a second before she answered. "Okay. I will." There. She sounded better. Friendly. Grateful. Didn't she?

She hung up the phone and sat there, on the twin bed that wouldn't let her sleep. At the camp that was the only steady place she'd had growing up. With snowflakes beginning to fall again. In the company of a woman she didn't know, who clearly had ghosts of her own, whose space she was inarguably infringing upon.

"How the hell did I get here?" she whispered to the empty room. She should just pack up her shit, get back in her rental, and get the hell out of there. Go home. Back to the West Coast. Back to warmth and sun and unchanging weather. Back to crazed days and working well into the evening and having zero time for anything or anybody else...

Yeah.

That's what had gotten her where she was now, wasn't it? And the weirdest part of it was that she—workaholic, woman-on-the-move, entrepreneur extraordinaire—had absolutely no desire to go back to that. She should miss her company right now. She should be missing the hustle and bustle, the endless phone calls, the travel and sales meetings and pitches. She should be worried about who was handling what because she felt better doing most of it herself. But the truth was, she wasn't. Not even a little tiny bit. And that scared the hell out of her.

Her gaze wandered from her clasped hands in her lap over to the dresser where the wooden box sat. She had so many things she wanted to say to Mason. So many questions. So much catching up. So many apologies.

Except it was too late now, wasn't it?

"I'm so sorry, Mason." The words seemed loud in the quiet house, the quiet bedroom. "I'm so sorry I wasn't there for you." Her vision swam as her eyes welled up, irritating her, but she was unable to stop it. The gentle knock on the door startled her. She flinched where she sat and used her fingertips to wipe the tears. "Yeah? Come on in."

The door opened and Frankie peeked in. It was clear she saw Cassidy's emotion, which had to be apparent on her face. "You okay?" Frankie asked, surprising her.

Cassidy gave one nod and a shaky smile.

Frankie let a second or two pass, and Cassidy had to make a conscious effort not to squirm under that dark-eyed gaze. "It's a commonly known fact that doughnuts make everything better."

Cassidy blinked at her.

"I have some."

"Oh!" A laugh burst out of her. "I had no idea what you were saying."

Frankie smiled that smile, the genuine one from yesterday, and again, Cassidy felt it in unexpected places. "Eden dropped them off. Baked Expectations in town makes them and sent some up."

"The town bakery just"—she made a sweeping gesture with a hand—"sends you doughnuts for no reason?"

"They do."

"How do I get in on that?" Cassidy pushed herself to her feet.

"You stay on my good side, and I share my spoils." Frankie opened the door wider, and Cassidy followed her out and down the stairs.

"Stay on your good side, huh?" They hit the bottom of the staircase and headed to the kitchen where Cassidy could smell a fresh pot of coffee brewing. "I guess you'd better teach me to chop wood then."

Frankie's eyes lit up like she'd just won the lottery. She picked up the box and held it out to Cassidy. "Cruller?"

"Nope." She let her hand hover over the box before choosing a doughnut covered in powdered sugar.

"Oh, she goes for the jelly. That was unexpected."

"Yeah? How come?" Cassidy bit into the doughnut, which was soft and sweet and filled with raspberry.

Frankie lifted one shoulder as she chomped down on the Boston cream. "Jelly doughnuts are messy. And you're...not."

Cassidy tipped her head, feeling a flush of something she didn't want to examine too carefully. "Was that a compliment?" she asked, making sure to keep it light. Playful.

"Maybe." Frankie shrugged.

"Interesting."

And they stood like that, on opposite sides of the stainless-steel counter, looking at each other, smiling, and eating doughnuts.

It was the best morning Cassidy had had in longer than she could remember. "You were right," she said.

"I was? About what?"

Frankie had a tiny glob of Boston cream filling at the corner of her mouth. Before Cassidy could think better of it, she crooked a finger, gesturing Frankie forward, and then swiped her fingertip against Frankie's lips, wiping away the custard. Frankie instantly turned red, and Cassidy rolled her lips in so she wouldn't smile openly about that.

"Doughnuts do make everything better."

CHAPTER EIGHT

The snow let up by early afternoon but was forecast to get worse later, so Cassidy decided to take a trip into town. Frankie had disappeared after their little doughnut moment, and Cassidy had no idea where she'd gone, so she left a note, got into her rented Infiniti, and headed down. Which was the only way to describe leaving Camp Lost and Found. You went down.

The snow had packed into the bumps and ruts and made the driveway much smoother than when she'd come up. At the bottom, she made a right and headed into the tiny town of Shelton.

It really was like a little storybook town right out of a Hallmark movie. One traffic light, one strip of shops, bars, and restaurants down the center of town. The sky had cleared, and the sun was shining now, and Cassidy slipped on her Ray-Ban aviators, parked the SUV, and decided to wander. A cute little gift shop had journals and nice pens and stationery in one display, and she thought about how she used to journal as a teen, how the therapist she'd had for a while suggested it in order to empty her head of all the confusing thoughts that clogged it. She'd taken to it, much to her own surprise, found it really did help. She'd always had a journal with her, but only one because she never knew where she'd end up or who might go through her stuff. The last thing she wanted was anybody else reading her private thoughts, worries, frustrations, anger, taking them out of context, using them against her. So she'd kept a small journal in her bag at all times, jotted in it regularly, and then when it was full, she'd find a dumpster or public garbage can somewhere, tear the pages out, crumple them up, and throw all of it away. As she stood in front of the window, she wondered what it would be like to have kept those old journals, to look back and read where her head was at during different times in her life. Where her heart had been.

Into the shop she went.

About twenty minutes later, she came out with a bag and continued down the street. She didn't realize she was following her nose—and the wonderful smell of cinnamon—until she ended up at the glass double doors of a place called Baked Expectations. She remembered the name from Frankie and the doughnuts earlier.

"Well, of course, I'm going in," she said to nobody and pulled the door open.

And walked into heaven, apparently.

How in the world did a tiny town like Shelton warrant such a glorious bakery? That was her first question. It wasn't huge, but every square inch was used. Packed, really. Small display cases gleamed in the overhead lighting, showcasing cookies and muffins and doughnuts, oh my. Not a huge selection, but a handful of each that all looked delectable.

"Hi there," came a friendly voice.

Cassidy glanced around, saw nobody, and was about to question her own sanity when a redhead popped up from behind the cookies, a smiling woman that Cassidy put somewhere in her forties.

"Hi," she said back, smiling because it was impossible not to smile at this woman.

"Started out kinda gross, but it's gorgeous out there now." The woman slid a tray of macarons farther to one side, making a space for an additional tray. She turned away, then back with a tray of what looked like chocolate chip cookies with M&M's pressed into them. Cassidy's mouth watered.

"It is. The sun is making the snow sparkle. I love that." She pointed. "I also love chocolate chip cookies, especially when they have M&M's on them, so I'm going to need a couple of those."

"Good choice," the woman said. "Fresh out of the oven."

"Well, if they're half as good as your doughnuts, I'm in for a treat."

The woman squinted slightly at her, and then her eyes opened wide. "Oh, you're up at the camp, right? With Frankie?" Cassidy's surprise must have shown on her face because the woman shrugged, shot her a look of sheepish apology, and said, "Sorry, small town," by way of explanation. "Everybody knows everything."

"Listen, I have no idea if those doughnuts were meant to be shared, but Frankie was nice enough to let me have my pick."

"And you went with…?" The redhead's eyes danced, her cheer infectious.

"Jelly. I mean, duh." Cassidy laughed. "And it was friggin' delicious, can I just say?" Then she looked more closely at the display case where the doughnuts were but saw no jelly.

"You can just say that all day long. In fact, feel free to stand out on the sidewalk and say it. Loudly." The woman reached over the display case and held out her hand. "Margaret Brookstone."

"Cassidy Clarke." They shook.

Margaret seemed to understand Cassidy's search. "I only make three kinds of doughnuts each day. Town's pretty small, and if I made all of them every day, too many would go to waste. No more jelly today, but the Boston cream is pretty good, if I say so myself."

"Sold."

"What brings you to our little hamlet, Cassidy Clarke, because you're clearly not from here." She didn't go so far as to rake her eyes over Cassidy's outfit as she boxed up a doughnut, but her quick sweep of a gaze was clear, and Cassidy wondered what it was that gave her away. She'd only been here a few days and had already met local people of color, so she didn't think it was her race. "It's the boots," Margaret said before she could wonder any longer.

Cassidy glanced down at her leather knee-highs with the slight heel. No, they were definitely not for trudging through snow, but they were so pretty…

"I have other boots," she said with a grin that she hoped covered her slight embarrassment.

"Thank God." Margaret laughed. "You'd be screwed in those if you went off the road and had to walk."

Cassidy blinked. "Does that happen often?"

"Where *are* you from?"

"I live in San Diego."

A laugh shot out of Margaret like a bullet. "Well, no wonder. Look, as long as you've got four-wheel drive, you're fine."

She managed not to let her sigh of relief seem obvious. "I do."

"No worries then." There was a second or two of quiet before Margaret asked, "So? What else can I get you? Oh! The cookies." She grabbed a small white box and folded it. "How many?"

Cassidy proceeded to point to the coconut macaroons, the pecan sandies, and the salted caramel macarons, causing Margaret to construct a second box.

"Frankie loves the pecan sandies, FYI," Margaret said as she taped the boxes closed. "Are you guys friends?"

Somehow, she'd known this question was coming. How was it that everybody seemed to know Frankie? She'd been there for four days, and Frankie hadn't left the camp. She shook her head. "Not really, no."

Margaret did nothing to hide her surprise. "What are you doing up there then? That place is falling apart. I assumed you were a friend who was visiting her." A grimace followed immediately, as if she knew she'd spoken out of turn, and she held up a hand, then swiped it once in front of her like she was erasing a whiteboard. "I'm sorry. Ignore me. That's none of my business."

"Oh, it's okay," Cassidy said. "I used to go to Camp Lustenfeld when I was a kid. We called it—"

"Camp Lost and Found." They said it together, then laughed. "I went there, too."

Cassidy looked at her in wonder. "You did?"

"I mean, well before you, I'm sure. But yeah. They did a span of weeks each summer where foster kids from all over could come have a camp experience." She raised her hand and gave it a little wave.

"Oh my God, you were a foster kid, too?" Cassidy was thirty-seven years old and had only met a handful of other foster kids in her entire adult life. And suddenly, she had a new affinity for this baker.

Margaret nodded as she rang up Cassidy's cookies. "I loved it here so much, I relocated here after school. I actually worked for the Lustenfelds for a couple years doing odd jobs until I was able to save up and get myself a small business loan to open this place. I owe them. Big-time."

"That's amazing."

"Yeah, I love it here. It's a great little town." She ran Cassidy's credit card and handed it back to her. "What do you do?"

"I run a business, too," she said, not wanting to overshadow Margaret's small bakery with her national brand. Instead, she held her fist toward Margaret and said, "To women business owners everywhere." Margaret bumped her.

"Well, I sure am glad to meet you. I don't know how long you're staying, but I hope I see you again."

Cassidy smiled back at her. "I hope so, too." And then she took her boxes of way too many cookies and doughnuts and left the bakery, feeling just a little bit sad to do so. Once tucked back into her car, she hit the ignition and got the heat going, then opened a box and took out a chocolate chip cookie. It had mostly cooled, but the chocolate chips were still warm and the M&M's were still melty, and it was every single thing she hoped it would be. "Oh my God," she said. "So good."

She ate the whole thing—and it was not a small cookie—then tried one of the salted caramel macarons before shifting the car into gear and heading back toward Camp Lost and Found. She'd come here for a reason. Well, for a couple reasons, and it was about time she started to focus on those things.

The sun had disappeared behind the thick clouds that were moving in, and she found herself wondering what Frankie was up to. It was going to snow again, she could see it in the sky, and the last thing she wanted was to be jinxed by Margaret and end up having to trudge through snow in her five-hundred-dollar leather boots. She was glad to be heading back to camp and to Frankie.

Wait. What?

She glanced at the enormous amount of baked goods she'd purchased, specifically to share, and thought about the quiet warmth of the living room, fire roaring, snow falling outside the window, and something in her just…settled. It was the only way to describe it.

She turned onto the driveway that would take her up.

❖

Frankie often wondered if she'd still be a chef if what had happened hadn't happened. She hadn't loved the hours, so there was that. She'd worked in a couple different restaurants but never really gelled there. She'd never been a night owl, so working into the wee hours was rough. When she'd found herself tempted to use a little pharmaceutical help, she knew she should probably start making some changes. And then the accident happened, and everything had changed anyway.

She lifted the ax over her head and let the weight of it lead her swing down. The log split like it was made of clay, not wood. She'd gotten really good, thanks to Luthor's lessons. Her dad would be proud. And not only was it a good workout, but it was a great way to take out frustrations. And Jesus, Mary, and Joseph, did she have some of those.

The sound of tires crunching on the snow made its way around the house and back to her, and she knew Cassidy had likely returned. Which made her happy. Which, in turn, made her feel guilty.

She swung the ax again, then turned the log, then swung again, did her best to lose herself in the physical activity until her arms felt rubbery and her shoulders burned. When she stopped to catch her breath, there was no sound other than nature. No crunching tires. No idling engine. No footsteps through the snow. Only birdsong and an occasional shuffle of branches where a squirrel jumped from tree to tree. She glanced up at the house.

Cassidy was watching her out the kitchen window.

She apparently didn't want Frankie to know that, though, if the way she jumped out of view was any indication. But she must've known Frankie saw her, as the door opened a few moments later and Cassidy stood there in jeans, tall black boots, and a cream-colored V-neck sweater. She folded her arms across her chest, likely against the cold. The hem of her sweater danced a bit in the breeze that had picked up, and her breath came out in puffs of vapor that dissipated in the chilly air.

"Hi," she said with a small smile. "Need help?"

"Just working through some head crap," Frankie said, then instantly wondered why she'd admitted to such a thing.

Cassidy nodded as if she completely got it and then said, "I visited your friend Margaret the baker. Brought some goodies to share if you're hungry."

It used to be that Frankie would pay close attention to what she ate. And then after the accident, she'd nearly stopped eating altogether. Now? Every day at the camp was so physical that she had to eat if she didn't want to fall over, and she no longer worried about eating too much or the wrong thing. Her mother had worried about how much weight she'd lost and had made her promise to cook meals for herself during her time on the mountain.

She would never make a promise to her mother and break it. She just didn't have it in her.

"Sounds great," she said to Cassidy as she leaned the ax against the chopping stump and wiped her hands on her jeans. She followed Cassidy into the kitchen, and a laugh burst out of her as she took in the open bakery boxes that held four doughnuts and what looked to be a dozen cookies. "Wow. Did you clean out Margaret's display case?"

"I mean, I came pretty close." Cassidy looked slightly sheepish at the confession, but her smile was pretty.

"You do know there's only you and me here, right?"

"I do. Yeah." Cassidy met her gaze. "Margaret said you like her pecan sandies. And sugar is the only thing that's never let me down in life, so…" She grinned as if wanting to take away the seriousness that statement could've carried.

"Margaret knows her client base very well," she said as she grabbed said pecan sandy and took a bite. "God. So good."

"Do you bake?" Cassidy asked, taking a tan-colored macaron from the other box. She took a bite and hummed in obvious approval. "Oh my God. So good."

"I *can* bake," she said as she chewed. "I prefer to cook. More freedom. Baking is all rules."

Cassidy nodded. "Makes sense."

"Do you bake?"

A snort. "God, no. I can barely boil water."

"But…" Frankie crossed the room to the corner where Cassidy's dry goods were lined up and grabbed the can of chocolate frosting. She held it up in question.

"Oh." Cassidy's blush deepened. "That."

"I noticed frosting, but"—Frankie made a show of looking around the kitchen—"no cake mix. No brownie mix."

"Yeah." Cassidy wet her lips and finished the cookie in her hand before continuing with, "That's my stress reliever."

Frankie tipped her head.

Cassidy sighed and gave what sounded like an embarrassed chuckle. "Some people choose ice cream or chips or whiskey. I eat frosting with a spoon when I'm stressed out."

"That is *fantastic*," Frankie said with a laugh.

"A good sugar coma is always helpful." Cassidy laughed along with her and then, as if proving her point, grabbed another cookie. "Also, I think Margaret might be a fucking goddess in disguise."

"You may be right about that." Frankie reached for a coconut macaroon and bit into it, the chewy sweetness coating her tongue in deliciousness. They ate cookies in silence for a moment, and it felt like something had loosened between them. Cassidy was studying her as she chewed.

"What are you doing out here all by yourself?" Cassidy asked, just blurting out the question, giving Frankie no warning. There was no accusation, nothing that made it feel like she was prying. Just innocent curiosity. Gentle. Nonthreatening.

To her own surprise, Frankie answered immediately. "I'm trying to lose myself." It was the most honest statement she'd made in months, and she followed it up quickly with her own question. "What are *you* doing out here all by yourself?"

Cassidy's eyes softened and there was a ghost of a smile as she answered, just as quickly, "I'm trying to find myself."

Frankie nodded slowly. "Interesting."

"You, too," Cassidy said. And they stood and looked at each other and ate cookies in silence. It wasn't uncomfortable. At all. It wasn't weird. In fact, it felt exactly right.

Who was this woman? Where had she come from?

And why?

CHAPTER NINE

They'd fallen into a sort of easy rhythm with each other over the next few days. It was almost as if they understood each other a bit, knew when conversation was welcome and when one or the other of them needed to be in her own head.

It was the following Wednesday and Cassidy had spent the morning on her laptop in the living room, sitting on the couch with her feet up on the coffee table and crossed at the ankle. Frankie was outside filling her bird feeders, and Cassidy watched as she moved around the yard. Her dark hair was pulled into a low ponytail, and she wore a black knit hat. Her coat was zipped, and her gloves stuck out of the pockets—it must've been harder to fill the feeders with gloves on. A few inches of snow had fallen overnight, and she left footprints around the property as she moved from feeder to feeder.

There was something incredibly relaxing about watching Frankie move. Cassidy couldn't put a finger on exactly what, but she was riveted.

Something strange had been happening in her head lately, and she didn't know what to do about it. She needed to talk to Jenna, but not until she was able to iron things out in her own brain more. Her work, her business, which had been her sole focus for several years now, suddenly felt like a burden. She was annoyed by the expectations her company had of her while she was away. Her emails were a nuisance. Phone calls that needed returning were irritations. She'd never, ever felt that about her own company before, but now, it was insidious. And she didn't understand it.

She'd been working on a couple of pitches that Jenna was going to give next week, typing away for more than an hour before a line in an email from Jenna caught her eye: *With production being shut down until Monday—*

Shut down until Monday? What?

Just as she was about to fire off an email, she glanced at the date on her screen, and it all clicked into place.

"Tomorrow is Thanksgiving."

She said it aloud to the empty house, shocked by how she'd completely forgotten it was the holiday season. The holidays had never meant all that much to her, likely because of her upbringing. But Thanksgiving was—duh—important to other people, and she couldn't believe it had simply slipped her mind the way it had.

With another glance out the window, she wondered if it mattered to Frankie. She'd heard her on the phone yesterday—couldn't make out the conversation, but registered Frankie's voice as slightly sad and a little apologetic. She wondered about her family. Did she have one? Parents? Children? A spouse? It seemed unlikely, her having a husband—or wife—and kids at home while she lived up here indefinitely, chopping wood and feeding wildlife. But she'd never asked. Maybe she should.

Another half hour went by, and Cassidy had buried herself deep in work when she heard Frankie coming in the back, stomping snow off her feet by the sound of it. When she entered the living room, she had olive-green socks on and was sliding out of her coat.

"Did you know tomorrow is Thanksgiving?" she asked.

Frankie stopped what she was doing and stood frozen in place as if she'd suddenly become a statue, except for her eyes. Those went wide, and she blinked several times before movement continued. "Oh. Wow. It is, isn't it?" She hung her coat up on the wooden coat tree in the corner that looked like it had belonged to somebody's grandmother once upon a time. "I completely forgot."

"Me, too." She gestured to her laptop. "My business partner was going on about production shutting down and I was all, Why the hell is production shutting down? And then I saw the date and it clicked."

"Weird."

"Very." Frankie stood with her hands on her hips looking out the window. Cassidy watched her for a long moment before asking quietly, "Do you have family?"

A slow inhale was followed by an even slower exhale before Frankie answered. "I do. My parents. My sister and brother."

"No...spouse? Kids?"

Frankie shook her head. A beat passed before she turned her gaze to Cassidy. "You?"

She shook her head. "Nobody. The holidays are just regular days for me. Always have been."

"I'm sorry to hear that." And Frankie really did sound sorry.

She shrugged. No big deal. It didn't matter that she'd always wanted a fairy-tale Christmas. A Thanksgiving at a huge table, surrounded by family and people who cared about her. She'd learned long ago that it was safer for her heart if she just let go of all that. Maybe it would happen one day. But the older she got and the more years that passed without it, the less hope she held out. Hey, she'd already defied the odds by becoming a hugely successful businesswoman. What more did she want?

"I take it you're not going home tomorrow?"

Frankie shook her head and a shadow of something dark passed over her face.

"Your parents will miss you." She didn't know how she knew this, but she was sure of it.

A nod. "Yeah. My mom's not happy."

"Where is home?"

"Newburgh. Downstate, closer to New York City."

Cassidy nodded. "I know where it is. I'm from Peekskill."

Frankie's eyes widened in clear surprise. "I thought you lived in California."

"I do now. But I grew up in New York."

And Frankie smiled at her. God, why did she love that smile so much? "Small world."

"Sure is."

Their gazes held for a moment before Frankie broke it. She lifted her arms out and let them drop to her sides. "I'm gonna grab something to eat before I head out to clear snow. You hungry?"

"I could eat," she said and closed her laptop. Work could wait.

❖

"Fair warning," Frankie said as she walked into the kitchen and pulled a pot from a lower cabinet. "I'm making oatmeal. Because I love it. Make fun of me all you want, I'm happy to make you something else. But I am in the mood for a big bowl of oatmeal."

Cassidy looked sexy this morning, and Frankie didn't like that sexy was the first descriptor that had popped into her head, but it wasn't a lie. She was casual in a pair of black joggers and a white hoodie with a cat on the front. Her hair was sleek, shiny, and she wore little makeup, her face looking freshly scrubbed. On her feet were cozy-looking white socks. She was the epitome of Sunday morning at home. Even though it was Wednesday. And she was far from home.

"Listen, I have no oatmeal hate. Only love."

"Yeah?" Frankie set the pot on a burner and reached for the big cardboard cylinder of oats. "How do you like it?"

"Mine usually comes in a little pouch, and I pour hot water on it and *bam*! Like magic, it has flavor." She grinned then, and did it light up the entire kitchen? Because it seemed like it did.

Frankie shook her head and sighed and pretended to be appalled by Cassidy's words, but she did it with a grin. "After you have my oatmeal, those instant pouches won't even come close to comparing."

"Big words."

"You'll see."

Cassidy pulled herself up onto the stainless-steel island and sat there, feet swinging gently. There was something kind of thrilling about Cassidy's eyes on her while she cooked, and she found herself almost performing. An extra flourish here, a little flounce there. She'd made oatmeal enough times that she had no need to measure. Water, salt, boil. Oats, stir, timer. While the oats cooked, she got out chopped walnuts from the cupboard and threw a handful of frozen blueberries in a cup, then into the ancient microwave to thaw.

Into bowls went the oats, topped with warm blueberries, a touch of cream, a sprinkle of walnuts, and a drizzle of honey. She sank a spoon in and slid the bowl across the counter to Cassidy. "Madame, your breakfast."

Before she had a chance to take one bite, though, the back door opened, causing them both to jump in surprise.

"I smell oatmeal," Reiko said as she pushed the fur-lined hood of her parka off her head. "Did you save me any?"

Frankie watched Cassidy's face for a moment, wondering if she'd be annoyed by the girl's sudden presence, but she only smiled and said, "Hi, Reiko. How's life?"

"Meh." She leaned her forearms on the counter.

Cassidy nodded as if that one word said it all. And it kinda did.

Frankie slid her own bowl toward Reiko. "Here. I can make more. Why aren't you in school?"

"We're off the rest of the week."

"Text your mother."

Reiko groaned like Frankie had asked her to clean the entire kitchen, but she pulled out her phone and tapped out a text.

"So, how long have you guys known each other?" Cassidy asked, looking from one of them to the other.

Frankie had her back to them, making another batch of oatmeal as she spoke. "Pretty much the first or second day I was here, she popped up. Scared the hell out of me."

Reiko laughed. "No, *you* scared the hell out of *me*." Frankie turned and grinned at her as she continued to talk. "I always came up here. Since I was young." Cassidy chuckled at that. "Anytime my mom drives me crazy. This is my escape place. Imagine my surprise when I made a regular trip up here to clear my head—*alone in the quiet*—and found this *loser* in my happy place."

"Meanwhile," Frankie added, "I'm up here trying to be *alone in the quiet* and *this* weirdo shows up out of nowhere." She gave Reiko a playful shoulder shove. "And she didn't tell her mother. So, we're sitting here chatting. Or, rather, Reiko's chatting and my ears are bleeding"— Reiko flipped Frankie the bird, which made her laugh—"and Eden comes screeching up here at eighty miles an hour, completely frantic."

Reiko rolled her eyes dramatically and made a *pfft* sound.

"That's how Eden and I met."

"And the rest is history?" Cassidy asked. She took a bite of her oatmeal, and Frankie watched her face as it went from happy surprise to delicious contentment. "This is amazing," she said to Frankie. "Seriously."

Praise from Cassidy went right into Frankie's heart...and then shot south. She rolled her lips in and bit down on them. Thank God the oatmeal on the stove needed stirring and she could turn her back. Because what the hell, Francesca?

"Are you escaping your mother right now?" Cassidy asked, and Frankie was grateful she clearly hadn't noticed the effect her words had.

"When am I not?" Reiko shoved a huge spoonful of oatmeal into her mouth, and Frankie watched with amusement as she clearly tried to pretend it wasn't burning her mouth.

"That just came off the stove, you know," she said.

Reiko shrugged, even as her eyes watered.

Kids, man. Frankie shook her head.

"Anyway," Reiko said once she'd swallowed the bite, "I keep trying to get Frankfurter here to take me back to New York City with her, but she keeps ignoring me."

Frankie stirred the new batch of oatmeal and said nothing.

"See?" Reiko said.

Cassidy laughed. "I suspect your mom would have something to say about that."

Reiko made a sound very close to a snort. "She wouldn't care."

"Spoken like a true twelve-year-old," Frankie said.

"Twelve and three quarters," Reiko corrected her firmly. There was quiet for a moment before Reiko added, "Oh, Mom wanted me to remind you about tomorrow. She said we eat at one." She pointed her spoon at Cassidy. "And you're supposed to come, too."

Cassidy's gaze met Frankie's, her dark brows raised in question, and it took Frankie a few seconds of blinking to remember what tomorrow was.

"Oh! We were invited to Thanksgiving dinner. I forgot."

"Mom said you probably did. Thus"—she stepped back from the counter and bowed deeply—"me."

Frankie looked at Cassidy, their gazes held, and it felt almost as if they were having a wordless conversation just with their eyes. She asked Cassidy if she wanted to go, and Cassidy replied with a smile and a very subtle half shrug coupled with one nod.

And for the first time in many, many months, Frankie found herself looking forward to something.

What to do with that?

CHAPTER TEN

I can't believe ur not coming home for Thanksgiving.
Frankie blinked at the text from her sister, Ashley. It was barely eight o'clock in the morning. She didn't need to be scolded by her big sister, true, but she'd expected it. Before she could respond, another text came through.

Are you trying to break Mom's heart?

That was followed by a broken heart emoji, just in case she wasn't getting the point Ash was trying to make, and Frankie felt the intensity of her own guilt. She sighed, debating whether to answer her sister or just call her mom. She definitely needed to call. Had planned on it. Of course she had. Holidays were important in her family, and her absence would be keenly felt, especially by her mother.

She listened for Cassidy moving around upstairs but heard nothing. Maybe she was still asleep. Frankie closed the door to her room and sat on the edge of the bed, gearing up. She watched the time on her phone click from seven fifty-seven to seven fifty-eight and let a small groan escape. It wasn't going to get easier just because she waited longer. Best to get it done.

She dialed.

"Frankie?" came her mother's voice after barely one ring. "You okay?"

"I'm fine, Ma. Hi." Her shoulders relaxed and she felt at least a fraction of the tension she'd been carrying for the past eight months ease up just a touch. Her mother's voice could do that for her. Always had.

"Hi, baby. How are you? I'm doing my best not to call and bug you all the time, but I worry. You know? How are you?"

"I'm okay. I'm doing okay."

"I don't like that you're up there all alone. Keeps me up at night."

They'd had this exact conversation no less than ten times since Frankie's arrival at the camp, but she knew it made her mother feel better to voice it, so she nodded and reassured her as best she could.

"I know, Ma. But hey, listen, I'm not alone anymore."

"What? Who's there?"

"There's a guest here. A woman who used to go to camp here when she was a kid."

"Really?" There was a pause, and she could totally picture her mother's face, brow furrowed, lips pursed. "I thought the place was closed up. Run-down."

Frankie let go of a small laugh. "Yeah. It is."

"So why is some woman there then?"

"Your guess is as good as mine, Ma, but she's here and I'm not by myself anymore. I thought you'd like knowing that."

"I do. I do. Definitely." There was a pause. "Do you think you'll make it home for Christmas?" The question was quiet. Soft. There was no pleading. No begging. Not even a lot of hope. Maybe that's what made Frankie say what she did.

"I might. Maybe."

"Oh, honey, I hope so." She was restraining herself, Frankie could tell. She knew her mother well. She was the middle child, but she and her mom were the closest. Their bond was tight, and she knew her mother struggled with her decision to retreat. But she'd clearly learned over the past several months what worked with Frankie and what pushed her farther away. So she stayed calm at the tiny possibility of her daughter coming home for Christmas. "Nobody blames you, baby. You know that, right?" The same thing her mother had been saying for months. Her voice was soft and tender, and tears sprang into Frankie's eyes before she even had a chance to feel them coming.

"I blame me, Ma."

"Well, you're going to have to stop that sooner or later, you know." Still gentle. Still tender.

"Yeah." And then there was another silence. She could feel her mother's presence, could feel her love, and that was enough. "Happy Thanksgiving, Ma."

"Happy Thanksgiving, baby. I love you more than life."

"I love you, too."

They hung up, and Frankie sat with the phone in her hand for a good three and a half minutes before she started to cry.

❖

Cassidy was nervous.

Well, a little nervous. After all, holidays weren't really her thing. And spending one with essentially a bunch of strangers wasn't something she'd normally ever do. At all. Pretty unconventional situation overall, right?

At the same time, it was kind of cool, actually spending Thanksgiving with people. Not that she never did. Of course she did. Jenna had her over often, hated to think of her spending any holidays alone. But Cassidy knew it was more for Jenna than for her. She was fine alone. Jenna hated the idea of her BFF spending a holiday by herself and felt like a bad friend if she didn't make her join them. And Cassidy was fine with it. She always went—she adored Jenna's family. And Jenna had been thrilled on the phone that morning to know that Cassidy wouldn't be alone today.

Frankie seemed nervous, too, though Cassidy wasn't sure why. These were her friends, right? But then she remembered that Frankie had only been here about a month and a half before she had arrived, so how close could they be?

They met at the door in the living room. Frankie looked great, casual and sexy. She wore soft-looking jeans and a black V-neck sweater. Her hair was partially pulled back, the rest down in dark curls around her shoulders. She'd applied mascara and lip gloss and she smelled wonderful—both spicy and woodsy—and it was all Cassidy could do not to stare.

"Do I look okay?" Frankie asked, pulling at her sweater. "I didn't really bring anything that dressy."

"You look fantastic," Cassidy said with a smile, and she meant it.

"Good." Frankie's relief was apparent. "And you..." Her eyes roamed over Cassidy, and it felt…God, so many things. Exciting. Familiar. Wanted. Nerve-racking. Like Frankie, she hadn't packed anything dressy, not expecting to need to wear anything nice while traipsing around at a defunct summer camp in the mountains. She wore a pair of black leggings, a button-down top in a deep green that fell to her thighs, and her tall black boots. Her hair was styled, and she'd put large gold hoops in her ears, which went a long way toward dressing things up. "You look incredible. And you smell amazing. One of your concoctions?" Frankie smiled at her, and honest to God, did everybody melt at that sight? Because Cassidy felt like she might.

"As a matter of fact, yes. It's Champagne and Strawberries. Inspired by the movie *Pretty Woman*, believe it or not."

"Well, it's awesome."

"Jenna—that's my business partner—likes to tease me because the majority of the ideas I have for scents are centered around food."

Frankie chivalrously held her coat while Cassidy slipped her arms in. "I don't see the problem," she said seriously.

"Thank you," Cassidy replied with a laugh. "Because there isn't one."

"I mean, I'm a chef by trade. My entire existence centers around food. I might be exactly your target audience."

"You really are." They stepped out onto the front porch, and Frankie locked the door behind them. "I have some samples in my room if you'd like to try any." Something about Frankie looking carefully at, using, products that she invented herself gave her a wash of happy that she didn't quite understand.

"I'd like that."

They took Cassidy's rental, since Frankie's car was parked in a pole barn about two hundred yards to the side of the property that Cassidy didn't even remember existed, and they rode mostly in silence. Comfortable silence, which was one of the things she was finding most surprising about being around Frankie. She didn't talk much, and that was okay. The only conversation was Frankie giving her directions, and in about fifteen or twenty minutes, they pulled into the driveway of an adorable red bungalow.

"Ready?" Frankie asked, sitting with her hands on her thighs, clearly in no hurry to open the door.

Cassidy looked at her and smiled. "I actually am. Which is weird."

"Yeah? How come?"

"Because I didn't expect to be spending Thanksgiving with anybody. Holiday gatherings aren't really my thing. Figured it would just be me." Frankie's gaze seemed to embrace hers. Gently. Softly. "This is better."

With a nod and that gorgeous smile, Frankie opened her door and slid out, then opened the back door and grabbed the three bottles of Cassidy's wine they'd brought.

"They're here!" Reiko's shout startled them both so much that they each flinched, then looked at each other and laughed.

"Kids, man," Frankie said quietly to her with a grin, and then Reiko was there, wrapping her arms around Frankie's waist and jumping up and down, very much not a too-cool-for-physical-affection twelve-and-three-quarters-year-old in that moment.

Cassidy snagged two of the bottles of wine from her as Reiko pulled Frankie by the arm along the cleanly shoveled sidewalk and up to the front door. Cassidy followed, unable to quit smiling over how much Reiko adored Frankie.

Eden met them at the front door and ushered them inside with hugs and Happy Thanksgivings, and when the front door closed behind her, Cassidy found herself inside the kind of warm, welcoming home she'd always dreamed of as a kid. It wasn't fancy by any means. The furniture was basic but looked inviting and comfortably lived-in—an overstuffed brown couch that looked like you could just drop into and stay in for the night, a well-worn recliner in the corner, facing the mounted flat-screen TV. A fire crackled in the brick fireplace along the side wall, the subtle scent of woodsmoke just vaguely detectable among the other wonderful smells of food. A large, framed baby picture of Reiko hung on the wall, surrounded by various school pictures at different ages, her expression more and more bored with each one.

"Your house is lovely," Cassidy said as Eden took her coat. "Thank you so much for having me."

Frankie held up the one wine bottle she held and gestured to Cassidy's two. "I feel terrible that I didn't make something to bring, but we brought alcohol."

Eden laughed. "Always welcome. Sometimes, more than food." She hung up their coats, took the wine from Frankie, and gestured to them to follow her. "This way."

Two hours later, there were five very, very full people sitting around Eden's dining room table. They'd plowed through a lot of turkey, much of a ham, a huge bowl of macaroni and cheese that Frankie hummed her approval over and said it was the best she'd ever had—high praise coming from a chef, sweet potato pie, and collard greens, which Cassidy'd had seconds of and was contemplating thirds. There had been much wine, lots of joking, and some fun and interesting conversation. Eden's father-in-law, Luthor, was one of those men who seemed quiet and happy to sit and watch his family, and every now and then, he'd pull the pin with his teeth and toss a zinger of a grenade into the conversation that cracked everybody up.

"Okay," Eden said, once the table had been cleared and they were all back in their seats with more wine and dessert. "We are now all sufficiently lubricated, as Luthor would say." Luthor held up his recently refilled wineglass. "The kid has abandoned us for the cooler atmosphere of...well, anywhere but near her mom. So, Cassidy. What are you doing here?"

Cassidy blinked. She'd had a couple glasses of wine and was feeling warm and pliable. Not drunk, but in that pleasant place that existed just before drunk. She'd had the best time, laughing and talking with this lovely family. She'd felt closer to being at home than she had in a very long time, and maybe that's why her defenses were so low. She knew it, but she didn't fight it. She picked up her wineglass, studied the ruby color of the cab as she said softly, "I suffered a loss recently, and Camp Lost and Found holds a lot of memories for me. I'm...searching for something, I guess."

She wasn't even aware of the warm hand on her knee until it squeezed her firmly, and she looked up into Frankie's dark eyes. They were filled with sympathy and an understanding that surprised her.

"Oh, wow," Eden said. "I had no idea. I'm so sorry."

"Thanks." There was more to the story, but she wasn't sure she wanted to go into detail about it. She wondered if Frankie understood that because she changed the subject immediately.

"Hey, Luthor, there's a new tree down on the south end of the property. Think you can come by with your chain saw and help me slice it up?"

"'Course," Luthor said with a nod. And then they were off talking about wood and other things around the camp that Frankie might need help with. "How's that furnace?"

Frankie lifted one shoulder and took a sip of her water—when had she switched?—before answering. "I mean, it's hanging in there. Still working, but I don't think it has long. Thing's older than me."

"Well, if it goes, those pipes'll freeze damn quick." Luthor had one of those deep voices that rumbled in Cassidy's tummy when he spoke.

"That's what I keep telling Ethan. Guy's just busy." Frankie's frown made a small dimple near her chin visible, something Cassidy'd never noticed before. It was cute. She stared at it until Frankie turned and met her gaze.

Okay, maybe she was a teeny bit drunk.

She set the wineglass down and reached for one of the macarons on a plate in the center of the table. "Did these come from the bakery?"

Eden smiled and nodded. "Yep. Margaret makes the best macarons on the planet, as far as I'm concerned." Turning to Frankie, she asked, "Have you ever tried to make them?"

Frankie shook her head, her curls bouncing. "Nah. I don't bake."

"Too many rules," Cassidy added, then tossed Frankie a grin.

"Exactly." Frankie smiled at her again, and Cassidy could swear she felt it all the way down to her toes. And in other places. Naughty places. Naughty places that hadn't felt anything in quite some time.

Was Frankie feeling it, too?

The house was cold by the time they returned. It had snowed the entire time they'd been gone, and Frankie had gone out ahead to brush the snow off the car and warm it up while she took the opportunity to cool down. Because, yeah, Cassidy had made her hot. There was no other way to describe how she felt right then.

She was a little bit tipsy, Cassidy was. Frankie could tell by her flushed cheeks and the way her smile never quite left her face. She seemed happy, like she was having a good time, and Frankie wasn't sure what to do about the fact that seeing Cassidy happy made her happy. What the hell was that about?

Frankie had driven them home. Slowly. Very carefully. The roads were slick, and the flakes made visibility less than ideal. She'd never driven a car this expensive before, so she was hyperaware of that fact as well. It would be just her luck to slide off the road and into a tree, wrecking Cassidy's very expensive luxury rental. But Cassidy hadn't seemed worried at all. She sat quietly in the passenger seat with the ghost of a smile still hanging out on what was—Frankie had finally let herself admit—her very beautiful face.

"Have fun?" Frankie'd asked, and her voice sounded loud in the quiet of the cab.

"So much," Cassidy said and turned to look at Frankie. Then a warm hand was on her thigh. "Thanks for being my date. And for driving. I feel okay but probably shouldn't be driving."

Frankie nodded, forcing herself to focus on the road rather than on the hand that was still on her thigh and seemed like it was going to stay there. The driveway was approaching, and she slowed down with plenty of time, then stopped completely as a herd of deer leaped across the road, one after the other.

Cassidy had gasped softly and whispered, "Oh, they're so beautiful," and in that moment, Frankie liked her even more. With a big smile, Cassidy turned to Frankie, squeezed her leg, and said, "I bet they're headed for your salt licks. Ya think?"

"Maybe they are." She turned into the driveway and drove them up.

And now they were in the house, and Cassidy had turned on the living room lamp and wrapped her arms around herself, and Frankie had immediately said, "I'll grab some wood," and headed out to do that. Because Cassidy was cold. And that wouldn't do.

Jesus Christmas, what was happening to her?

Back inside, she had a fire roaring in under five minutes.

"You're good at that," Cassidy commented from closer than Frankie expected. Then she stepped forward and held her pretty hands out toward the flames, rubbed them together, and sighed. "There's nothing like a good fire."

"Agreed."

They stood there in silence as the fire crackled and the room warmed up.

"Hey, can I make a request?" Cassidy asked.

"Sure."

"Can you make some of that amazing hot chocolate for us?" Frankie must've looked as surprised as she felt by the question because Cassidy went on to say, "I just think sitting by the fire with your fantastic hot cocoa and watching the snow sounds like the most relaxing thing in the world right now. Don't you?"

She totally did.

"I'm on it." Frankie held her gaze for a beat before retreating to the kitchen.

"I'm gonna run upstairs and change into cozies," Cassidy called. "You should, too."

Twenty minutes later, wearing gray sweats, a navy-blue hoodie, and thick socks, she carried two very full steaming mugs, brimming with frothy, chocolatey goodness. Cassidy had changed into black joggers and a long-sleeved ribbed white T-shirt. She'd also clearly discarded her bra, and Frankie couldn't decide if the shirt was teasing her or helping her by leaving very little to her imagination.

Cassidy had shoved the chair and ottoman up next to the hammock chair so they could sit side by side, the ottoman centered in front of them. "I thought we could share the stool. If you didn't want to swing in your swing chair." Her teasing tone was clear.

"Hey. That's a *hammock* chair, ma'am."

"Oh, right. Forgive me. If you didn't want to swing in your *hammock* chair." Frankie handed one mug over, and Cassidy took it carefully in both hands. "I mean, seriously, who decides to *hang* a chair in a living room?"

"That is an excellent question to which I have no answer, sadly. It was like that when I got here." She glanced at Cassidy as she circled around to sit. "Meaning, it wasn't me. The chair hanger."

"I cannot describe my relief." Cassidy chuckled.

"It's crazy comfortable, though. I admit I've fallen asleep in it before."

Cassidy looked at her with a smile but said nothing and sipped her hot cocoa. Then she sighed in what sounded a lot like bliss. "I'm happy to report that the first hot cocoa I had was, in fact, not a fluke. Chocolate heaven in a mug, right here. That's what I'm drinking." She took another sip. "Decadent. That's the best word for it. It's magical decadent chocolate heaven in a mug. You should market it. Seriously.

This stuff could create world peace. No, I'm sorry, we can't drop any bombs or fight any wars when there's magical hot cocoa to be sipped."

Frankie chuckled quietly. "I'm glad you like it."

"Like it? Are you not hearing me? I love it. I'm in love with it. I might wanna marry it—it's that good. I could be Mrs. Decadent Hot Cocoa. I could pull that off. I'm the right color, first of all."

Frankie laughed some more. "And you've got the scent down, if that bubble bath from the other day is any indication."

"*Yes*." Cassidy pointed at her. "I so do. See? It may be my destiny."

"Mrs. Cassidy Decadent Hot Cocoa. I like it."

"Same."

And they were quiet, sipping and watching the snow fall and it was the most peaceful Frankie had felt in months. Literal months.

She wasn't sure how much time had passed with only the sound of the crackling fire before Cassidy spoke, her voice soft. "Tell me why you're here, Frankie."

And Frankie turned and met those dark, dark eyes and saw the tenderness in them, the safety, and there was no way she couldn't answer.

"I killed someone."

CHAPTER ELEVEN

Cassidy could feel herself blinking at Frankie. She almost laughed, but the seriousness of Frankie's expression kept the sound in her throat.

"You what?"

Frankie looked down into her mug. Swallowed hard. Glanced back up and out the window. Looked like she wanted the floor to swallow her up.

"Okay, you can't say something like that and not follow up with details." Cassidy forced a chuckle. "'Cause, you know…" She gestured to the window, to the dark and the snow. "Isolated cabin. My phone upstairs. Alone with you. You're not planning to murder me, are you? Please say no."

Frankie turned to her, wide-eyed, as if just realizing what she'd said and how it sounded and held up her hands. "No. Oh God, no." She shook her head, hard, and looked mortified.

"Okay. Good. Yeah, you can't just drop that on a girl like that." What she didn't say was that she hadn't even been the tiniest bit afraid of Frankie. Which was totally weird because, oh my God, she should've been.

Frankie shot her a ghost of a sheepish grin. "Yeah. Sorry about that."

"You wanna tell me what happened?"

Frankie sighed and sounded like she was resigned to telling her story. And maybe she needed to. Cassidy kind of felt that in the air somehow. Frankie cleared her throat and began to speak, her voice low and gravelly.

"It was last March. I'd been working at a restaurant. Busy night. A Friday. We'd been packed, and I was going a hundred miles an hour from four o'clock." She took a sip of her hot cocoa. "The late hours of a chef are the thing I hate most about the job. I thought I'd get used to it, but I always felt so beaten up by the end of my shift."

Cassidy watched Frankie's face. She couldn't see more than shadows and outlines accented by the firelight, but her eyes held so much. She reached out and closed her hand over Frankie's forearm, hoping to bolster her, offer comfort.

"We'd had a large party that way overstayed, so by the time I got out of there, it was close to two in the morning. I was exhausted. And an ice storm had come through sometime that evening. I stayed an extra twenty minutes to clean up some stuff so I wouldn't have to deal with it the next day, and then I left. I was the last one there."

Cassidy nodded, catching a vague idea of where this was going.

"I was driving home, and I was tired, and I just wanted to take a hot shower and fall into bed." She stopped and Cassidy saw her throat move as she swallowed. "I hadn't even gotten half a mile away from the restaurant. I was driving along, and all of a sudden, these headlights were blinding me, and I realized a car was coming right at me with its high beams on. I couldn't see and I tried to swerve, but I must've hit a patch of black ice, and we crashed. Head-on."

Cassidy gasped and covered her mouth with a hand as she squeezed Frankie's arm. "Oh my God."

"My airbag went off, and I remember hearing a scream, and then I think I blacked out for a short time. I don't know how long. When I came to, I couldn't get out of the car at first. I had to climb out the passenger side. It was the middle of the night, so nobody had come. I found my phone on the floor and called 9-1-1. And then I stumbled over to the other car and…"

Tears were silently falling down Frankie's cheeks, and the anguish on her face was so clear, even in the dim lighting. Cassidy wanted to wrap her up in her arms but somehow knew she needed to let her finish.

"They were kids. Just a couple of kids. Teenagers. And they were both gone. I knew it. Could tell."

Oh God. Poor Frankie. Cassidy's own eyes welled up. She kept the physical contact. Wanted Frankie to know she was there. She heard her inhale, the breath shaky. Then she seemed to steady herself.

"They said later that they were drunk. They'd been going too fast. That I wasn't to blame. That it wasn't my fault."

"But you blame yourself." It was now as clear as glass to Cassidy what Frankie was doing up there at a deserted camp all by herself.

Penance.

Frankie nodded. "I do. Of course I do. If I hadn't been there, if I hadn't worked so late..."

Cassidy spoke softly. "If there hadn't been an ice storm, if the kids hadn't been drinking, if the party at your restaurant hadn't stayed so late..." She tipped her head to try to catch Frankie's gaze. "Can you see how many variables there were that had nothing to do with you?"

"They were kids, Cassidy. Sixteen and seventeen years old. Dead before they even lived. Because I hit them."

Because they hit you, Cassidy wanted to say, but it was clear to her that Frankie had heard all of this before, and that anything she said wasn't going to magically absolve her of all the guilt. But God, it had to be so heavy, carrying it everywhere she went—Cassidy knew a thing or two about that—so, instead of trying to contradict her words, Cassidy simply leaned closer to Frankie until she could wrap her arms around her and hug her close. To her surprise, Frankie let her, and as they hugged, she whispered, "I'm so sorry you went through that, Frankie. I'm so sorry you hurt so badly."

She felt Frankie stiffen, but just as quickly, she seemed to melt into Cassidy's arms, and in the next moment, she was crying softly.

Cassidy held on.

❖

Frankie was torn.

She cracked eggs into a bowl, added a little milk and a little cinnamon, and whisked it together with a fork while her brain felt like it, too, was being whisked, all her thoughts and feelings jumbled into a confusing mixture until she had trouble sorting them out.

Shame was first and foremost. Hot embarrassment. Not only that she'd shared her story, but that she'd cried on Cassidy. Frankie wasn't a crier. She hated crying. It made her feel weak, needy. And she'd airbrushed the story ever so slightly. She didn't tell Cassidy about their eyes, what she saw in them.

At the same time, there was a sense of relief having shared her situation. Now she wasn't hiding anything from Cassidy. There was no looming secret hanging over them. She didn't owe Cassidy anything—it was true. She was a virtual stranger. But still, she had to admit that sharing her burden with somebody else had its advantages. She felt just a little bit lighter today.

Not a lot—*let's not get crazy*—but a little. Of course, she knew from experience that it wouldn't last. All it would take was another nightmare and she'd be right back to drowning in her own guilt.

"Shake it off, Francesca," she whispered to the empty kitchen. She could hear Cassidy above her, moving around, the sound of the water groaning through the old pipes and into the bathroom, and hoped she was hungry. When Frankie had woken up that morning, she'd felt like cooking. More specifically, she felt like cooking french toast.

Camp Lustenfeld had cast-iron cookware. Some might look at that as being old, not updating their pots and pans, but Frankie loved it. Cooking in cast iron was awesome. She'd already made herself several frittatas in the time she'd been there, and she knew from experience that the french toast would crisp up on the outside nicely, thanks to the seasoning of the iron.

"Good morning." Cassidy breezed into the kitchen on the scent of warm caramel, and Frankie smiled to herself as she recalled Cassidy telling her she leaned toward scents that were food-oriented.

"Morning," Frankie said and glanced her way. Today, she wore jeans and a blue-and-white-striped sweater. "Making french toast. You in?"

Cassidy poured herself coffee from the pot Frankie had brewed. "Does a bear crap in the woods?"

"Pretty sure he does."

"Then I'll have some french toast."

"You got it." She pointed her spatula at the stools by the island, silently telling Cassidy to grab a seat. She got to work, dipping bread, flipping it over, dipping it again, then into the hot pan.

"God, that smells good," Cassidy said from her seat. She pulled her phone from the back pocket of her jeans. "It's like, warmth and cinnamon and..." She squinted at Frankie.

"Eggs?"

Cassidy's laugh was almost musical. "I mean, yes, but that's not really a selling point for smell."

"Vanilla."

"Yes! Is there vanilla in it?"

Frankie nodded. "A little bit in the batter, yeah. Just a taste." She glanced over her shoulder to see Cassidy typing away on her phone.

"You like vanilla. It's in the hot chocolate, too, right?"

"It's a good way to add some depth of flavor." It didn't escape Frankie's notice that neither of them had spoken about the previous night's conversation. And maybe that was best. "Got plans today?"

Cassidy finished what she was typing, set down her phone, and sighed as she picked up her mug again. "I've got a phone call with my business partner that I'm kinda dreading. Then I'm gonna wander some more. Think some more. Question my life choices some more." And then she chuckled, which smoothed the serious edge in her voice just a touch.

"I was thinking of making soup tonight. Eden sent so many leftovers home with us." It wasn't until the words left her mouth that she realized how presumptuous they were. How domestic. But before she could backpedal, Cassidy spoke.

"That sounds fabulous. This is definitely soup weather."

"Good." And then there was quiet, the sound of the spatula against the pan the only noise.

Half an hour later, they had eaten, the kitchen was clean, and Frankie was alone again, Cassidy headed upstairs for her business call. There was something about having her there, something…comforting. Nobody was more surprised than Frankie, given how resistant and annoyed she was when she learned Cassidy was coming. But now? Her change of heart surprised even her.

She stepped into her boots and pulled on a coat. A storm was coming, and she wanted to bring in enough firewood to keep her from having to go out later. Besides, some physical activity would be good.

❖

Cassidy was not proud of herself.

She stomped through the snow, glad she was leaving tracks so she could find her way back to the camp, since she was walking with no clear direction, just irritated at herself.

Jenna was pissed. Rightfully so. She wanted to know when Cassidy was coming back. Rightfully so. She was overwhelmed, carrying the load for both of them, not to mention there were certain clients that wanted Cassidy. Expected Cassidy. It didn't mean Jenna was any less competent, but clients got comfortable. They didn't like change. And forcing them to meet with, Zoom with, or talk with Jenna instead of their usual contact—Cassidy—irritated them.

What she should've done was offer to Zoom with them herself. Or call them. But the signal at camp was iffy at best, and the last thing she wanted was to promise contact and then not deliver.

"Tell them I'm having a family emergency," she told Jenna.

"You don't have any family," was Jenna's reply. It stung, yes, and it was probably meant to. And she deserved it. "Look, Cass, I love you, and I'm happy to cover for you when you need it. But you've been gone for over a week. You can't Zoom with clients. You won't tell me when you're coming back. It's the beginning of December, and the great news is, we're busy. I want you to do what you need to do out there, but I'm frustrated. *I* would like to be able to take some time off for the holidays."

Cassidy sighed now, her breath visible in vapor form. Damn, it was cold. She'd been wandering for a while now, her brain a jumbled mess. The sky was low, heavy. Snow had begun, but not pretty, fat, slow-falling flakes. No, these were small and they stung her face, and they blew sideways because *the wind.* God, the wind. She'd always been here in the summer, and it was always lush and green and *hot*, so the wind was praised. Needed. Not today. Today, it only made everything colder. It made her face hurt, for God's sake.

The trees being bare, and all the vegetation being gone for the winter made it harder for Cassidy to identify familiar landmarks. Well, that and the twenty years that had passed. She kept trying to picture different clearings, specific trees or rock formations. That cliff had been easy to find because, hello? It was a cliff. But she and Mason had had many other secret spots they'd sneak off to.

And right then, she was standing in one. The giant tree trunk right where the hill got really steep pinged all kinds of memory alarms for her, and when she looked up into the tree, there it was, the tree stand.

They used to sit in that stand all the time and talk. About everything. School. Their foster homes. Where they thought their parents might be. Well, Cassidy's dad, because they knew where her mom was. And then there was that one time when they were seventeen...

Cassidy had to work harder than she'd expected. Twenty years past seventeen meant she wasn't nearly as flexible, but the boards nailed into the tree were still fairly solid, and she pushed and pulled and got herself up so she was eye level to the stand, able to inspect it enough to see if it would hold her weight. Deciding it would, she climbed the rest of the way, took a seat, and blew out a long, slow breath. The base was made of two-by-fours and was just wide enough to hold two people. She got comfortable—or as comfortable as she could be, sitting out in weather that was definitely below freezing—leaned back against the solid trunk of the tree, and remembered the last time she'd sat there.

"What'll you do in the fall?" Mason asked.

"I'm gonna go to college." She felt him turn her way more than saw it. The dark was deep. "I looked into some grants and scholarships. I think I can manage to afford some classes at the community college."

"Where will you live?" They both knew as soon as she turned eighteen, her foster parents would cut her loose, her presence no longer worth it to them.

"I have a couple friends looking for a roommate. And I got that waitressing job. If I bump up my hours, I think I can make ends meet."

She'd been so naive back then. She'd made ends meet, but barely. And her roommates were basically big children. She shook her head now at the memory of just how filthy that apartment had been, how many times the rent had been paid late. Yet she'd stayed for nearly three years because she had nowhere else to go.

"What about you?" she asked Mason.

His sigh was heavy. "I know a guy who owns a garage. He said a while back that he might be willing to take me on as an apprentice. Teach me cars."

"That's amazing. You're so good with that kind of stuff. Taking things apart and putting them back together." It was true. Mason had a science brain, and being a mechanic would be perfect for him.

"I mean, it's not for sure."

"Still."

They'd gone quiet then, just listening to the night, the gentle breeze through the leaves on the trees, the rustling of brush on the ground that told them some small animal or other was on the move. She turned to ask Mason a question, and before she even had a second to comprehend what was happening, Mason's mouth was on hers and he kissed her.

She gasped and pushed away from him. "What are you doing?" she asked. Which was a stupid question because it was pretty obvious what he was doing.

"Come on, Cass. It's you and me. Right?"

She didn't like to remember the rest of that night because the look on his face when she'd rebuffed him...He wasn't angry. He was hurt. Deeply. Even after she'd been honest with him about her growing attraction to girls, it didn't seem to lessen his pain. Add some embarrassment to that and it was just a mess. She'd taken a really nice moment between the two of them and made it into a painful memory for them both.

No, this wasn't the place.

How long had she been sitting there? Had it gotten colder just in that time? Sure felt like it. With a sigh of frustration, she finally lowered herself out of the tree stand and headed in what she thought was the right direction back to the camp. Her footprints were still slightly visible, but the snow had picked up. She needed to get back before it got too cold. A quick check of her phone told her it was after three. How the hell had that happened? Frankie was going to be worried.

Wait, what?

She tipped her head to the side and examined that thought, where it had come from. Would Frankie be worried? Would she be worried if the situations were reversed and Frankie had been out walking in the cold, snowy woods for hours?

Yes. The answer to that was a resounding, unhesitating yes. She absolutely would.

She followed her footprints and picked up the pace.

CHAPTER TWELVE

The wind had picked up and felt like it was slicing right through Frankie's pants. She'd cleaned up some fallen brush, broken it up for kindling, chopped a little bit of wood, but mostly worked on stacking it.

And the later it got, the more aware she was that Cassidy hadn't returned. She'd gone for one of her walks. What she did on those was beyond her, but this was not weather to be out in the woods. It was snowy, windy, and getting dark. Frankie loved the change of seasons, couldn't imagine living anywhere but the Northeast. But what she didn't love was the time change in the winter, the way it started to get dark by four in the afternoon. Especially at Camp Lustenfeld, where the only light was from the house. No streetlights to help illuminate the property. If Cassidy wasn't back soon, she could get lost out there in the dark.

Why was she worrying about this person she barely knew? That was the question, wasn't it. As she sighed and stacked up the last couple of logs she'd tossed in a pile a couple days ago, she heard barking. Duke.

The dog came bounding out from behind one of the cabins, tail wagging, excited to see her. She dropped to her knees and gave him all the love a good boy deserved.

"What are you doing over here? Huh? What are you doing out in this snow?" She used the baby talk voice people always used with dogs, and he ate it up, rolling onto his back in the snow. Because cold be damned if there was a belly rub to be had.

A minute or two later, Jack followed, Cassidy with him. They trudged through the snow, which was accumulating pretty quickly. Cassidy looked less than thrilled.

"Hey there," Frankie said as they came close. "Everything okay?"

"Yup," Jack said. "Just out walking and ran into your friend here."

Cassidy sighed. "I got lost." She was clearly a combination of embarrassed and irritated, her cheeks flushed, her eyes a little flashy. Sexy. That's what she was. And it hit Frankie square in the chest, that realization. Made her breath hitch. What the fuck was that? She quickly turned her focus back to Duke, not sure what might be on her face. "I don't know why I thought I could remember my way around here after two decades. That was stupid of me."

"Hey, you found that tree stand, didn't you?" Jack asked, obviously trying to make her feel better. Because he was a nice guy.

Frankie smiled. "Well, I'm glad you're back. The snow's been picking up pretty steadily. And I need somebody to help me carry in wood." She tossed a half grin at Cassidy, who looked grateful, if she was reading it correctly. "Jack, you wanna stay for a bit?"

Jack was in his usual guy-who-lives-in-the-woods attire: heavy pants, boots, beat-up Carhartt jacket, and a hat with earflaps that Frankie's brain referred to as an Elmer Fudd hat, though she'd never said it aloud. His beard was thick and graying, but his eyes were soft and kind. "Appreciate the offer, but Duke and I gotta get back before it gets too bad out."

Exactly the answer Frankie had predicted, but she always offered anyway. She gave one nod. "Okay then."

"Thanks, Jack," Cassidy said quietly, "for not letting me get too lost. And for not laughing at me."

He smiled at her and—was he blushing?—Frankie watched as he gave a quick nod and turned away, whistling for Duke as he walked quickly back into the woods. She waited until she was sure he was beyond overhearing before she turned to Cassidy with a big smile. "I think somebody has a crush on you."

Cassidy snorted a laugh. "Please. He thinks I'm a pathetic city girl. I had walked in the same circle three times before he rescued me." She sighed. Her eyes were darker than usual, and there was a slight furrow to her brow.

"You okay?" Frankie asked.

"Yeah. Just annoyed with myself." Cassidy held out her arms. "Load me up, boss."

They spent the next half hour carrying firewood into the house, as Frankie was pretty sure the furnace was on its very last legs, and she did not want them to get caught with no supplies for heating the house.

"I put a call in to Ethan Lustenfeld in the hopes he'll step up the timeline on a new furnace." Frankie dropped her last armload of wood on the floor near the fireplace, then turned and helped unload Cassidy's arms.

"The furnace dead?"

"Not yet, but I don't think it has long. It's been making some weird noises today. The fireplace will keep us warm, but it will only do so much when it comes to the pipes."

"Yikes."

"Yeah." She stood and wiped her hands on her thighs. "I bet you don't worry so much about things like furnaces and firewood in Southern California."

Cassidy smiled for the first time since her return from the woods. "Not so much, no."

"Well, if he's gonna put the place on the market, he's gonna need to dump some money into it. I keep telling him that, and he keeps not addressing it."

"He's selling the camp?" Cassidy looked surprised.

"That's what he said, though I have no idea when. It's kind of why I'm here, to keep it standing until he's ready."

Cassidy looked around, seemingly taking the whole place in. "You know, if you put some money into it, it'd make a great bed-and-breakfast. A great getaway for people."

"I guess it would." Frankie shrugged, then looked down at her dirty jeans and hands. Yikes. "I'm gonna get cleaned up. The soup has been simmering for a while, so we can eat whenever."

"I meant it when I said it smelled like fucking heaven in here." It was the first thing Cassidy had said when they brought in their first armloads. "It has been a *day*, and when it has been a day, it doesn't get any better than soup."

"I made bread, too."

"As I was saying, it doesn't get any better than soup and homemade bread." Cassidy stood there and held her gaze—Frankie couldn't have looked away if she'd wanted to. Which she did not. "Thank you, Frankie. I mean it. Thank you."

There was a beat of silence. Of...something. Connection? Understanding? Kismet? Whatever it was, it was warm and solid. Frankie cleared her throat. So many things she wanted to say. Instead, "You're welcome," was all that came out of her mouth.

"I'm gonna go change, too," Cassidy said, jerking a thumb over her shoulder toward the stairs. "Meet you in the kitchen in twenty?"

"Deal."

She stood there and watched Cassidy head upstairs and into her room, then shook herself into motion. She was feeling things she shouldn't be feeling. Things she didn't deserve to feel.

But goddamn it, they felt good. It had been too long.

She headed to the kitchen, gave the soup a stir, and took a taste—and patted herself on the back because wow, that was good—and tipped the bread out of the pan to cool on a wire rack.

She hadn't so looked forward to dinner in a really long time.

Cassidy was quiet tonight.

Not that she was ever loud, but she seemed more reserved than usual. Frankie chuckled internally when she thought that, though. More reserved than usual. What was usual for Cassidy Clarke? Frankie had no idea. Maybe this was really her. Maybe the real Cassidy Clarke *was* reserved and quiet.

Somehow, she didn't think so.

They'd eaten, and Cassidy had oohed and aahed over the soup and the bread. She'd eaten a decent amount. But she hadn't talked much. Frankie's realization came then, that she'd gotten used to Cassidy's presence, to her voice, in just over a week, and now that it had gone quiet, she missed it.

So. Weird.

They sat now in the living room. The fire was roaring. Frankie sat in the hammock chair, not swinging, but moving gently. Cassidy was on the couch—not the chair that she usually pulled up next to the hammock to look out the window this time—and Frankie found herself strangely disappointed. Cassidy had her laptop, her tablet, her phone, a notebook, and a couple novels all piled up nearby, but she hadn't stayed with any one of them for very long. Yes, Frankie had been watching.

"You know," she said, and her voice seemed loud in the lengthy quiet, "this chair is weird and silly and does not belong in a living room." She spun herself with her toes so she was facing Cassidy, who'd looked up from the book that she was supposedly reading but hadn't turned a page of in almost twenty minutes. "But it has really grown on me."

"Yeah?"

"I might put one in my place."

"House or apartment?" Cassidy set her book down, seemingly relieved to do so.

"It's just a little house. A bungalow."

"You miss it?" Cassidy sat back and crossed her legs. She'd changed into leggings and a super-soft-looking oversized hoodie, her hood up covering her head. Casual. Relaxed. Inviting. That's how she looked.

Frankie inhaled and thought about the question. "Yeah, I do. I didn't for a while, but I'm starting to." Then she quickly stood. "Here. Come here. Try this." She gestured to the hammock chair.

Cassidy hesitated for a beat, then pushed to her feet. "Fine. I'll give your silly hanging chair a whirl."

Frankie held it still for her and tried not to inhale audibly when Cassidy got close. "You smell good. What's this scent?"

Cassidy sat. "What do you smell?"

Permission was what she'd been given, so she did. Took in every molecule her nose could. "Nutmeg."

"Mm-hmm. What else?" Cassidy sat in the hammock chair.

Frankie tipped her head to the side. "Hmm. Vanilla? Or cloves. No. Vanilla. Wait. Both."

"And what do all those scents make up?" Cassidy held her gaze, and Frankie felt a weird wave of courage. It hit her out of nowhere, grabbed her by the nose and pulled her forward until she was so close to Cassidy, she could see the tiny flecks of gold in her brown eyes. She inhaled again and it hit her.

"Eggnog."

Cassidy's smile blossomed on her face. "Winner, winner, chicken dinner."

"You weren't kidding about your scents all being food-related."

Cassidy sighed. "I know. It's a problem. Jenna wants me to branch out, but I always seem to be dragged back to things I can put in my mouth." Frankie sat with those words doing naughty stuff low in her body while Cassidy used her toes to push herself around in the hammock chair. "You're right. This is surprisingly comfortable."

Frankie pulled the other chair close and then asked if Cassidy was up for a glass of wine.

"The answer to that question is going to be yes about ninety-five percent of the time," was her response, and ten minutes later, they were sitting quietly, sipping a lovely Montepulciano and watching the continuation of the storm that had begun that afternoon. Cassidy's rental car was already covered. "The animals must all be hunkered down against the cold," Cassidy said quietly as they gazed out the big window where nothing moved but the snowflakes and the tree branches in the wind.

"When I was a kid, I used to worry in the winter. About the animals." Frankie sipped her wine, then let the glass dangle in her fingers. "My parents had to constantly reassure me that the deer and the squirrels and the raccoons were built for winter, that they could handle it just fine."

"Aww, little baby Frankie sounds like a sweetheart."

"Or a dope." Frankie chuckled.

"Worrying about other living creatures does not make you a dope."

Frankie turned and met Cassidy's gaze. Smiled.

"Mason was like that." Cassidy looked back out the window. "He was always looking for the animals when we were here. Squirrels. Chipmunks. Birds."

"Mason?"

The sigh Cassidy let go of was so many things right then. Frankie could hear them all. Tired. Sad. Guilty. "He's the reason I'm here."

The moment felt important, and Frankie wanted to offer whatever support she could. She gave one nod and waited. Cassidy wanted to talk about it, she could tell, but in her own time. In her own way.

Cassidy took a sip of her wine, then gazed into the glass as if everything she wanted to say was in there. "He was my best friend here. Our foster families were in different towns, and we emailed each other here and there throughout the year, when we had computer access. School. The library. Wherever. But when we got here, it was like we'd never been away from each other. Mason just…got me. We got each other." Cassidy's voice was soft, held almost a dreamlike quality. Frankie listened quietly but kept her eyes on this beautiful woman.

"Mason was in the system from way early on. He was left on some church steps when he was just a few days old. My mom was a drug addict who got busted for possession when I was three. She went to jail and then died in there. I never knew my dad or any other family. I'm not sure there was any. Social services couldn't find any."

Frankie's heart squeezed as she tried to imagine how hard it would be to have no family. Nobody who knew you. No history.

"Anyway. I survived. A couple different foster homes, but coming here? It changed me. There was something about this place, about being here with three dozen other kids who were just like me. I wasn't alone. Finally, I knew I wasn't alone. And Mason felt the same way. In the grand scheme of my life, the time I spent here is so small, so short, but had the most impact on me. If I ever meet Mr. Lustenfeld, I'll tell him that."

Frankie'd had no idea the effect the camp had had. To her, it was just a handful of run-down buildings owned by some family with too much money. She felt her perceptions shifting.

"So." Cassidy took a sip of her wine as if fortifying herself. "The last year I was here was when I was seventeen. A few months before my eighteenth birthday. I was starting to feel a bit resentful of what life had handed me. I was determined to make something of myself. To prove everybody wrong." She looked at Frankie for the first time since she'd begun her story. "The statistics around foster kids becoming big successes—especially kids of color—are pretty unimpressive. But I was on fire. I had a bug up my ass, as Mason used to say, and I was going to make something of myself. Show everybody who didn't believe in me." Her gaze was out the window again. Far away. Frankie was afraid to disturb her momentum with words, so she stayed quiet and waited for Cassidy to continue. "Mason and I always waited until everybody was asleep, and then we'd sneak off into the woods." A small chuckle. "I doubt we were the only ones, but it felt like we were. That's what I've been doing on my walks recently. Trying to find those spots, to revisit them." She looked at Frankie then, and the anguish in her eyes was almost too much. Frankie felt her own breath catch in her lungs as Cassidy whispered, "I need to find the right place to scatter his ashes."

That took Frankie by surprise. She hadn't expected the main character of the story to be dead. Wow. "I'm so sorry," she said quietly. "It sounds like you were close."

Cassidy inhaled slowly, deeply, then blew it out. "We were. For a while. I…" She blinked several times and seemed to be looking for the right words. "I could've been a better friend."

Okay, Cassidy was clearly struggling with some stuff, and Frankie was both sympathetic and empathetic. She wanted to offer some great advice, but she came up with zilch. They were quiet for a long while before she remembered something Cassidy had said a while back. "You told me you were here to find yourself again."

A nod. "Yeah. And you wanted to lose yourself." She turned those dark eyes on Frankie.

"I told you why I wanted that. Why are you trying to find yourself? When did you get lost?"

"That *is* the question, isn't it?" Cassidy looked down into her now-empty glass, then held it toward Frankie with a soft smile. "I'm gonna need more wine for this."

She took both glasses into the kitchen and refilled them, then returned to the living room where Cassidy sat gently swinging.

"Want your chair back?"

Frankie shook her head. "No, you're having too much fun."

"It is fun. I didn't expect it to be this comfortable."

She sat back down, took a sip, and waited. Cassidy clearly wanted to talk, but she wasn't going to push her. She'd start when she was ready. If there was one thing Frankie had learned in her time alone here, it was patience and the value of silence.

"The tree stand Jack mentioned?" Cassidy began.

Frankie gave a nod.

"That was the first place Mason kissed me."

Not the words she'd been expecting. Nope. Okay.

"I sat up there today for hours, remembering. That night. The look on his face when I pushed him away."

"You pushed him away?"

Cassidy turned to look at her, her eyes slightly wide. "I mean, I was only seventeen, but pretty sure I was into girls."

Frankie was not proud of the relief she felt at those words. Not even a little bit.

"I was so stupid, though," Cassidy went on. "Here I was, thinking of Mason like a big brother, and he was thinking of me as girlfriend potential. I hurt him. Badly."

"It wasn't your fault, though. What were you supposed to do? Pretend?"

Another sigh from Cassidy. "No, I know. You're right. But Mason, he couldn't let go. And I threw myself into school and work and making myself successful. I wanted out of the stigma that foster kids can have and I went for it. Hard."

"Again, you did nothing wrong." Frankie wasn't really sure why Cassidy was beating herself up.

"Mason got into drugs not long after our last summer here. I felt kind of responsible for that."

"Cassidy. What? How in the world would you be responsible for his decision to do drugs?"

"Like I said, I could've been a better friend. I stuck by him for a while, helped him get into rehab. The first two times." Cassidy stopped, took a sip of wine. "And after that, I just couldn't. My business was growing and I moved to San Diego and we sort of drifted apart—" She seemed to catch herself and wiped her hand in front of her like she was erasing her words. "No. *I* drifted. Away from him. I started answering his texts more and more sporadically. I let days go by between contacts. Then weeks. He finally got himself clean and together and learned cars and became a mechanic, and I think we both tried to focus on our lives." The room had gone dark and neither of them had moved to turn on any lights. But the snow outside the window reflected what light there was, and Frankie could see the unshed tears pooling in Cassidy's eyes as she turned to her. "Do you know what his ex said to me at his funeral? When she told me I should be in charge of his ashes?"

Frankie shook her head.

"She said, *You know why we broke up? Because I wasn't you.*"

"Ouch."

"Yeah." Cassidy blew out a breath as if unloading her story had taken a weight off. "So I brought him here because I think this was the place he was the most at peace. But honestly? There were so many years we were out of touch, maybe I'm wrong." She turned panicked eyes to Frankie. "What if I'm wrong? What if I scatter his ashes in the place that he hated most in the world? God, this is too much pressure." She shook her head and seemed to run out of steam.

"Do you wanna know what I think?"

"I do." Cassidy's response was quick, instant. "I really, really do."

"It sounds to me like, despite your troubles and your drifting, you likely knew him better than anybody. And because of that, I think you should trust your heart and, more importantly, your gut. Something made you think you should bring him here, so I'm willing to bet you're right." She sipped her own wine and added, "And if you're not religious and you want to get into the whole, he's gone and probably has no idea and doesn't care what happens to his ashes, I can go there, too."

Cassidy's laugh was soft, but it was there, and Frankie gave herself a point for causing it.

"I guess you're right. But this whole thing has really made me think about what's important. I've given everything to Scentsibilities. Everything. I never vacation. I haven't had a relationship in years, and I barely date. The holidays mean nothing to me, as you saw. So, yeah. I'm here to try to find myself. Somehow. Which seems like a really ridiculous thing now, as I sit here in a hammock chair on a mountain."

"We are quite a pair," Frankie said after a bit. "Sitting here on a mountain, as you said, battling our demons."

"Certainly is kind of a perfect setting, isn't it? Snowy. Cold. Falling apart."

"At least we have wine." Frankie held up her glass.

"Amen to that." Cassidy leaned toward her and touched her glass to Frankie's.

And then they were quiet. Each lost in her own thoughts, probably. At least Frankie was. Her thoughts about herself. Her thoughts about Cassidy. After many minutes went by and both their glasses were empty, she turned to Cassidy. "You know," she said softly, then pushed on because she knew if she hesitated, she wouldn't say what she was thinking, "I took this job because I wanted to be alone. Because I thought I deserved to be alone. And while I haven't necessarily changed my mind about that, I'm really glad you showed up. I like having you here."

Cassidy's expression changed slightly. Her eyes went soft, and the corners of her mouth lifted just a little. "Weird as it's all been, I'm glad I'm here, too." Their gazes held for a second or two before she added, "Do you want your chair back? I know you end up staying out here all night sometimes."

That was news. "You do?"

"When I do sleep, it's not very soundly. I get up a lot. I've seen you down here in the wee hours."

Frankie lifted one shoulder. "Yeah, I don't sleep much. Bad dreams."

"I'm sorry."

"What can you do, right?" She waved a hand at Cassidy. "You enjoy the chair. I'll sit in it when you head to bed."

"I'm not ready yet. Is that okay?"

What Frankie wanted to say was that she would be perfectly happy to sit there next to her forever. She honestly hadn't felt so at peace in another person's presence in longer than she cared to remember. But she didn't. Instead, she simply said, "Totally okay. I'm not either."

As if orchestrated to match their conversation, a deer walked into view. Then another. Then a third and a fourth.

"Looking for some salt, I bet," Cassidy whispered, as if afraid of scaring them away. "Have you named them?"

And suddenly, it felt like such a travesty that she hadn't. "No, but we should."

"Right?" Cassidy sat forward in her chair.

"You think about it, and I'll put another log on."

What was it about this night? Frankie couldn't put her finger on it. Couldn't explain why she suddenly felt completely at ease with this woman she'd met barely a week ago. Was it their shared traumas? Did they make them feel like kindred spirits? She tossed a log onto the fire, which was burning so hot now that she couldn't stand too close for more than a couple seconds. *One more oughta do it.* She tossed another log, which caught her hand just right to puncture the skin in the side of her palm.

"Son of a bitch," she muttered.

"What happened?" And then Cassidy was right there next to her.

"Sliver," she said, turning her hand at an awkward angle trying to see it, but failing. "I can't see it very well."

"Here." Cassidy grabbed her phone and turned on the flashlight. "Hold this." She gave the phone to Frankie, then took her hand and gently turned it so she could see.

She swallowed hard. The warmth of Cassidy's hands and the fact that their heads were practically touching were doing things to her. Sexy things. Naughty things. She could smell that eggnog scent up close, but also Cassidy's hair, which smelled coconutty. Her face was smooth, almost shocking in its perfection. And her lips. God, don't get her started on those lips…

She swallowed. She had to. It was involuntary and it was loud. If Cassidy noticed, she didn't show it, just used the nails of her forefinger and thumb and worked until she got a grip on the sliver and pulled it out from under Frankie's skin. She was so distracted by every other aspect of Cassidy that she barely even felt it.

"There. Got it." Cassidy looked up, and the world froze.

Just froze.

The crackling of the fire faded away. The rest of the room blurred. Did they stop breathing? 'Cause it sure felt like they had. Frankie's gaze held Cassidy's, her long, dark lashes moving as she blinked, and neither of them looked away. Neither of them seemed to want to stop what was about to happen.

And oh, did it happen.

Frankie hardly had to move, they were that close together. But there was no way she could *not* kiss Cassidy right then. It wasn't possible. Even if she'd wanted to avoid it somehow—which, to be honest, she did not—she couldn't have. It was like it had been set in motion the second that sliver of wood had slid under her skin. Like the Universe had it all planned out from the beginning, right down to this very moment, even when the phone slipped from Frankie's hand and landed with a thump on the floor, the flashlight still on and aimed at the ceiling. They were meant to kiss. Right here, right now. And it was their first, but it wasn't tentative. No, there was nothing tentative about it. They crashed together, kissing hard. Deeply. Thoroughly, like they'd been doing it for months.

How the hell did one woman taste so good?

The question shot through Frankie's head without her even realizing she was thinking it. Cassidy's lips were slick and sweet. Her tongue was hot and wet and held the tang of the wine, and all Frankie wanted was more. More, more, more.

Cassidy whimpered. It was a quiet sound. If the room hadn't been so silent otherwise, Frankie might've missed it. But she didn't. She caught it in all its sexy glory, and it ratcheted her arousal higher. And then Cassidy's hands were in her hair and tugging her head back so she could launch an all-out assault on her neck, kissing and licking and sucking and oh my God had she ever been this turned on this fast in her entire life?

No. The answer to that was a resounding no. She had not. Ever.

By unspoken agreement, they'd shuffled to the couch and sat, and for a moment, they simply looked at each other. Cassidy was so fucking beautiful, her lips kiss-swollen, her eyes way darker than they usually were. Her cheeks were flushed—Frankie could see that even in the dim light of the fire.

And then they were kissing again, but this time, a little more slowly. Frankie wanted to savor it, the feel of Cassidy, the taste of her, the warmth, the way she moved. She didn't want to think of anything beyond that. Just the kissing.

Cassidy was a little smaller than Frankie, and when she pushed in to her, they lay back onto the couch, Frankie on her back, Cassidy on top. And it was perfect. The fit. The feel. Frankie closed her eyes and let go of everything in her head except how she was feeling in that exact moment. Her hands were on Cassidy's back, and just a little movement of her fingers allowed her under her shirt, the skin of Cassidy's back warm and soft, and was that a groan? Was it hers? She felt Cassidy smile against her lips and knew that it likely was.

"I like the way you sound," Cassidy said on a whisper.

"I like the way you feel," Frankie responded. And they lay there, looking at each other for what felt like it might've been a long time. But probably wasn't.

"I didn't expect this," Cassidy said. She shifted her weight slightly so she could bring one hand up, and Frankie felt the backs of her fingers caressing her cheek.

"Same."

"You're a fantastic kisser, by the way."

"Yeah? Well, I think that's something that takes two, and you are no slouch in the kissing department."

"I should get that printed on a T-shirt." And then Cassidy kissed her again, and Frankie was lost. In the best of ways. Just happily, sexily, completely thrilled to be lost.

CHAPTER THIRTEEN

Cassidy was warm.

Not in a bad way. Just in an unfamiliar way. She'd gotten used to waking up in the cold of the camp house, but that wasn't the case as she slowly came to life. She was warm. And comfortable.

And there were warm, strong arms around her.

And then she remembered.

A big inhale coupled with a big smile happened next and when she lifted her head, soft brown eyes were gazing at her.

"Good morning," Frankie whispered.

"Morning. When did we fall asleep?" She lay back against what she now knew was Frankie's shoulder, her arm draped across Frankie's middle.

"We didn't. You did."

Cassidy snapped her head back up, suddenly horrified. "Oh my God, I'm so sorry." But when she tried to push herself up, Frankie's arms tightened around her.

"No, no, it's okay. Lie back down."

Cassidy held her gaze for a moment before relenting and relaxing. "I'm sorry."

"Why? Because you fell asleep?" She could feel Frankie's smile against her forehead. "No reason to be. You fell asleep and then I wasn't far behind. I only woke up a few minutes before you."

The words hung there for a beat before Cassidy made the connection. She lifted her head again so she could see Frankie's eyes. "You slept?"

The smile was slow in coming, but it came. A slight nod. "I did. A good couple of hours."

She glanced down at their bodies, smooshed together on the couch, her body half on, half off Frankie's, and she frowned. "With me lying all over you like this?"

"Yes, ma'am." And then Frankie's face grew serious. "It was a nice change, to be honest."

Cassidy blinked at her before settling back down with a "Huh."

"You will need to charge your phone, however."

Cassidy looked up at her, and Frankie indicated the floor a few feet away where her phone lay, facedown. She remembered the flashlight, the sliver.

"It went off eventually."

"How's your hand?" Cassidy lay back down and grasped Frankie's hand when she raised it. "We should've put a Band-Aid on it."

"Yeah, well, we were a little busy."

And it wasn't that she didn't remember what had happened merely hours before, but there was something about Frankie's words that seemed to open floodgates. And flood she did. Her body flushed hotly, her underwear dampened, and she had to swallow down the lump of arousal that appeared in her throat out of nowhere. "We were, weren't we?" Then she waved a hand dismissively in the direction of the device on the floor. "Who needs a stupid phone anyway?"

She felt Frankie's laugh under her more than she even heard it. The rumble in her chest. The way she moved just a bit underneath her. She lifted her head so they were face to face, their noses just about touching, and she brought her lips softly to Frankie's. Tentative. Gentle. She'd absently wondered if kissing Frankie would feel different in the light of day, but it didn't. It was still wonderful. Hot. Sexy.

The sound of the back door banging open and loud, likely booted footsteps clomping through the house made her jerk in surprise.

"Hey, where's break—" Reiko stood there in her snow-covered boots and puffy coat and blinked at them.

Frankie was the first to move and tried to push herself up off the couch, which made Cassidy scramble off her.

"Sorry," Reiko said. "Didn't mean to interrupt your"—she waved her hand around—"whatever you were doing."

"No, no, you're fine." Cassidy pushed to her feet. "I was just going to go shower anyway." She grabbed her phone off the floor—yup, dead—and found herself unable to look Reiko in the eye. Not because she'd done anything wrong, but simply because of the circumstances.

"I'll get breakfast started," Frankie said, and she seemed way more relaxed than Cassidy, which helped her calm down a bit. "You want some?"

She nodded. "Breakfast would be great. I'll be quick." And she headed for the stairs, forcing herself to walk at a normal speed and not sprint. *You are in control. You have nothing to be ashamed of.* The mantra ran through her head as she climbed the stairs. What she did not have control over was her hand, which went to her mouth, her fingertips dancing across her lips, still slightly swollen from all the kissing.

She also couldn't control the smile.

"Well. That was interesting." Reiko went to the back door to kick off her boots, then slipped out of her coat. Then she came to the counter next to Frankie and pushed herself up so she was sitting on it and could watch Frankie mix pancake batter. "You guys have sex?"

Frankie gaped at her. "Excuse me? You're twelve."

"Exactly. I'm twelve. Not five. I know what sex is. And I know what gay is."

"Oh my God." Frankie shook her head, unable to find anything else to say. Was this really happening? Was this *kid* asking her about her sex life?

"It's just a question."

"A question that's none of your business."

Reiko sighed the way only a preteen could, making it sound like the weight of the world was upon her. "Fine. I will assume that's a yes then."

"No," Frankie blurted. "It's a no." Too late, she realized the trap Reiko had neatly laid to get an accurate answer to her question, and it was her turn to sigh.

"Well, she sure is pretty. You've got good taste."

"We are not having this conversation." She whisked the pancake batter with more fervor than required while the cast-iron skillet heated up on the stove. "What are you doing up here so early anyway? Did you have another fight with your mother?"

"Another fight? No. Same one as yesterday. Same as the day before. And the day before that. She wants me to see a therapist." She said the word *therapist* like it was a swear word. Distasteful.

"Maybe you should. Why are you so against it?"

"Because a therapist is gonna make me talk about my dad, and I don't want to. Don't you have stuff you don't wanna talk about?" She reached for a chocolate chip from the bowl of them Frankie had poured for the pancakes.

"Well, sure. But…" She spooned batter into the pan, four perfectly round pancakes. Yeah, she couldn't begin to tell a child the things she kept hidden.

"I've been in therapy." Cassidy came into the room wearing yoga pants and an oversized hoodie that hung to midthigh. Her hair was newly shiny and neat, and she smelled like eggnog again. Frankie's grip tightened on the spatula. It was all she could do to keep from reaching out for her, pulling her close, burying her nose in Cassidy's neck. "Here's the thing about it that's good." She, too, grabbed a couple chocolate chips and popped them into her mouth. "The therapist? She's on your side. She's not on your mom's side. She wants to help you. And whatever you say is between you two. So it's private." She shrugged. "It really helped me."

Frankie glanced at Reiko, who was watching Cassidy carefully, a slight squint to her eyes like she was concentrating.

"Is it hard?" It was the first time since she'd arrived that she actually sounded twelve years old, and Frankie knew then that Cassidy was getting through. She flipped the pancakes and stayed quiet, let the two of them talk it out.

"It can be, sure. You talk about tough stuff. But that's the point. Talking about the tough stuff so that you can understand it better."

"Huh."

A few seconds of quiet went by before Frankie said, "Plates," and Reiko slid off the counter to get them. She put two pancakes on each plate and told them to sit and eat while she made more. Syrup and butter were taken from the fridge, and a third place was set at the stainless steel island. Frankie flipped the pancakes and turned to look at Cassidy and Reiko, and for a split second, the scene was shockingly domestic—the two of them sitting side by side and talking about pancakes and various toppings, arguing the virtues of blueberries versus chocolate chips—and something in her heart grew. For just a moment, it swelled. Sent a lump into her throat that almost choked her. Cassidy's eyes met hers, and she smiled, and Frankie quickly turned back to the pan, both intensely comforted and freaked the hell out by what she'd just felt, and how could both those feelings exist together?

And then Reiko was laughing. Frankie didn't know at what, but Cassidy joined in, and the two of them were cracking each other up, and Frankie's smile was something she couldn't control. The sound of that laughter was like warmth. Like life. Like joy. It nearly overshadowed the nightmare she'd had early that morning—the reason she'd been awake so early. She hadn't felt such wonderful things in a really long time, and she let it all wash over her as she stood there with her back to the other two. Listening. Smiling. Feeling, for the first time in eight months, something other than dread and self-loathing and sorrow and guilt, able to tuck the nightmare into a dark corner, at least for now. Two pancakes went onto a plate for herself, and she scooped one more to each of the other two, then watched Cassidy cut hers in half and give half to Reiko. She sat, doctored up her pancakes, and looked from Reiko to Cassidy and back.

"Do you think I should go?" Reiko asked her then.

"To therapy?" She forked a bite into her mouth. "Wow, I make killer pancakes." At Reiko's eye roll, she grinned and said, "What can it hurt? Right?"

"Why does your mom want you to go?" Cassidy asked, and Frankie was shocked when Reiko answered with no hesitation.

"My dad died last year, and my mom thinks I"—she made air quotes—"haven't dealt with it yet."

"Have you?" Cassidy chewed some pancake, her eyes on Reiko, and Frankie had to admire her directness. The question was matter-of-fact, no hesitation. Frankie had spent many mornings tiptoeing around the subject with Reiko, afraid to upset her, but Cassidy was simple and no-nonsense. Her voice held no accusation, only curiosity.

Damn, she could learn a thing or two from this chick.

Reiko sighed and looked off into the middle distance as she chewed, as if really thinking about it. "I guess…I don't really know." She turned to Cassidy. "I mean, what does that mean? How do you *deal with* a death?" More air quotes. "Are there instructions?"

Both Cassidy and Frankie snorted.

Frankie said, "Please…"

And Cassidy said, "I wish," and then they looked at each other and laughed.

"Exactly," Reiko said, shaking her head.

"You seem wise for a kid, though," Frankie said. It was something she'd always thought about Reiko, since the first time they'd met.

"Yeah, she's definitely one of those." Cassidy nodded.

"One of what?" Reiko looked from one to the other of them and back.

"An old soul," Cassidy said.

"Ah." Reiko nodded. "My grandpa says that, too."

"You want my opinion?" Cassidy asked. When Reiko nodded and ate the last bite of her pancakes, Cassidy said, "I think you go. To therapy. Give it a try. Don't be stubborn, be honest. It only helps if you're open and honest."

A twelve-year-old sigh. "Won't they just tell my mom everything I say? 'Cause that's sus."

Cassidy glanced at Frankie as if looking for corroboration. "Like I said, I don't think so. I'm pretty sure that unless you tell her something that's dangerous—like you're thinking of harming yourself or somebody else—everything is kept confidential."

"You can ask," Frankie added. "In your first appointment, just ask her. How much of this session are you going to tell my mom? And then you'll know, and you can make an informed decision."

Reiko was nodding slowly, squinting just a bit like she was thinking it over. "Okay," she said finally. "I'll give it a shot."

"Good." Then Cassidy wrapped one arm around the kid's shoulders and gave her a squeeze. Frankie was pretty sure Reiko blushed.

"Could I…" Reiko shifted in her seat as if unsure of her words. "Maybe, could I tell you about it after I go?"

"Absolutely." Cassidy gave her another hug, and Frankie grinned at her across the stainless-steel surface of the island counter.

"Cool." And with an expectant glance at Frankie, she asked, "Is that it for the pancakes?"

Frankie jumped up. "God, no. I was just resting, Your Highness." And when her eyes met Cassidy's and held, she understood what it meant to say somebody's eyes were sparkling.

CHAPTER FOURTEEN

That was the thing about guilt. About anger. About frustration. It was never gone for long.

Breakfast finished up, Reiko headed home, and Cassidy headed upstairs to deal with some work stuff. Frankie's phone buzzed with her daily text from her mother—*Just checking in*—but Frankie knew there was likely an element of *Just making sure you haven't done something like offed yourself up there*. Because of course there was. Why wouldn't there be? Why wouldn't her mother be scared out of her mind? Frankie told her she'd be fine up here alone. That she needed the space. The solitude. That it was what she wanted and that she didn't have a time estimate. She'd terrified her parents. She knew that.

So, yeah, there was extra guilt on top of the main guilt she carried regularly.

The texts and calls from her parents were cautious, as if they were afraid of scaring her off and having her never contact them again. Which would never happen, of course, but Frankie knew the fear was there. Conversely, the texts from her siblings were angry, mostly because of what she was putting their parents through. Her younger brother, Sam, was a bit gentler in his scolding. Her older sister, Ashley, had no qualms about telling her she was being a selfish bitch.

Was she?

Sometimes, she thought maybe Ashley was right. Maybe she was being utterly selfish in her inability to get past things, to move forward with life. But then she'd have the nightmare and she'd see the eyes—the cold, unseeing eyes—and she just couldn't bring herself to be around anybody.

It was super cold today, in the teens. She wasn't quite used to the winter getting so cold and snowy this early. It was the beginning of December, definitely the beginnings of winter, but she was from the southern part of New York State, just north of New York City. Things didn't often start to get really cold and snowy until Christmas. Sometimes, not even then.

She pulled her gloves off and blew on her hands. She had heavier gloves but couldn't hold the ax properly with them on. The last thing she wanted was to have it slip and chop off her own leg, so she wore lightweight ones with rubber grippy stuff. She pulled them on, set a log up on the stump, hefted the ax over her head, and neatly split the log in two.

"God, you look satisfied when you do that."

Cassidy was standing in the doorway when she looked up. She wore her coat and hat and came down the stairs. Her brows were knit together above her nose, and she ordered, "Show me," once she was next to Frankie.

"Need to blow off some steam?"

"You have no idea." Cassidy folded her arms and took a step back to observe. "I was gonna eat some frosting, but I'm too full from the pancakes. And this looks much more satisfying. Show me."

"Okay." Frankie went through the motions the way Luthor had taught her when she'd first gotten here, and he'd come up to check on her. "I didn't know a whole lot about chopping wood when I got here. Luthor came up to deliver some paint Ethan had ordered for me, and he saw me struggling." She planted her feet shoulder-width apart. "Brace your stance like this. Now, the key is to let the ax do the work. The head is heavy. Here. Feel." She handed the ax to Cassidy, who hefted it and nodded, then gave it back. "You're not going to chop with your arms. You're gonna chop with your whole body. You bring it up, hold it toward the end of the handle, like this, and then let it slice down. Use your legs, your back, and the ax's momentum." She split the log, and the pieces fell on opposite sides of the stump. "See? Here. Give it a try."

Cassidy took the ax, and Frankie placed another log, then pointed to a spot in the center of it.

"Aim for right here."

Cassidy took her time, never said a word, just did her best to mimic Frankie's movements. She didn't get enough of a swing, tried to use her arms too much, and the ax stuck in the log. She glared at it.

Yeah, something had pissed her off. Frankie could tell by the look on her face. She loosened the ax free and said simply, "Try again."

They worked on it together for around twenty minutes, using the same log, Cassidy hitting it in several spots, but never hard enough to split it. It was only when her frustration got the better of her that she did exactly what she needed to do. With a growl, she used perfect form. The ax hit the log in just the right spot, and it split neatly down the middle.

Cassidy's eyes went wide, and she looked at Frankie. Blinked. "I did it."

"You sure did."

"I did it!"

"Yes, ma'am."

"Oh my God, that felt good. I see why you do this so much. Gimme another one."

For the next hour, they chopped wood, hardly saying a word, except for Cassidy's small, satisfied laughs when she did it right. Soon, there was a sizable pile of split logs scattered around the stump.

"I think that's probably good," Frankie said, dropping the ax-head to the ground and leaning against the handle, slightly breathless.

"My arms feel like spaghetti, so probably a good call." She looked at Frankie. "Why were you chopping?"

"My guilt reared its ugly head in the form of a worried text from my mom and a bitchy one from my sister. What about you?"

"My guilt came out to play, too, in the form of my business partner calling me selfish and my daily realization that Mason is dead, and I wasn't there for him."

They stood there in the cold air, looking at each other. Frankie had worked up a sweat, and she figured Cassidy likely had, too, if her flushed face and ragged breathing were any indication. Their gazes held for a moment before Cassidy looked away, off into the trees.

"We're pretty much both trying to run from our guilt, aren't we?" She didn't look at Frankie when she asked.

Frankie shrugged. "Yeah, I guess we are."

When Cassidy turned back to her, her eyes had welled up, and her voice went soft, cracked as she asked her next question. "Is that even possible?"

Frankie inhaled deeply and let it out very slowly, shaking her head as she did so. "I don't know, Cassidy. I really don't know. I wish I did."

"Yeah. Well." That seemed to end the conversation for her, and she started to load up her arms with logs. "I'll help you stack these, and then I think I'm gonna walk."

Frankie nodded. She wanted Cassidy to stay with her. They didn't have to talk. They could just curl up with books or something. But Cassidy was far away now—she could tell by the expression on her face. By the sadness in her eyes. Whatever had been said in her conversation with her business partner, it had bothered her, sent her to a place of solitude, a place Frankie wasn't asked to accompany her to. And she got that. If there was one thing she understood, it was the desire to be left alone. She couldn't blame Cassidy for that. She knew it all too well.

They carried their split logs to the stack of wood in silence. Once they were stacked, Cassidy turned to her.

"Thanks for letting me crash your wood-splitting party. It helped. I see why you do it so often."

"Anytime," Frankie said, and she meant it. She knew how cathartic it could be. And the way Cassidy looked doing it? All sexy and powerful? Yeah, she was definitely going to revisit that in the very near future.

"Okay. Gonna walk."

"Be careful, okay?" Frankie looked up at the iron sky. "It's gonna snow soon. Don't go too far."

"Yes, Mom," Cassidy said with a wave over her shoulder as she walked toward the cabins, and Frankie couldn't help but chuckle. She watched until Cassidy had disappeared behind a cabin, then shook her head at herself.

"She's not staying," she whispered to herself. "Get your head out of your ass." But then she remembered kissing Cassidy the night before, how warm and sensual and fucking perfect it was, and all she could do was shake her head some more.

❖

"Look, I'm all for taking some time to get your head straight, but you've been gone two weeks. Meanwhile, I'm running around like a chicken without a head, picking up your slack, and I have no time to take care of my own stuff. Christmas is only a couple weeks away..."

Jenna had been pissed. And Cassidy couldn't really blame her. Nothing she said was wrong. And the worst part was that Cassidy didn't care. Well, no, that wasn't entirely true. She did care. It was her company, after all, and she didn't want it to fall into any kind of real trouble. But she just couldn't. Just...didn't. She didn't have it in her, and she couldn't quite grasp why. It was like she'd lost all sense of motivation around her job, which was crazy because her job had been *everything* for the majority of the past ten years. She'd foregone vacations and holidays and relationships for it. And almost overnight, she felt like she'd simply let it go.

It all came back to Mason. She did know that. She just wasn't sure what she was supposed to do about it. How she was supposed to deal with it. Why this was happening. What was the point? Was she going to spend the rest of her days walking through these woods trying to find the right place to scatter his ashes, but never quite settling on it? Was she a fable now?

With a loud sigh, she pushed a branch out of her way and felt the tightness through her shoulders.

"Oh, those are gonna hurt tomorrow," she said to nobody. But then her brain tossed her an image of Frankie chopping wood, and why the fuck was that so sexy? Cassidy didn't really go for masculine of center, but Mother Mary and a chocolate chip cookie, Frankie was sexy when she was swinging an ax.

Yeah. Frankie. Because they'd both seemingly brushed under the rug that they'd spent the evening on the couch together, making out and then falling asleep in each other's arms. And more making out this morning until *kissus interruptus* by a twelve-year-old. Which meant half the town would have heard about it by now. Maybe the whole town, 'cause Shelton wasn't that big. God, she was confused. What the hell was the point of it all?

"What the hell is the point?" Mason asked, tearing open a bag of M&M's and pouring a few into Cassidy's hand. "I mean, we'll age

out, and then we'll be on our own, and how? Why? What's the fucking point anyway?"

Cassidy studied him in the light of the moon as they sat with their backs against the solid trunk of an enormous maple tree. *"Dude, don't talk like that."*

"Why not? It's true. We're on our own. We always have been."

"So? Does that mean we can't make something of ourselves? 'Cause I'm gonna." She was getting mad at his gloom and doom attitude. It was recent, only since their failed kiss. He'd been different. Angrier. Not at her, but in general. Frustrated with life.

"You're smarter than me, Cass. You can have a future."

"What the fuck, Mason? What are you talking about? You've got the garage thing. The mechanic apprenticeship."

His turn to study her, and he did. She could feel his eyes on her in the moonlight. *"Yeah, you're right,"* he said finally. *"I'm just being dramatic."*

Relief flooded through her, even though she only partly believed him. Mason had always been prone to extremes. Hyperbole. Things were the best ever or the worst ever, rarely anything in between, and her rejection of him had only exacerbated that personality trait. *"Listen, if you'd rather, I can help you find ways to go to college, you know. There are grants and scholarships for people like us. You just have to find them. You have to search. I think the mechanic thing is perfect for you, but you sound less excited than you did at first."*

He shrugged and pushed against her with his shoulder, then smiled at her. She knew it was forced, but she let him think she bought it. He made a pfft sound. *"Ignore me. Like I said, I'm just being dramatic."* He popped a handful of M&M's into his mouth. *"So, what kind of classes you gonna take?"*

The snow was coming down heavily now, and Cassidy was kind of amazed at how easily and deeply she could get lost in the memories of Mason. She could still hear his voice in her head, even after all these years, as if she'd spoken to him on the phone just yesterday. The way it cracked here and there as it changed while they were here at Camp Lost and Found, and then the deep timbre of what she called his man voice. The thought made her smile, and she pushed off the tree she'd been standing next to and glanced at her watch, shocked to see she'd been walking for over an hour. Frankie was going to worry.

Um, what?

She literally stopped in her tracks—and there were tracks, thanks to the quickly falling snow—and replayed what her mind had just said. For the second time, she'd been out walking and absently noted that Frankie would worry if she didn't return soon. And as soon as the slight panic eased up, she smiled. Because it was true, and she knew it.

Frankie *would* worry.

She glanced around, finding it interesting that she had very little concern about getting lost in those woods again, even though in reality it was probably something she should think about, since it had already happened once. But she could still make out her footprints, even though they were quickly filling with snow, and she made her way back to parts she recognized pretty easily. The wind had picked up significantly, and she pulled her hat down more tightly on her head and bent slightly forward against it. There was the cabin called Coyote—she rolled her eyes at the overt sexism that the boys' cabins got badass names like Coyote and Wolf and the girls' were frilly things like Bluebird and Butterfly—and made her way between them and toward the main house. She could smell the woodsmoke in the air, which told her Frankie had the fire going, and something about that simple fact did things to her, body and mind. Things she wasn't used to. Things she hadn't felt in a very long time.

She hurried past the wood-chopping stump and glanced up at the house, and there was Frankie in the kitchen window. Their eyes met, and Frankie left the window, and the back door flew open.

"There you are. I was getting worried. Get in here and warm up." She held out an arm and Cassidy didn't even hesitate. She walked right up the back stairs and into Frankie's personal space and kissed her. Solidly. With certainty. She pulled back and looked into those brown eyes, which were colored with both surprise and something deeper. Something warmer. Something that made them darker. Arousal.

"I made brownies," Frankie croaked.

"Perfect."

❖

"Have you found the right place yet?" Frankie was slicing up some Manchego to add to the sharp cheddar and the crackers on the makeshift charcuterie board she was putting together. There was a hunk of brie melting in the oven, and she'd made a cranberry compote out of cranberries Eden had sent home with them, leftover from Thanksgiving. She was warming that in a small pot on the stove to pour over the brie. She and Cassidy were having a charcuterie and wine dinner, they'd decided.

"The right place for what?" Cassidy was opening a Beaujolais, pressing down on the arms of the corkscrew.

"For your friend's ashes." Cassidy had been gone for a long time, and Frankie had spent most of it trying hard not to notice how long Cassidy was gone. And also trying not to get lost in the sense memory of making out with her the night before, of falling asleep with Cassidy in her arms, of how her first act of the morning had been to kiss her. Failing miserably on all counts, of course. And the heavier the snow got, the higher her worry ratcheted up.

"Oh." Cassidy sighed and poured the crimson wine into two glasses. "Not yet."

"Are you actually finding familiar places out there? I'm surprised."

"Me, too," Cassidy said and laughed that soft, musical laugh of hers that Frankie had decided she didn't hear nearly enough, and oh my God, what was happening to her? "I just walk and then a memory hits." She shrugged as she carried the wineglasses to Frankie and handed her one. "My summers here were some of the most special of my life, so I think that's why my memories are so strong."

"Makes sense." Frankie lifted her glass and touched it to Cassidy's. "Wanna take this stuff out to the fire? Brie's almost done."

"Definitely. It's cold in here."

Frankie had noticed that, too. "I think it's supposed to snow pretty steadily for the next twenty-four hours. I might have to get the snowblower out."

Cassidy blinked at her in surprise. "You're not planning to try to snow-blow the entire driveway, are you?"

Frankie barked a laugh as they set the charcuterie and their wineglasses on the coffee table. "God, no. I'd be snow-blowing for a week. No, Luthor will plow the driveway, but I'd like to clear around the house a bit, make a path to the pole barn and the woodpile and some space around the feeders."

"You're so cute with the feeders, you know that?"

Frankie lifted one shoulder and felt herself blush at the words. "Animals gotta eat, too."

"You're such a chef." They sat down. "Wanna cook for everybody."

"I always did," she said, putting a slice of cheddar onto a stone-ground wheat cracker. She popped the whole thing into her mouth and savored the creamy sharpness of the cheese. "Even as a kid. My mom tells a story about me in my little plastic kitchen when I was, like, three, making dinner for everybody."

Cassidy made a quiet squealing sound of delight. "Oh my God, little baby Frankie must've been *so* cute. Tell me, did you have all those curls back then?"

"I did."

"I bet your baby pictures are adorbs."

Frankie shrugged again, and they ate their cheese and sipped their wine and watched the snow fall. It was relaxing and beautiful, and while Frankie had fully expected to spend the winter here alone, she had to admit that having somebody to talk to didn't suck. The fact that it was a beautiful woman who also wanted to kiss her made it suck even less. But as had been happening all day, when she got that little flare of joy, that blip of happiness, she'd remind herself exactly why she was there, why she'd chosen isolation, and those tiny sparks were extinguished with a hiss, as if her brain doused them with cold water.

Of course, then Cassidy would walk into the room or, in today's case, come tromping out of the woods through the falling snow, to Frankie's great relief, and those little flames would ignite all over again.

"I like that you and I can sit in silence, and it doesn't feel weird," Cassidy said after a few moments. Then she wrinkled her nose and added, "And I realize I am doing the opposite of sitting with you in silence by talking about sitting with you in silence."

Frankie grinned at her. Cassidy's sense of humor was one of her favorite things. "I like it, too."

"I need a refill. Gonna grab the bottle." Cassidy pushed to her feet and headed for the kitchen, and yeah, Frankie totally watched her walk away. God. She shook her head at herself and stared into her wineglass, at the small amount of wine left.

They hadn't talked about the previous night. At all. Not before Reiko had busted in and not after. Probably not a good thing, pretending it didn't happen, because if Frankie was being even the tiniest bit honest with herself, she wanted it to happen again. She didn't even try to pretend.

"Hey, Frankie?" Cassidy's voice pulled her back to reality as she called her from the kitchen.

"Yeah?"

"It's *really* cold in here. Like, more than usual, I think."

Frankie set her glass down and followed Cassidy's voice, and she was not kidding. The temperature change from the fire-warmed living room to the icy kitchen was significant and noticeable. "Uh-oh." She grabbed a flashlight from a drawer and headed for the basement door. It didn't take more than a five-minute examination to confirm her fears, and she headed back up the steps. Cassidy stood there, wine bottle in hand. "Furnace is dead."

"You called it."

"I did." She slid her phone out of the back pocket of her jeans and sent a text to Ethan Lustenfeld. "Problem's gonna be that it's Thanksgiving weekend. We might have to wait until Monday before we can get anybody up here."

"Yikes. What about the pipes freezing? Didn't you mention that could be a problem?"

Frankie scrolled on her phone and was pleased to see solid cell service. She chose the weather app and scrutinized the forecast. "Well, once this storm moves out in the early morning hours, it looks like it's going to stay above freezing until Tuesday." She glanced up at Cassidy. "Not a lot above freezing, but above freezing. So the pipes *might* be okay. We'll need to keep the fire going pretty hot."

"Good thing we chopped all that wood, huh?"

"Damn right." She glanced out the window at the still falling, still wind-whipped snow. "We'd better bring some more in."

"Good idea."

"I can do it," Frankie said as Cassidy found her coat.

"And I can help."

"Yeah, but..." Frankie frowned. "You're supposed to be, like, a guest."

"Frankie." Cassidy dropped her arms to her sides and tipped

her head. "I completely crashed the Winterfest of Isolation you had planned. You're not the concierge. You don't have to wait on me. In fact, I'd prefer it if you let me help. There's no reason not to. Four hands are better than two." But she said it with a smile and her tone was kind. And then a mischievous glint appeared in her eyes as she added, "You can reward me later."

And yeah, Frankie felt that in all the lower parts of her body. God, did she feel it.

"I see by the expression on your face that you're thinking of very *specific* rewards." Cassidy leaned in close and whispered, "So am I." Then she zipped up her coat, stepped into her boots, and pushed out the back door, leaving Frankie standing there, blinking and turned the hell on.

Jesus Christmas in Cincinnati, what was she going to do with this girl?

CHAPTER FIFTEEN

The next two hours were spent hauling in wood for the fire and stoking it up to a roar. Frankie was on her phone, texting with Ethan Lustenfeld as well as a couple different HVAC companies, none of which were open over the holiday weekend, but one had an emergency number. Frankie had left a message with an answering service but didn't seem terribly optimistic that they'd hear anything before Monday morning.

"The possibility of frozen pipes aside," Cassidy said when Frankie had finished her calls and texts, "this is kind of fun. Snowed in. Roaring fire. Wine and cheese." She gave Frankie an obvious up and down. "Beautiful woman."

Frankie nodded and grinned and blushed and looked like she wanted to say something else, but thought better of it.

Well, hell, I'll say it then.

"It's kind of romantic." Cassidy lifted a shoulder and tried to make it as nonchalant as she could, but the truth was, that's exactly what she thought. She felt like they were in some Christmas Hallmark movie— two lonely people find themselves snowed in together for a weekend.

Frankie gazed out the window at the snow for what felt like a long while before she began to nod. "It kind of is, isn't it?" And the way she looked at her right then, her eyes soft, her voice quiet, a glass of wine in her hand as she stood near the fire…Cassidy couldn't help it. She took the four steps between them, moved into Frankie's space, and pressed their lips together. Just once. Just for a beat or two. Just to see if last night had been some sort of fluke.

They hadn't talked about last night. But Cassidy knew somehow that they would. Eventually. They were both in very cerebral places in life, and this crazy attraction they had for each other was yet another complication. She knew that. She suspected Frankie did, too. But that didn't make it go away. As it was, she'd been trying hard not to ogle Frankie since she got back from her walk. The well-worn jeans that hugged her ass like they were tailored specifically for it. The soft, black V-neck sweater that she wanted to hook her finger into and tug down just enough to get a peek at more cleavage. And the kiss? The soft, quick one? Became less quick when Frankie gently cupped her chin and deepened it.

Yeah, not a fluke. Not even close.

Cassidy felt every ounce of moisture in her body drop south.

"Should we change into cozier clothes before it gets too cold?" Frankie whispered as the kiss ended.

"Probably not a bad idea."

And just like that, they set down their glasses and headed in different directions, like they were choreographed. Frankie headed for the back of the house. Cassidy took the steps two at a time. In less than ten minutes, they were back in the living room, Frankie in joggers, a long-sleeved thermal T-shirt, and a zip-up hoodie, Cassidy in leggings and a tunic-length sweatshirt with a pouch pocket in front. Frankie had two pairs of thick socks in her hands and held one out to her. "Eden recommended these the first week I was here, and they're super warm."

"Thank you." Cassidy took the socks and exchanged her thinner ones for the chunky soft wool ones. "These are great."

"So," Frankie said after a moment, "I was thinking."

"Uh-oh."

"Funny." Frankie met her gaze with a smile, then glanced back to the front window where the snow had picked up. "It's getting super cold in the house. It's clearly not well-insulated."

"You're not wrong about that. My room already feels like the inside of a fridge."

"What if we pulled a mattress out here?"

Cassidy frowned, not following.

Frankie jerked a thumb behind her. "There are three bedrooms back there, mine included. What if we took the mattress from my bed, the blankets and the pillows, and dragged them all out here so we can sleep by the fire? Might be more comfortable than the couch." Then she glanced down at her feet and all the confidence she'd just spoken with seemed to dissipate as she cleared her throat. "Or we could drag two mattresses out here. I don't mean to be presumptuous."

Cassidy barked a laugh before she could catch it. "Frankie." She waited until brown eyes met hers. "I practically slept on top of you last night. Do you think I'm scandalized by your suggestion that we essentially sleep in the same bed tonight?"

Frankie blinked at her for a second before saying, "No?" in a question form.

Cassidy shook her head. "God, you're cute. Yes. I think that's a fabulous idea. Let's do it."

She followed Frankie toward the kitchen, but then they took a left instead of going straight and Cassidy found herself in a part of the house she'd never seen before, even as a camper. A hallway with four doors, three of them closed. She could smell Frankie's...whatever it was she wore. Perfume or lotion or soap. It was a woodsy smell, soft and inviting, but with a subtle tang underneath. It was only when she crossed through the doorway and into Frankie's room that she realized that's what it was. She'd drifted off last night to the comfort of it, and for a moment, she was kind of stunned. Her life was scent. Her livelihood was smells. And she'd totally spaced on this one. That's how far from her job she felt lately, how removed, and it made her sad.

"You okay?" Frankie was standing next to her bed, looking at her expectantly.

Cassidy shook herself free of the sudden emotions of confusion and disappointment. "Yeah. Yeah, I'm fine." She made a show of looking around. "This is nice." To the right was a small en suite. "Your own bathroom and everything. I think this must be where the head of the camp lived in the summers."

Frankie was pulling the bedding off the mattress, everything but the fitted sheet, which was a soft cream and light blue striped flannel.

"I expected scratchy utilitarian white sheets," Cassidy said with a grin.

"Yeah, those are in the closet if you'd prefer them."

"Ha. No, thank you." She ran her hand over the cotton. "This is lovely and soft and pretty."

"Brought it from home."

Not only was she going to sleep next to Frankie tonight, she was going to sleep on Frankie's sheets, and something about that made her entire body tingle.

Together, they hauled the mattress off the box spring and tipped it up onto its side, then shimmied their way with it into the living room and plopped it down in front of the fire.

"Not too close or we'll roast," Frankie said.

"It *is* a damn good fire," Cassidy agreed as they pulled it a few feet away.

"Maybe we should roast marshmallows."

"Great idea, but I think we're out. The hot chocolate? Reiko?"

Frankie made a face then, one that said, *Who do you think you're dealing with?* "You think I don't have a hidden stash?"

"Oh, please tell me you do."

"I do."

"You just got so much sexier," she said before she could stop herself. "And you were already way ahead of the curve as it is."

Frankie just stood there for a moment, smiling at her, blushing just a bit, and the sight of her—that sight right there—was so much. She didn't understand what was happening. Why. How. But she was there. She was down. She was in it.

Their gazes held for what felt like a long time but was likely only a few seconds before Frankie sprang into action. "I'm gonna run out and find a couple of good sticks."

Cassidy gaped at her. "Um, have you seen it outside? It's a blizzard, and you're gonna go stick hunting?"

Frankie's laugh was deep. Husky. "In the kindling pile, weirdo. I'll be back in five minutes."

"Oh, phew." She watched Frankie head for the back door, pictured her stepping into her boots and sliding her arms into her coat. It held her there, the vision, before she was able to finally shake herself free. "Lord in heaven," she whispered as she headed back to Frankie's room to grab more blankets and the pillows. By the time Frankie came stomping back in the house, she had the entire mattress made up very much like the bed it would've been back in the bedroom. Sheets, pillows, comforter. It looked super soft and inviting, if she said so herself.

A minute or two later, Frankie walked in carrying two long sticks and a bag of marshmallows. "Success."

"Where were you hiding the marshmallows?"

Frankie gave her a look of mock indignation. "I can't tell you that. It's a secret."

Cassidy laughed and reached out a hand, wiggled her fingers. "Fine. Gimme."

Half an hour later, she looked around and was shocked by how perfect it all was. Roaring fire, roasted marshmallows, cheese and crackers, wine, and a beautiful woman. "Not gonna lie," she said softly as she looked at Frankie, her smooth face bathed in firelight. "This is kind of perfect."

Frankie glanced at her, then looked around at their surroundings. Her smile was slow and sexy. "Kind of the ultimate date night, isn't it?"

"It really is." She poked her stick into the center of a marshmallow. "The only things missing are graham crackers and a Hershey bar."

"Seriously."

Several moments went by. She ate her marshmallow and decided that was enough for now. She picked up her wine and studied Frankie's profile. Her straight nose and full lips. The prominent chin and long eyelashes she envied. "Tell me about your family," she said quietly, then sipped her wine.

Frankie turned to her, blinked a couple times, and Cassidy could feel it, could feel her eyes. "What do you want to know?"

Cassidy lifted one shoulder and inhaled deeply. "I don't know. Everything. I don't have family, so I always want to know about other people's. You said you have siblings. What are they like? What are your parents like? Do you have a big extended family? What do they think of you being out here alone?"

Frankie's shoulders moved slightly as she chuckled. "Oh, just that?"

"Just that."

Frankie took the marshmallow she'd been roasting out of the fire and blew on it. Then she gingerly used her fingers to take it off the stick, and Cassidy watched. Watched her hand. Those fingers. Hands were one of the first things she looked at on a person, and Frankie's were beautiful. Long, tapered fingers, neat nails, hands that were pretty but also looked strong. She thought about those hands on her body, couldn't help herself. A pang of arousal hit her stomach.

"Let's see." Frankie popped the marshmallow into her mouth, then seemed to ponder as she chewed. Using her feet, she pushed herself backward along the floor until she hit the edge of the mattress where Cassidy sat, got comfortable next to her, and picked up her wine. "As I said, I have two siblings. An older sister named Ashley and a younger brother named Sam. Ashley is a pain in the ass. Sam is the sweetest guy on the planet. I love them both deeply. My mom is a worrier. Everything I do worries her, whether I'm taking a shower or living on a mountain in the woods alone. She texts me every day, and I don't call her nearly as often as I should. My dad is a stereotypical Italian guy, a little bit sexist, though he's aware and he tries and he doesn't get mad if I call him on something he says. They've been married for almost forty years. I envy their marriage. They are a true team. My extended family is pretty sizable. My parents hate that I'm out here alone, and my mom asks me to come home every single time I talk to her." She grimaced at Cassidy. "Circling back, that's likely why I don't call nearly as often as I should." And then she sighed, and Cassidy got a sudden, crystal-clear vision of just how tired Frankie's mind was.

She thought about Frankie's entire situation. The accident, the self-blame, the inability to do anything at all to help things, the penance, the knowledge that her parents were endlessly worried about her. It all had to add up to one indescribably heavy load, and Frankie was carrying it all by herself.

"How?" she asked quietly. When Frankie turned to meet her eyes, she asked again. "How can you possibly shoulder it all and not have it flatten you?"

Frankie's throat moved as she swallowed, and when her eyes welled up, Cassidy only saw it because of the firelight making them shimmer.

She opened her arms. "Come here."

❖

This was the second time Frankie had ended up crying in Cassidy's arms, though this time, she didn't sob. It was more tears flowing down her cheeks than emotion ripping through her heart. It was always guilt, but this time it was more about her mom, her mom's worry, and how much Frankie really did miss being home.

Cassidy excelled at hugs, a fact Frankie had understood the last time that was only solidified this time. She held her tightly, pressed gentle kisses to her head, and just waited her out. When she finally lifted her head from Cassidy's shoulder, she let go of a small chuckle. "That's becoming a habit of mine," she said as she wiped her nose with a tissue she found in the pocket of her hoodie.

"I don't mind," Cassidy said softly. "Seems like you need it."

She took a deep breath, and when she felt steady, she reached for her wine and said, "What about you? Tell me about your life now. Do you have a house? Do you love your job? When was your last relationship?" She realized she was assuming Cassidy wasn't actually in one, and it occurred to her that maybe she was. Frankie really had no way of knowing, did she?

Cassidy sat up a little straighter and took a sip of her wine before she spoke. "I don't have a house, but I have a really nice apartment in San Diego. Ninth floor. Great view of the water. I used to love my job. I poured everything I had into it, into starting the company and keeping it running, keeping it growing. To the detriment of anything else. My last relationship ended about a year and a half ago. She told me I was not only emotionally unavailable, but"—she made air quotes—"*completely* unavailable. And you know what?" Her eyes met Frankie's in the firelight.

"She wasn't wrong?"

"She wasn't wrong." The slight bitterness in Cassidy's laugh was clear. "Nope. She was not wrong. I focused so hard on my company that I forgot to pay attention to anything or anyone else. Which sounds ridiculous and impossible. Like a contrivance for a rom-com or something, right? The workaholic who has no time for a love life." She scoffed. "But that was exactly me. And then I found out about Mason dying, and I have no idea how or why it happened, but I suddenly found myself at the complete opposite end of the spectrum." Her eyes were wide with clear disbelief. "Like, how is that even possible?" Then another laugh born of sarcasm as she stared into the fire. "My biggest client has left me four voice mails I haven't returned. My business partner is ready to kill me. I have a mailbox full of emails I need to answer. And you know what? I don't give a shit. I seriously couldn't care less." And then her eyes welled up and she turned to Frankie. "Why don't I care?" And she covered her mouth with one hand as a sob burst out of her.

In a flash, Frankie set her wine down, took Cassidy's from her hand and set it down, then wrapped her in a hug. "I happen to know the answer to that," she said quietly as she held her.

"You do?"

A nod. "Yup. It's guilt. You said before that you weren't there for Mason the way you think you should've been. And now he's gone, and that guilt has swamped you. You think that because Mason can't have a successful company now, you don't deserve to either."

She could feel Cassidy nodding against her shoulder. "You're right. That's exactly it."

"I'm sorry. I know how hard it is."

They were quiet for several moments before Cassidy seemed to collect herself and sit up. She wiped below her eyes, clearly worried her mascara had run. Then she narrowed her eyes at Frankie.

"What?" Frankie asked.

"Do you ever wonder if the Universe put us together on purpose?"

"The Universe, huh?"

"Yeah." Cassidy reached for the bag of marshmallows. "The Universe. God. Fate. Whatever you believe in." She pushed a marshmallow onto the end of her stick and stuck it toward the flames. "I mean, it's a pretty big coincidence that we're both here. That we're both *the only ones* here. And that we're both dealing with major issues of guilt in our lives." She was quiet for a beat, then turned to look at Frankie. "You know?"

"It's definitely strange," she admitted.

"Not to mention," Cassidy added, waggling her eyebrows, "the physical attraction. I mean, what are the odds? Seriously?" She held her stick with the toasted marshmallow out to Frankie. "For you."

It was golden brown, just the way she liked it, and she smiled at the fact that Cassidy had paid attention.

"Take it, so I can burn one to a black crisp for myself."

"Okay, okay," Frankie said with a laugh and pulled the marshmallow off the stick.

The conversation died down then, in direct proportion with the heaviness of the snow, it seemed. Frankie kept the fire stoked, and the living room was warm, though any time either of them went to the kitchen or needed the bathroom, they were reminded harshly that the rest of the house was in a deep freeze.

Cassidy stood at the window sometime later, a mug in her hand, having switched out her wine for tea. Frankie studied her, let her gaze roam over her body, stopping at the more interesting places—her shoulders, her ass, her breasts.

"Not even the animals are moving tonight," Cassidy said softly, and there was something in her voice that drew Frankie, that pulled her. She stood and crossed to Cassidy, pressed her front against Cassidy's back, and wrapped her arms around her stomach.

"They're all hunkered down in their nests."

"I hope they're warm enough."

"They are. They're built for this." She echoed the words her parents had told her as a child.

They stood like that for a long while. At least it felt long. It also felt like they were made to fit together, as clichéd as that sounded. Frankie was just slightly taller, and Cassidy fit against her like a puzzle piece. It would've been unnerving if it wasn't so completely comfortable.

"This is nice," Cassidy whispered as if reading her mind, and was it the words? Or the tone? Or simply that she whispered it? Frankie had no idea. All she knew was that if she didn't kiss Cassidy right then, she might implode.

Cassidy must've felt it, too, because she turned in Frankie's arms before Frankie could say anything at all, and they stood there, like that. Noses almost touching, eye contact intense, bodies warm and inviting. Breathing the same air.

"Frankie…" Cassidy whispered, and that was all it took. Frankie crushed her mouth to Cassidy's and kissed her. Not tentatively. Not hesitantly. Deeply. Thoroughly. And they were familiar enough with each other at that point that there was no surprise other than how quickly Frankie's arousal ratcheted up and went crashing through the roof. Holy hell, how was it possible to be so incredibly attracted to somebody you'd known less than two weeks? How could she already know they were going to be a bonfire in bed? Because she did. She absolutely did. She knew it with every fiber of her being.

Cassidy gave as good as she got. There was no dancing around Frankie's mouth, waiting for permission to enter. No, she pushed her tongue right in like she owned the place, and Frankie loved it, loved everything about Cassidy's assertiveness. She was a woman who knew what she wanted, clearly, and she wanted Frankie. Which was totally fine because Frankie wanted her right back.

Cassidy pushed the hoodie off Frankie's shoulders, and it fell to the floor, leaving her in her long-sleeved thermal T-shirt. Frankie didn't even make an attempt to remove Cassidy's sweatshirt before sliding her hands up her sides and cupping her breasts in both hands. God, where had *those* come from? They were fuller than she'd expected. Heavy. Filled her hands. Beautiful. And then, yeah, she needed more of them. She grasped the hem of the sweatshirt and pulled it up, Cassidy lifting her arms to help, and then it was on the floor with her hoodie.

They looked at each other. Ragged breaths. Darkened eyes. Swollen lips. Frankie in her shirt. Cassidy in a black bra that did things to Frankie's lower body, sent flutters through her stomach, and dampened her underwear just by existing. And suddenly, her desperation was gone. That need to touch every part of Cassidy *right now* left her in favor of something less hurried. More relaxed. Still intense, but in a softer kind of way. She reached out a hand and ran her fingertips over the top of Cassidy's breast, just above the edge of her bra. The skin there was soft. Hot. When Cassidy's eyes drifted closed at her touch, Frankie's arousal cranked up another notch.

"God, you're beautiful," she said, so softly she wondered if she'd said the words aloud or simply thought them. Slipping her hands around Cassidy's torso, she unclasped the bra and slid it off her arms. Dropped it to the floor. Stood. Looked.

Cassidy's breathing had increased a bit, her chest rising and falling more quickly. The firelight bathed her naked torso, her dark nipples making themselves known. Frankie's gaze focused on them, then roamed over her skin, down to her stomach and back up to those beautiful breasts, and then she couldn't wait anymore. She reached out, had to touch them.

They did not disappoint.

Full. Soft. Cassidy's breath hitched as Frankie bent and took a nipple into her mouth, sucked on it gently, then more insistently, rolled her tongue around it. Hands were in her hair, and when she glanced up, Cassidy's head was thrown back, the long column of her throat beckoning Frankie. She ran her tongue all the way up to Cassidy's chin and then they were kissing again.

By unspoken agreement, they shuffled toward the mattress as they kissed. When Frankie's feet hit the edge of it, she sat and pulled

Cassidy down with her, on top of her, and she never wanted their lips to be apart again.

After long minutes, Cassidy pushed herself up on her elbows so she could look down at Frankie. "You sure about this?"

"Are *you* sure about this?"

Cassidy smiled at her. "The weird thing is, I am. Completely sure."

"Same."

It was like they'd been making love for years. More clichés, she knew, but there was no other way to describe how easy it was to be with Cassidy. She ran her hands over every inch of her. Softly at first, then more insistently. They undressed each other until they were both naked in front of the fire, rolling on the mattress, battling for the top, letting each other win. Cassidy was responsive…and vocal. Frankie knew exactly when she was doing something right, and that was new for her—and awesome. She spent a long time exploring all of Cassidy's gorgeous body before settling between her thighs. She glanced up— Cassidy was propped on her elbows and looking down her body at Frankie, and the sheer arousal clear in her eyes sent a rush of wetness between her legs. With a dip of her head, she tasted Cassidy slowly, felt her drop flat onto her back, and heard her moan her pleasure.

She was tangy and sweet, and Frankie had to make a conscious effort to take her time because the truth was, she wanted to devour this woman. *Devour her.* She hadn't been this turned on in…ever. Not ever. How was it possible to fit so perfectly with somebody you'd lived thirty-three years without? She felt like she knew exactly what to do, where to touch her, what kind of pressure, how to draw things out. All Frankie wanted was to give. To give and give and give. And then she wanted to give some more.

Cassidy's thighs were soft and smooth under her hands, and Frankie watched her as she worked. Her head rolled from side to side. She bit her bottom lip, hummed as she did, and Frankie filed every little thing away. For future reference. Which she didn't allow herself to stop and think about. No. This was about Cassidy and making her feel wonderful. She moved her hand down and pressed two fingers into her, and Cassidy's hips rose up off the mattress, a small cry escaping her throat.

"You're so beautiful," Frankie stopped to whisper.

"Please, Frankie," Cassidy said back and lifted her head so her gaze met Frankie's. "Please."

Frankie smiled at her. She couldn't help it. And with one nod, she gave the woman what she wanted. She pressed her tongue to the spot she'd been avoiding, and it was like she'd hit a switch. Cassidy cried out, this time loudly and to God. Her hips rose again, up off the mattress, and she fisted Frankie's hair in one hand, hard, and the pain Frankie felt was delicious and sexy and she felt herself smile against Cassidy's hot wet flesh as she held tightly to her hips, as tightly as she could with one hand, pushing her fingers rhythmically in and out of her as she came, only slowing when her hips began to drop and Cassidy's hand fell from her hair and onto the mattress like a branch falling from a tree. Frankie slowed her fingers to a stop, stopped moving her tongue, but kept it pressed to Cassidy, and watched her for a moment.

God, had any woman ever been sexier, more beautiful than Cassidy Clarke was right then in the afterglow of sex? Frankie didn't think so.

She moved her tongue slightly, and Cassidy's whole body twitched. Cassidy's quiet laugh filled the room, and her hand met Frankie's face, gave her a little tug under her chin.

"Come up here," she said, her voice hoarse, and Frankie obeyed, crawling up her body slowly as Cassidy's knees dropped and her legs lay flat. Frankie kept her leg between Cassidy's, gently pressed a knee into Cassidy's center as she settled alongside her naked body, and Cassidy sighed. "Oh my God, you're fantastic. Did you know that? That you're like some kind of sexual dynamo in the sack?"

Frankie chuckled. "I did not know that, no. But I'll be adding it to my résumé, that's for sure."

"And your business card. It's important information."

"Noted." Cassidy's arms tightened around her, and Frankie inhaled deeply, the scents of nutmeg and cloves filling her lungs. "God, you smell good."

"Since scent is my livelihood, that's a good thing." Cassidy smiled and ran her fingertips up and down Frankie's arm, causing goose bumps to emerge along her skin. "You cold?"

"Not even a little." Frankie lifted her head and looked down into Cassidy's eyes. There were so many things she should say. So much she wanted to say. But the words stayed lodged in her throat, and all she could do was stare.

Cassidy reached up, stroked her fingers down Frankie's cheek, along her jawline, and Frankie could have sworn she saw the same thing in Cassidy's eyes that she felt in her own heart. No words were spoken, but the eye contact was heavy. Deep.

"Something you should know," Cassidy said finally.

"What's that?" Frankie asked, settling back down and nestling against her.

"We're not finished."

The fluttering in her belly that had eased a bit kicked right back up again. "No?"

"Not by a long shot."

CHAPTER SIXTEEN

Cassidy woke up slowly, gradually taking stock of her body before she opened her eyes. Legs? Yup. They were there, sore in places they hadn't been sore in a very long time, and she tingled all over at the realization. Her body was warm, but her nose was cold, the way it was when the bed was toasty, but the room was chilled. The silk scarf she'd slipped out of her sweatshirt pocket and wrapped around her head was in place, and her head was pillowed on a couple of very soft breasts that were lifting gently and evenly up and down, up and down. She slowly lifted her head and looked at her own personal human body pillow.

Frankie was asleep.

That alone was amazing, and it kept Cassidy from moving much because she didn't want to wake her up. She knew how fleeting sleep had been for her, and she wanted her to get as much as she could. So she lay back down and snuggled back in.

She was awake, but it was okay. She was happy to lie wrapped up in Frankie. The longer they stayed this way, the longer they could put off having to do any kind of discussing of what was happening—what had happened—between them. She couldn't deny their chemistry. Mother Mary in gym shorts, it was off-the-charts hot. She'd never been so sexually compatible with anybody. Ever. Never, ever, ever. Frankie had taken her to new heights. Heights so high, she hadn't known they even existed. If she hadn't still been wet from their last bout—which had only ended about ninety minutes ago, according to her Apple watch— she'd be surprised to find herself soaked just from the flashbacks.

This isn't why I'm here! her brain screamed at her. Like she didn't already know she'd veered horrendously off course. She was here for

Mason. She was here for herself. She was supposed to be grieving and reminiscing and figuring out her shit. Trying to rediscover her passion for work. Not having mind-blowing, limb-melting, indescribably hot sex with a woman she just met. This wasn't her. She didn't do this.

From her spot on Frankie's chest, she could see the fire. Frankie had tossed a couple big logs on before they'd begun their last round of lovemaking, but they'd pretty much burned down to embers. The longer she was awake, the more aware of the cold she was. She was gearing up to slide out from under the warmth of the blanket when she felt Frankie stirring beneath her. Her breathing changed and her muscles tensed. When Cassidy lifted her head, she met Frankie's smiling eyes.

"Good morning," she said quietly, not wanting to disturb the peace in the air.

"Good morning," Frankie said and gave her a squeeze. "My nose is cold."

Cassidy grinned at her. "Yeah, I think we need to build the fire back up and hope we hear from the heat guy today. 'Cause yikes." She chattered her teeth.

Frankie looked around the room. "Seen my clothes?" Then she arched an eyebrow seductively at her.

"I would ask if you really needed them if it wasn't about fifteen below in here." With a laugh, she stretched to her left and grabbed the long-sleeved thermal shirt Frankie'd had on last night. Then she pointed at her pants, which were out of reach.

Frankie shrugged into the shirt, then slid out from under the covers and padded several feet—all bare legs and bare ass—to where her pants lay in a heap.

"Nice buns," Cassidy said, and Frankie comically put her hands over her rear end.

"Stop ogling me."

"No way."

Once in her pants, Frankie got to work on the fire, and within minutes, it was roaring again, throwing off heat, and Cassidy felt her own muscles, which had tensed up in the cold, start to relax.

"Coffee?" Frankie asked.

"I mean, I was gonna go make it."

"No worries. I got you." And Frankie disappeared into the kitchen.

Cassidy sat up and scanned the room for her clothes, finding them just as scattered as Frankie's had been. It wasn't a bright morning, she noticed as she slipped off the scarf and slipped into her clothes, the snow still falling. She moved to the window, her arms folded across her chest because the cold was much more obvious away from the fire. Her rental was completely covered in what looked like a solid foot of snow, and she hoped Luthor was planning to plow the driveway, or the heating guy would never be able to get to them. That's if he even called. There were some tracks—likely deer—that led to the bird feeders and then away. She made a mental note to go out and dig out Frankie's salt licks at some point.

"Wow, it's still coming down, isn't it?" Frankie said quietly, coming up behind her. "M'lady." She handed a mug of steaming coffee to her, and Cassidy wrapped it in both hands.

"Yeah, I think we are truly snowed in." They stood quietly for a moment, just watching the show nature was putting on for them.

"I want to go check on Jack at some point today," Frankie said.

"In this?" Cassidy's worry was clear in her voice—clearer than she'd intended—and she wasn't sure what to do with that.

"There are snowshoes. I'll wear those. It won't take long. I just want to make sure he's okay, warm enough, that he doesn't need anything."

Cassidy wanted to say something like, *The guy lives off-the-grid in the woods, on his own, he's likely fine*, but there was something about the concern on Frankie's face that made her close her mouth before the words could exit. Frankie was a good soul, and the fact that she wanted to check on somebody else's well-being wasn't something to be mocked. "Do you want me to go with you?" she asked.

"No, no. You stay here and keep the fire going." And when Frankie looked at her, right then, with a tender smile on her face and a happy sparkle in her eyes, Cassidy felt herself go all mushy inside. Frankie leaned in and kissed her softly, then whispered, "Last night was amazing."

Cassidy nodded because it was. It absolutely was.

Frankie shifted her gaze back to the window and was quiet for a moment before saying, "It was very…not me."

A head tilt. "How so?"

Frankie rolled her lips in, bit down, and took a few seconds, as if trying to figure out the words. It was clear when she had because she met Cassidy's gaze. "I don't normally fall into bed with somebody I only just met." And then she frowned, made a sort of grimace like she was worried she'd said something insulting, but Cassidy barked a laugh at her.

"Oh my God, me neither! I was thinking about that this morning before you woke up. Like, I *never* do this. Never." And just like that, they were on the same page, and Cassidy felt relief. "So weird."

"So weird," Frankie agreed. And they stood there, smiling at each other, their shoulders touching. "I'm glad you're here," Frankie said, her voice just above a whisper.

"Me, too." And she knew, in that moment, that neither of them had expected to feel that way. That they'd both come to this place expecting solitude, not company. And certainly not sex. Good sex. Excellent sex.

They spent the next hour or two discussing the pros and cons of showering when you had hot water, but the bathroom itself was below fifty degrees. Frankie offered up her bathroom, which shared a wall with the living room and might have a tiny bit of warmth. Cassidy decided she'd venture there after Frankie headed out to check on Jack, which she decided to do before she showered, thinking she'd likely want to come back and get right under the hot spray to thaw out. So Cassidy helped her bundle up in layers of shirts, her heavy coat, hat, gloves, boots, and snowshoes from one of the back rooms.

Cassidy had charged their phones overnight and checked hers now. "Spotty service at best," she said as she handed Frankie her phone. "Take it anyway."

Frankie slid it into her coat pocket and zipped it closed. She was ready. "With the snow, maybe twenty minutes to a half hour to get to his cabin. He'll want me to visit a bit, so give me time for that. I shouldn't be more than maybe two hours."

"How long after two hours do I come looking?"

"You don't." Frankie's voice was firm. "I don't know these woods that well, but you haven't been here in twenty years. I don't want you getting lost. There's a lot of snow. Too much."

Cassidy wanted to point out that yes, it had been twenty years, but at least she'd had experience in these woods, which was more than they could say for Frankie. But Frankie was adamant, and to be honest,

Cassidy kind of liked deferring to her in this situation. Which was another thing that was very unlike her, and she'd need to revisit it later. "Okay. But please be careful."

"I will. Luthor will probably be along with the plow soon. And I'm gonna snow-blow later."

And then there was a beat. Quiet. Eye contact. Then Cassidy pushed up on her toes and kissed Frankie's mouth. "Hurry back."

A nod from Frankie and she was out the door.

The kitchen was freezing, but Cassidy stood there and watched out the window as Frankie headed back toward the cabins. Breaking a path in snowshoes was slow, but it would have been impossible without them—the snow would be close to knee-high. It had been a long time since Cassidy had lived in New York. She both missed the snow and did not miss it at all.

She watched until Frankie was out of sight, seemingly absorbed into the woods, and then she stood there for a few more moments, replaying the previous night in her head. Every touch. Every groan. Every kiss. Every orgasm. They all flooded her mind, spinning and diving and washing over her in waves of both pleasure and confusion. Because what the actual hell? How had any of this happened?

With a sigh, she headed back into the living room and made up the mattress so it was neat and tidy. She picked up any clothes they'd left lying around, along with the leftover cheese and their empty wineglasses. She was just putting another log on the fire when she heard the scraping of a snowplow, and then the red pickup truck pulled into view out the window, Luthor sitting in the driver's seat.

She opened the front door for him, and he stomped his boots on the snowy front porch before coming inside. His deep brown eyes went immediately to the mattress on the floor, and he raised one graying eyebrow.

Cassidy felt herself blush to the roots of her hair. A clear of her throat. "Heat went out," she said without meeting his eyes.

"Mm-hmm." When she looked back at his face, there was a tiny ghost of a grin. "Knew it would. Frankie was expecting it."

"She was. We have a call in to a couple of heat places."

"Might not hear until tomorrow. It's a small town, and this is a holiday weekend."

Cassidy nodded and because Luthor was looking at the mattress again, she blurted, "Coffee?"

"Don't mind if I do. Got one of those travel mugs? I got a few more drives to do. Love to take it with me and get it back to you."

"I'll see what I can find." Anything to get out of that room and away from Luthor's knowing eyes. Why was she sweating? She had nothing to be ashamed of. She and Frankie were grown women. They'd both consented. So why did she feel like a teenager who'd been caught doing something wrong?

She went through several cabinets in the kitchen and found an old plastic travel mug with a tractor logo on it and filled it with the rest of the coffee from the pot. "Luthor?" she called. "How do you take it?"

"Just black is fine," he called back, and a few moments later, she handed the cup to him. He hadn't moved from his spot and was still looking in the direction of the fireplace. "Snow should stop soon," he said, and he seemed more like he was just saying it out loud rather than informing her. But finally, he met her eyes again. "Frankie around?"

"She went to check on Jack." Firm. Yes. That was better. That's the Cassidy who'd built her own company from the ground up. She straightened her posture a bit, gave Luthor a smile.

"She's a good girl," Luthor said as he turned to leave. "She deserves the best."

He left her with those words, held up the coffee, presumably in thanks, and got back in his truck. As he plowed a bit around her rental, made a turn, and headed back down the long driveway, plow on the ground clearing more of the snow, she wondered at his words. And if they were a warning.

Frankie loved winter.

She loved the crisp chill in the air. She loved the falling snow. She loved that a fresh coat of snow overnight could look like a clean slate, like you could start all over again, leave all your crap behind. She loved the way the cold air in her lungs made her feel alive, the way sunshine could make the snow sparkle like it was made of tiny little diamonds.

But this current snow? Yeah, this was not the snow she loved. This was not the winter she loved. This was teeny pellets whipped through fucking freezing cold air and making her face hurt. This was snow so deep that simple walking took a hundred times more effort, made her lungs heave and her body sweat under all the layers she wore.

Was it the fact that Cassidy was back at the house waiting for her? Was that why she couldn't seem to focus on the beauty of nature the way she usually did? Because there was a gorgeous woman standing in the building she was actively walking away from?

"Walking," she snorted, the word floating away on a breath of vapor. "Trudging is more like it." But she needed to make sure Jack was okay. There was something about the man that had drawn her from the very first time she'd met him several weeks ago. Maybe it was Duke and what a squishy, furry love monkey he was. He certainly added to it. But there was something in Jack's eyes that made her know they were kindred spirits. He'd been through something. She didn't know what, and she didn't feel she had any right to ask. In fact, she'd likely never know. But here they were, the two of them, living on a mountain, pretty much off-the-grid, and alone. She was punishing herself, plain and simple, and she had a feeling Jack was, too.

She saw few tracks from animals during her trek through the woods. It was too windy, likely. They were all hunkered down somewhere. Smarter than her, clearly, but it was only a bit farther before she smelled the woodsmoke that must have been from Jack's fire. His cabin came into view in the next couple of minutes, and she heard Duke bark, likely hearing her or smelling her or both. She knocked on Jack's door and unclipped her boots from the snowshoes as he answered.

"Girl, what are you doing way the hell out here in this?" he asked, eyes wide behind all the facial hair.

"Just wanted to make sure you were okay," she said.

He stood aside and waved her in. "Well, get in here and warm up and catch your breath."

Jack's cabin was small, one room with a bed, a small table, and two chairs. A countertop of sorts ran along one wall, and some primitive shelves held a few dishes and some canned goods that she knew Eden had delivered to him every so often because the tiny town of Shelton knew he was there and did what they could for him. Several gallon bottles of water were stacked in a corner. He had no running water and no indoor plumbing, but there was the pond nearby and a well somewhere close that she knew about but had never seen. Jack was a true man of the woods, and off-the-grid barely scratched the surface of just how isolated he was. The smell in the cabin wasn't pleasant. Sweat and wet dog, mostly. Jack had a story, Frankie was sure, but she never asked. And he never asked her what the hell she was doing out here alone. It was an understanding between them, and they both knew it. No questions. No discussions. But they checked on each other periodically. It was an unspoken thing that Frankie would probably never understand.

"No heat in the house," she told him as she slipped off her gloves and held her hands out toward his woodstove while Duke pushed his snout against her, asking for attention.

"Furnace finally went, huh?"

She nodded.

"Got someone comin'?"

"Holiday weekend."

Jack's bushy eyebrows furrowed. "Is it?"

"Thanksgiving." Frankie wasn't surprised he didn't know. A calendar wasn't something he had hanging around, and he probably didn't really care.

He grunted his recognition. "Your company still there?"

Frankie nodded. "Keeping the fire going, I hope." She scratched Duke behind his ears and absently wondered if she should get a dog, and the thought surprised her.

"How long she staying?"

"No idea."

"Long as it takes, I imagine."

It was funny, the way they conversed. They didn't really look at each other. They spoke in short handfuls of words. Like two old men, Frankie thought, not for the first time. Few words. Right to the point. "You're probably right."

"Tell her to check by the pond. Might find what she's looking for."

"Yeah? Okay. I will."

They were quiet for a few moments, the only sounds in the cabin the crackling of the fire and little soft whines from Duke, asking for more scratches.

"You need anything?" she asked him finally, rezipping her coat, ready to head back. Jack was fine—that's what she wanted to know, and now she did. She could get back to the house. To food and warmth and better smells. Back to Cassidy.

"Nope. I'm good. Thanks for checkin', though."

"Of course." And that was the whole visit. Frankie clipped back into her snowshoes, gave Duke one last scratch, and slid her gloves back on. "Stay warm, okay?"

"Will do, Frankie."

She began her trek back, her path still visible, surprisingly. She heard Jack's door latch, and she plunged back into the woods, her brain whirling as it always did after she saw the way Jack lived.

He was lonely. How could he not be? You could be a person who was fine on their own, but at some point, human contact became a necessity. And that's where the punishment came in. She knew this from experience. When you thought you deserved to be isolated, loneliness was just part of the program. It was why she'd been so annoyed when Cassidy had shown up. She'd ruined the loneliness.

It was also why Frankie had reached for her. Why she wanted so badly to hold tight to her. But should she? Did she deserve to?

That was the question.

CHAPTER SEVENTEEN

Shockingly, Cassidy got a bunch of work done while Frankie was off on her mission. The signal stayed steady on her phone, and she was able to use it as a hot spot to get online for a while. She checked some inventory, placed a few orders, answered more than a dozen emails, then sent a text to Jenna, telling her so.

And in the back of her mind, the whole time, she listened for Frankie's return. Waited for the crunching of footsteps in the snow, the stomping of boots, the opening of the back door.

She'd kept the fire hot and roaring and had even bundled herself up and gone out to grab several more armloads of firewood. The rest of the house was freezing. She'd taken a shower, taking Frankie up on her offer of using the downstairs bathroom, and while the water stayed hot, the bathroom itself—especially the floor—was icy. She'd dried herself off as quickly as possible, scooped up her clothes and toiletries, and headed for the living room. She'd lotioned herself up and got dressed right there in front of the fire, praying nobody came hauling up the driveway because the window was *right there* and anybody who looked in would get an eyeful.

Now, she was in joggers, a long-sleeved white T-shirt, and a flannel shirt in pink and purple plaid over that, sitting in the hammock chair, her laptop open. Every so often, she glanced up and out the window. The snow was still coming down, and the occasional gust of wind blew it sideways. Just as she was about to start to really worry about Frankie, she heard the back door open, and relief flooded into her like warm water rushing through her veins. She set the laptop down, padded in her thick socks through the very cold house, into the kitchen, to the back door, and wrapped Frankie in a hug that shocked both of them.

It took a beat or two before Frankie's arms went around her, but then Cassidy felt her squeeze, heard Frankie's breath near her ear, something that sounded very much like a sigh of relief, and she tightened her own grip.

"I'm so glad you're back," she whispered.

"Me, too."

They slid slowly apart. "Everything okay with Jack?"

Frankie nodded. "He's fine. All tucked into his cabin with Duke."

"Oh, good. I remember him from camp. He was always a nice guy, though he always seemed to have a..." She looked around the room for the right word. "A sadness about him."

Frankie nodded. "Yeah, I can see that."

"What's his story?" She watched as Frankie shed her coat, hat, boots. "Do you know?"

A head shake. "I don't. I've never asked."

She wasn't surprised by that. On some level, she wondered if Frankie and Jack were sort of kindred spirits, each knowing the other had some sort of backstory, and that it wasn't something up for discussion. She'd probably never know all the details, and she respected that. To change the subject and lighten things up, she asked, "Hey, you know what would be great right now?"

"Hot chocolate?" Frankie asked in reply.

"Exactly that." Cassidy clapped her hands together once. "I love that we're on the same wavelength."

Frankie gave her that quiet smile and gathered items together to make the hot chocolate. With her chin, she gestured to the rest of the house. "Go. Sit by the fire. It's freezing in here."

"You sure? I can help." But her folded arms probably gave away just how chilly she actually was.

"I got this. Go." As Cassidy turned to leave, Frankie added, "Oh, I almost forgot. Jack said to tell you to look by the pond." Their gazes met and Frankie shrugged. "About where to lay your friend to rest. He said you might find what you're looking for."

"Oh. Okay. Thanks." The pond. Huh. Back by the fire, Cassidy sat back down in the hammock chair and pushed it gently with her toes. She and Mason did spend time at the pond. A lot of time. Maybe because that was more of an open space, it hadn't yet occurred to her to check out how it felt. She'd been too busy looking at all their secret spots in the woods. But they'd had many talks sitting on the shore of the small, man-made pond, sitting with their backs against tree trunks and watching the water. Once the storm stopped, maybe she'd take a walk in that direction.

Which wasn't going to happen anytime soon, judging by the sight out the picture window. The snow, which had started to taper off, had picked back up again and was falling in big, fat flakes.

"More?" Frankie said as she approached, as if reading Cassidy's thoughts. "Wow." She handed Cassidy a mug of steaming chocolate goodness.

"Luthor plowed earlier, but you can hardly tell."

"Did he wave?"

"He came in, actually. I gave him a travel mug of coffee. Hope that was okay. He said he'd bring it back."

A shrug. "Of course." Cassidy watched as Frankie sipped her hot chocolate while her gaze roamed the room, stopping on the neatly made mattress.

"Yup. He saw that. Raised his eyebrows. Literally."

Frankie nodded slowly, and Cassidy was pretty sure she saw a shadow of a smile before the rim of the mug hid it from view.

The rest of the day was spent on various activities. Frankie braved the chill of the kitchen to throw together tomato soup and grilled cheese sandwiches for lunch. Then she went out to run the snowblower around the house, while Cassidy shoveled off the front steps and porch and cleared her rental with a branch of dead leaves, since the rental company hadn't left a snow brush in it. When she looked up, Frankie was walking the snowblower in some random direction that made no sense in the capacity of necessity, and she grinned, realizing Frankie was simply having a blast blowing snow.

The daylight began to fade around four that afternoon, something California transplant Cassidy was not used to. But at the same time, there was something super cozy about it, about being hunkered down in front of the fire, her with her laptop, Frankie's stack of books on the table next to the hammock chair. The murmur of Frankie's voice came from the kitchen. She was on the phone with her family, and things were getting a little heated, Cassidy realized. The more she told herself not to listen, that it was a private conversation, the harder she tried to hear.

"Yes, Ash, that's exactly what I'm doing," she heard Frankie say, her voice laced with sarcasm. "I'm up here feeling sorry for myself. You're right." There was a pause, clearly while the other party was talking. Then Frankie continued. "I know Mom wants me home. You think I don't? I just…I have to work some things through before I can come back. I—" Interrupted, then another pause, then, "Well, thanks so much for understanding, Ashley. Really. You're a fucking saint."

Silence.

Cassidy wanted to go in to see if she was all right, but that would make it clear she'd been eavesdropping, so she waited, and a few minutes later, Frankie came out.

"Everything okay?" she asked as Frankie sat in the hammock chair and groaned.

"You ever think that nobody in your family understands you? Like, none of them?"

"I mean…" She shrugged and then felt Frankie's head whip around more than saw it.

"Oh my God, Cassidy, I'm so sorry. Jesus, I'm an idiot."

Cassidy reached out and closed her hand over Frankie's forearm. "Hey. No worries." She gave what she hoped was a goofy grin. "This isn't the first time I've realized I don't have a family, okay?" When she felt Frankie relax, she asked, "Wanna talk about it?"

Frankie sighed. "I need to go home."

Cassidy blinked at her. Waited.

"But not yet. I'm not ready." Frankie kept her gaze on the window, and her voice got very soft. "It's hard on my mom."

"I can imagine it is."

"Especially this time of year. She decorates this weekend. Right after Thanksgiving, always. She puts up the tree and the lights and her Santa collection. I usually stop by and help."

"And this year, she's doing it without you."

A nod. "That's why my sister called to bitch at me."

They sat in silence for a long while. Finally, Cassidy spoke.

"If it makes you feel any better, my business partner is pretty pissed off at me, too. And I don't blame her."

Frankie used her toes to turn the hammock chair enough so she was facing her. "How come? Like, why are you here? I know you want to scatter your friend's ashes, but..." She let the question go unasked, so Cassidy asked it for her.

"Why am I still here?"

Another nod from Frankie.

"That is the question, isn't it?" She let go of Frankie's arm and sat back in the chair she'd dragged next to the hammock. "I'm still here because..." Finding the right words wasn't that hard, but saying them out loud was. "I'm still here because I let Mason down. I wasn't there for him. I got tired of constantly having to pick him up, of having to talk him off ledges. He was fucking exhausting." Her eyes welled up. "And I'm saying this out loud, and I never have, and now somebody else will know how I failed as a friend. Hell, I failed as a *human being*. Because he called me. He left me three messages in the weeks before he died. He was worried. He'd injured his back at work a few months ago, and the doctor gave him a prescription for Oxy, and Mason was in so much pain. He was worried he was taking them too often. And I didn't answer him. I was so tired of having to be his voice of reason, and I saw his name on caller ID, and I just...couldn't. He accidentally OD'd." Only then did she become aware of the tears rolling down her cheeks, and she swiped at them angrily.

"Is that it?" Frankie asked quietly. "You blame yourself for his death?"

She nodded, her voice now stuck in her throat. If she tried to speak, she'd start bawling. She knew it.

Frankie was suddenly out of the hammock chair and squatting in front of Cassidy's chair. She took both Cassidy's hands in hers, which were warm and soft, Cassidy noted. Frankie waited until she made eye contact. "His death was not your fault. It had nothing to do with you."

Cassidy took in a shuddery breath.

"You said he OD'd accidentally. You can't prevent an accident. You have no idea if answering his calls would've changed anything. You don't." When Cassidy raised watery eyes to her, she said it again and squeezed her hands this time. "You. Don't."

After another moment, Cassidy squeezed back. "We are the guilt twins, aren't we?"

"Damn right, we are." Frankie returned to her seat but kept one of Cassidy's hands in hers and brought it to her lips. She brushed a kiss across her knuckles, and interlaced their fingers, and they sat like that for a long while. Lost in their emotions. Together.

❖

They made love that night.

That's how Frankie looked at it. Because it was gentle and sweet and caring and much more emotionally engaged than having sex was in her eyes. They slept on the mattress in front of the fire again, as the HVAC guy wasn't coming to replace the furnace until the following day. It was warm and cozy, and Cassidy was fucking gorgeous in the firelight, and there was something about the admissions they'd made to each other that had Frankie feeling closer to her than she ever expected.

It happened by unspoken agreement.

They got under the covers around midnight, Frankie taking the outer side, knowing she wouldn't sleep much and would want to get up without disturbing Cassidy. They turned to look at each other and that was it. Frankie rolled over and kissed Cassidy and they were off and running.

Their chemistry in bed astonished her. She'd been turned on by many women in her life, but never like this. Never so strongly. She wanted to touch every inch of Cassidy, and she did her best to do just that, undressing her, running her hands along her smooth skin, her hands, her lips, her tongue. The soft sounds Cassidy made only ratcheted her own arousal higher, and while she tried to take her time, she ended up crouched between Cassidy's legs in no time at all, her arms under her thighs, her hands grasping Cassidy's hips. But before she plunged in, she raised her gaze, looked up the length of Cassidy's body to her face, and found Cassidy looking back at her. That eye contact held. It was intense. Solid. And there was more there that Frankie wasn't ready to put words to, and she imagined Cassidy felt the same. But it was there, and she knew they both felt it.

She dropped her head and ran her tongue the length of Cassidy's center. It was warm and soaking wet, and Cassidy dropped her head back to the mattress with a sexy moan. She took her time tasting Cassidy, explored in and around every curve, every fold, paid attention to every sound, filed away what type of pressure had what effect. She learned Cassidy's pleasure, and it had been a very, very long time since she'd been interested in doing that. With anybody.

When Cassidy came, it was loud. Louder than the last time, as if she'd thrown all her inhibitions out into the snow and didn't care who heard her. She grabbed Frankie's head in both hands and arched up off the mattress, a sexy cry ripped from her throat, and Frankie held on to her hips, did her best to stay with her, to draw it out, to make it last.

Hips finally back down on the bed, Cassidy's breath came in ragged gasps, and she uttered, "Holy shit," under her breath, which made Frankie chuckle against her center. "Are you kidding me with that?" Cassidy asked a moment later, still breathing heavily.

Frankie had her cheek against Cassidy's thigh and was just watching her come down. "Nope. No kidding here." She let a beat pass before adding, "You're fucking gorgeous. Do you know that?"

Cassidy met her gaze and replied softly, "Only when you tell me."

"Well, I'm telling you now. Fucking. Gorgeous. Wow."

And something about her words must've spurred on Cassidy's recovery, because the next thing Frankie knew, the tables had been turned and she was on her back, her clothes were gone, and her nipple was in Cassidy's mouth, being sucked and licked and nipped at, and shots of pleasure shot directly down to Frankie's core. Nobody had ever turned her on so much so fast. She grabbed Cassidy's head with both hands and pulled her up so their mouths met. Because kissing Cassidy? The best. The. Best.

And then Cassidy was moving down her body, stopping at each breast, running her tongue along Frankie's torso, her sides, then the inside of each thigh, before settling between her legs and getting to work.

Frankie saw stars. Colors behind her eyelids. Her legs quaked. Her stomach muscles quivered. Cassidy had all the control. All of it. Frankie was a useless pile of muscles and bones, and her orgasm hovered just out of reach for what felt like hours. Just when she thought she could grasp it, it would recede, and it actually took Frankie several moments to understand that Cassidy was doing that, doing it on purpose, that she had the ultimate control over her body.

"Please," she finally whispered, not sure how much more she could take. "Please, Cassidy."

She felt Cassidy's smile against her flesh and then she said softly, "Only because you asked so nicely."

And Frankie's body exploded in pleasure.

Did she black out? She seriously wondered if she had, because it felt like she'd lost a few seconds. It wouldn't surprise her, the climax had been so powerful. When she finally got her bearings, she turned to meet Cassidy's gaze. She was alongside her, propped up on an elbow, smiling and looking extremely self-satisfied. Frankie couldn't help but laugh.

"Well, don't you look proud of yourself," she said.

"Listen, that was some of my best work," Cassidy said, then tipped forward and kissed Frankie's lips with a sweet tenderness she hadn't felt in a long time.

"Lucky me," Frankie whispered against her mouth.

It would be so easy to fall into a routine with Cassidy, Frankie realized a bit later. They practically had. They ate together. They spent the evening in the living room together. They watched nature outside the window together. They made love together. They slept together. Just the two of them, insulated against the rest of the world.

It was wonderful.

It couldn't last.

Could it?

CHAPTER EIGHTEEN

All day Monday was spent with the furnace being replaced. Cassidy had stayed in the living room by the fire, as doors opening and closing had made sure the house stayed as cold as possible. The guys doing the replacing had been big and burly, and one of them spent all his time coughing, but they got the job done. Frankie was itching to help, and it made Cassidy grin to watch her bouncing on her toes like a little kid, pitching in where she could. The job was done and cleaned up and it was back to just Frankie and Cassidy by early evening, and by Tuesday morning, the whole place was toasty again.

Good thing because Wednesday morning turned colder. No snow, but colder temps.

"Holy crap, it's cold out there," Cassidy said as she stomped her booted feet after having filled one of Frankie's bird feeders.

"Your West Coast blood can't handle it." Frankie was on the mattress by the fire under a blanket, a book in her hand.

"You okay?" she asked, as Frankie was usually doing some kind of chore in the morning.

A sigh. "I don't feel great. I wonder if I caught something."

"Well, the furnace guy was coughing all over the place, so I wouldn't be surprised." She stepped out of her boots and crossed to the makeshift bed. She laid a hand across Frankie's forehead. "You're warm."

"I don't feel warm. I'm freezing."

"You might have a fever."

"Terrific. I don't have time to be sick."

Cassidy stared at her, and Frankie blinked back for a solid four or five seconds before they both burst into laughter. "Seriously, all we have here is time."

"It is kinda like a whole other world, isn't it?"

Cassidy sat on the edge of the mattress next to Frankie's hip. "Right? Like a meteor went by and we were spared for some reason, and now we're some of the only people left on Earth, living out here in the woods alone." She shrugged. "I mean, we'll probably have to defend our house at some point from nefarious gangs of other survivors who might want to take it for themselves."

"We'd better start whittling sticks into spears." Frankie's laugh morphed into a cough, and her grimace told Cassidy her throat hurt.

She touched Frankie's forehead again. Definitely warm. "I'm gonna take a drive into town and grab you some medicine."

"You don't have to do that. I'll be fine."

Cassidy made a stern face. "Fran—wait. What's Frankie short for? Francis?"

A sigh. "Francesca."

"Oh, I like that. That's pretty." Back to the stern face. "Listen, Francesca, I know I don't have to. But you're sick and I'm not, so I'm gonna go get some supplies." She softened her expression and her voice. "You've taken care of me since I got here. My turn." She pressed a kiss to Frankie's forehead, then stood and tucked the blanket more securely around her. "Be back soon."

Finally feeling productive, Cassidy carefully maneuvered her SUV down the driveway and into town. The sun was shining, and the roads were clear, but damn, it was frigid out. Thank God for the heated seats in the Infiniti. They kept her from freezing completely.

"I always wanted a hot ass," she said out loud to the car's interior, cracking herself up. "That one never gets old."

Shelton was bustling, the cold weather not stopping regular day-to-day business, clearly. Traffic zipped along. People milled up and down sidewalks. She passed a couple of cars with ski gear on their roof racks, and a truck with a snowmobile in the bed. No, people in the Adirondacks didn't let winter stop them. They lived for it.

She parked in the lot at Dobbs's, locked up, and went inside. Eden was stocking a low shelf and looked up as Cassidy entered. "Hey, you," she said as she stood, clearly happy to see her. "How's life on the mountain. Got heat?"

"Finally. Yes."

"Dad said you guys had a little slumber party in front of the fire." There was nothing at all teasing or knowing in Eden's tone, but Cassidy felt her entire face heat up, sure that the blush was obvious, and when Eden's grin grew wide, she knew she was right. "Oh my God, you're so cute," Eden said and pushed into her with a shoulder. "I think it's great. Frankie's isolated herself up there for too long now. It's not healthy."

Desperate to change the subject, Cassidy jumped on those words. "Speaking of not healthy, I think the furnace guy brought something in with him and left it as a gift. Frankie's got a fever and a sore throat right now. Little bit of a cough."

"Oh no. Okay. This way." Eden led her to the pharmaceutical aisle and loaded her up with cough medicine, cough drops, Tylenol, tissues, NyQuil. Then they moved up and down other aisles, Eden wearing her mom hat and handing necessities over to Cassidy. Orange juice. Bread for toast. Several cans of soup. "Otherwise, Frankie will try to make it herself." A couple suspense novels. A word search book. A deck of cards.

By the time Cassidy dropped everything onto the counter to be rung out, she was laughing. "You are thorough, I'll give you that."

"I'm just glad Frankie's got somebody up there to take care of her." A shadow crossed Eden's face as she started to ring up the purchases. "She doesn't talk about why she's here all alone or what she's searching for. Or hiding from. But I'm a pretty good judge of character. I can peg a person within the first few minutes of meeting them. And Frankie? She's the best kind of human. She's punishing herself for something, and I wish she'd stop."

Cassidy swallowed, astonished by Eden's accuracy. "Me, too," was all she said. The bell over the door jingled, announcing another customer, and as she glanced toward it, her eyes caught the items on another shelf, and an idea sparked. "Hey," she said to Eden, holding up a finger. "Let me grab a few more things."

Half an hour later—after having stopped at Baked Expectations, because of course she did—her car was full. Cold remedies, groceries, today's doughnuts—apple fritter, chocolate glazed, and powdered cinnamon, and a few special items. She turned into the camp's driveway and made her way up. A huge gathering of birds was on the ground below and all over the feeder, and they flew away in one swoop as she pulled in and cut the engine. And for a moment, she just sat in her car, looking at the beauty of her surroundings—the trees, branches painted in white, the fresh snow on the ground with tracks of so many different animals, and the quiet. That was the big thing. The quiet. Because she'd been here for camp as a kid, quiet wasn't something she associated with the place. There was always running, shouting, splashing, laughing. But now? Silence reigned, and the whole picture was nothing short of beautiful. She wondered what it would be like to live here year-round.

She gave herself another moment, then got out of the car and began to unload. She went in the front door and set down her first load, stepped out of her boots, and crossed to check on Frankie, who was sleeping like a baby on the mattress. She laid a hand on her forehead—definitely a fever. Deciding she'd unload and put things away, then wake Frankie up to give her some medicine, she got to work, being as quiet as possible while traipsing in and out.

Cassidy could tell Frankie was exhausted by the dark circles under her eyes and the fact that she seemed groggy and didn't talk much when she woke her up to give her medicine.

"I can get up," Frankie said, not moving.

"You don't need to. I'm taking care of things. Okay? You just rest."

Frankie met her eyes. "I don't rest well."

She grinned. "I know. Try."

Frankie must've been too tired to argue. She took the Tylenol and snuggled back under the blanket. Cassidy set up a spot next to her with a box of tissues, a glass of water, and some cough drops. She went back outside and brought in a couple armloads of wood. No, they didn't need it for heat anymore, now that the furnace was fixed. But there was something about the ambiance of the fireplace, about being with Frankie in front of it with snow outside. It was their own little world, that living room, and something within her wanted to hold on to it. So she brought in wood. Stoked up the fire to keep Frankie warm.

When everything else was put away and Frankie was sleeping soundly, she took the last bag of stuff she'd purchased from Eden and got to work.

❖

Frankie felt like shit. Like death warmed over, as her grandmother would say. Like she'd been run over by a steamroller that had then put itself in reverse and rolled over her again just for good measure.

When she opened her eyes, she had zero idea what time it was, but she was soaked. Covered in her own sweat. It beaded her upper lip. She felt it under her shirt, between her breasts. Her shirt was damp. She tossed off the blanket and sat up slowly, and then she sat there. Just breathing.

"Hey, you're awake. How do you feel?" Cassidy came in from the kitchen and crossed immediately to her to place a cool hand on her forehead.

"I feel gross."

"I think your fever broke. That's a good thing. How's the rest of you? Throat still sore? Stomach?"

"Meh." She was painfully aware of not only her appearance, but likely her scent. "I need a shower."

"Okay, sure." Cassidy grasped her arm to help her stand, and then they just did that. Stood. Frankie was a little light-headed, and it took a minute or two for her to feel balanced. "Maybe I should help you."

Frankie grimaced at that idea, and that apparently made Cassidy laugh.

"It's not like I haven't seen you naked, you know."

"I just feel gross," Frankie reiterated.

"Well, you're not, but I understand. You can shower on your own, but I'm going to stand right outside the door in case you crumple to the ground in a heap."

And she did exactly as promised. Frankie left the door cracked a bit, and she could see Cassidy's shadow out there. She took a quick shower, thankful that the bathroom was no longer on par with refrigerator temperatures, and she felt a little better once she was clean and had fresh clothes on. But she was still weak, and much as she wanted to be up and about and do stuff, the mattress won out. She returned to it, noticing that Cassidy had changed the sheets and blankets to fresh ones while she'd dressed.

"I'll throw everything in the wash," Cassidy said as she followed her back into the living room and gestured to the supplies next to the mattress and to the glass she'd set there. "And I got you some orange juice. I thought it might feel good on your throat. But maybe it won't be so good in your tummy, so it's up to you."

Suddenly exhausted, Frankie settled back onto the bedding and under the clean blanket. "Thank you," she said quietly. Cassidy was doing so much, and she wanted to be more exuberant in her gratitude, but the shower had taken all her energy, and she felt herself drifting off before she could think any more about it.

Several hours must have passed as she slept because when she woke up again, it was dusk. She lay there for a moment, getting her bearings, remembering exactly where she was and why. The fire crackled, and she felt warm and safe and almost human again.

"Hi," came Cassidy's soft voice. She was swinging in the hammock chair, laptop open, and she smiled at Frankie.

"Hey." Frankie sat up, shocked at how much better she felt.

"Doing okay?"

A nod. "Yeah. Must've been a twelve-hour thing or something. I feel a lot better."

"Good. Hungry?"

"Starving." She pushed herself to a sitting position, gearing up to head to the kitchen, mentally inventorying what was in there.

Cassidy closed her laptop and stood up, then held out her hand to Frankie. "First, I have a surprise for you. Come look."

"A surprise, huh?" Frankie took the offered hand and let herself be pulled to her feet and led to the front door where her boots stood as if waiting for her to step into them. Cassidy held her coat open, and Frankie slid her arms in, narrowing her eyes at Cassidy, who simply grinned at her and said nothing more. "Well, this is mysterious."

In coat and boots as well, Cassidy led her out onto the front porch. It was snowing lightly, and the crisp fresh air felt so good in Frankie's lungs. She closed her eyes and inhaled slowly, doing her best to feel every molecule.

"Okay," Cassidy said, pointing in the direction of where her SUV was parked. "Go stand out that way."

Frankie waved randomly and laughed. "Just...out that way."

"Shut up and walk. I'll tell you when."

"Whatever you say." Frankie shook her head and went down the front steps, walking the fifteen or twenty yards to where Cassidy's rental was parked. The night was deep, but the snow kept it from being pitch black.

"There's good," Cassidy called. Frankie turned around to see she was still on the front steps. "Ready?"

"I think so?"

Cassidy squatted down, and Frankie couldn't see what she was doing, but in the next moment, her breath caught in her throat as the porch, the pillars on it, and several nearby trees all lit up in tiny, multicolored lights.

She brought a hand to her lips and felt her eyes well up, a lump suddenly lodged in her throat. It was beautiful and festive and cheerful and the sweetest, kindest, nicest thing Cassidy could've done. And before she understood what was happening, Frankie began to cry.

"Oh my God. Oh my God." Cassidy rushed across the snow to her. "No. Don't cry. This was supposed to make you happy, not sad. I'm sorry. I—"

Frankie stopped her with fingers against her lips. "I'm not sad," she whispered. "I'm beyond happy. This…" She waved a hand toward the lights. The colors reflected off the snow and gave the entire area a warm, welcoming feel. "It feels like Christmas now. Like it's supposed to."

Cassidy blew out a breath, and Frankie could tell it was one of relief. "Okay, good. Yeah. *That's* what I was going for."

"I don't know what to say."

"That's okay. The tears are enough." Cassidy held on to her arm and leaned into her, and they stood there. Just stood there, looking at the lights.

"Thank you, Cassidy," she finally said, her voice quiet.

And when Frankie looked down at her, she couldn't not kiss her. She couldn't. It wasn't possible. She met Cassidy's cool lips with her own, and in the moment, in that exact moment, every single thing was perfect. And then Cassidy whispered, "There's more."

"I don't need any more than this," she whispered back, surprised by the deep truth in those seven words. But Cassidy laughed.

"Too bad. Come on."

Tugged by the arm, she followed Cassidy back to the house and inside where they shed their boots and coats. Then Cassidy went to the dining room and grabbed a bag off the table. "Okay, so. This might be going too far, crossing boundaries, so if it is, that's totally okay. Just tell me and I can back right the hell off."

Frankie narrowed her eyes at her. "You are so mysterious right now."

That seemed to delight Cassidy. "Yeah?"

"Totally. It looks good on you. Sexy."

"Okay, good, 'cause…while you were sleeping, I rummaged around in the attic and found a stand, and I thought tomorrow, we could go out and find a tree." She set the bag down on the ground by their feet and began to pull things out. Garland. More lights. A few inexpensive ornaments. A star. "We could string some popcorn and maybe some cranberries." Cassidy shrugged as her eyes searched Frankie's face. "I just felt so bad when you talked about your mom decorating right after Thanksgiving. You looked so sad, so I thought maybe we could do a little decorating ourselves." A shrug. A pause. Then, "But if that's not something you're comfortable with, I'm totally okay with that." She began putting things back into the bag, and Frankie stopped her.

When their eyes met, Frankie knew hers were once again filled with tears. Happy tears that made no pretense of not running down her cheeks in wet streams. "This…you…" She shook her head, her grasp of the English language somehow leaving her head completely for a few seconds, and she simply smiled at Cassidy. "This is amazing," she finally managed. "*You* are amazing."

"You like the idea?"

"I love it." Again with the sigh of relief, and it occurred to Frankie then what a chance Cassidy had taken. She had no idea how Frankie might've reacted. She could've been insulted. She might've felt forced into doing something she didn't want to. She might've gotten too homesick to bear. But she didn't feel any of those things. She didn't feel anything but warmth in her heart. "I know exactly where we can go tomorrow to find a tree."

"I'm ridiculously excited about that." And then Cassidy stepped close to her, and they hugged and it felt more perfect than she wanted to think about.

"Dinner?" she asked after a long moment.

"I was wondering when you were going to offer. You came dangerously close to having a Lean Cuisine, you know."

"Never," Frankie said with a shake of her head and a full-body shudder as they headed into the kitchen.

CHAPTER NINETEEN

For the first time in her adult life, Cassidy found jeans, boots, buffalo plaid flannel, and a handsaw indescribably sexy. Yes, she knew it had to do with the person sporting all of it, but still. Wow.

"Ready?" Frankie asked, and you'd have never known she'd been super sick just the previous day. Her cheeks were flushed with a healthy glow. Her smile was wide. She had a white knit hat on her head that only accented all the dark curls. And her eyes. God, those eyes. They sparkled in the morning sunshine. She truly was something to behold. "What? Why are you staring at me like that?"

"Because you are *stupidly* sexy right now. That's right. I said it." She skipped down the stairs to follow her sexy lumberjack girl. "Lead the way."

The sun was bright and the snow reflecting it just added to the brightness, and she'd grabbed her sunglasses from the car before they headed out. The temperature wasn't as cold as it had been—it was in the low thirties—but her California blood still balked, and it took time for her to get used to it. The sun at least made it seem a bit warmer, not to mention how much it lightened the mood.

They trudged through the snow in silence for the first few minutes before Cassidy said, "I know I can't speak for you, but I've been having flashbacks of last night for a solid fifteen minutes now."

"Only fifteen minutes?" came Frankie's response from a few steps in front of her. And when she turned back to look at her, she winked. And just like that, Cassidy's panties were damp.

Yeah, she was in big trouble with this woman. Big trouble.

The previous night had been... *Wild* was an understatement. She'd never met anybody who recovered from sickness so fast, but Frankie had been energetic and sexy and such a complete top. Their previous times together, they'd been on equal footing, trading the upper hand back and forth. But last night? All Frankie. Cassidy had ended up on her back and had stayed that way for hours, while Frankie explored every inch of her body. Every. Single. Inch. She'd lost track of how many times she'd come. Four? Six? Easily the sexiest night of her life. No comparison.

Shaking herself back to the present, she asked, "Where are we headed?"

"There's a big area of evergreens on the east side of the pond." Frankie said over her shoulder, her breath a cloud of white vapor against the bright blue sky. "I'm sure we can find something there. It's not too much farther."

Summers at Camp Lost and Found were the only times in her life that Cassidy found herself comfortable in nature. She was a city girl at heart. She liked being close to everything. Restaurants, stores, movie theaters, bars. She didn't want to have to drive for half an hour to find civilization.

Except here.

Here, the trees, the fresh air, the quiet—God, the quiet—had seemed to be just what she needed. As a teenager and now.

Her thoughts were interrupted by cheerful barking, and then Duke came bounding through the trees, meaning Jack wasn't far behind. They were just reaching a point where the woods opened up, and there was the pond.

"We called this a lake when I came here as a kid."

Frankie snorted and squatted down to love on Duke. "And now?"

"I can't believe how much smaller it seems." She wasn't kidding. She remembered it being huge, filled with canoes and kids swimming and splashing. "There was one of those rafts anchored in the middle and we'd swim to it and lie in the sun there." No such raft was there now. "Will the water freeze?"

Just as Frankie shrugged, Jack stepped out of the woods.

"It will," he said. "Just too early in the season right now. Usually by late December."

"Hey, Jack," Frankie said. When Jack eyed the saw, she explained, "We're looking for a Christmas tree."

"Well, isn't that cozy?" He squinted and let his gaze roam over the water, and Cassidy couldn't tell if his tone was happy or sarcastic. He turned his head and took her in. "You find your spot yet?"

She shook her head, knowing he meant a place for Mason. Jack jerked his head to the left and behind him but said nothing more, and she squinted at him.

"Might wanna check those trees."

Huh? Cassidy's gaze followed the direction of his head jerk. She walked toward the trees, feeling Duke jogging to catch up with her. She could hear Frankie and Jack chatting but didn't pay attention to what they were saying, as all her focus was on the edge of the woods.

She thought back, recalling how many times she'd met Mason to just sit there on the bank, watching the water. It was so chaotic during the day and so peaceful at night, and he'd been fascinated by the difference.

I'll never understand how a place I hate being around during the day can be the same place I'm drawn to in the dark, he'd said more than once. He wasn't a water guy. In fact, he had a fear of water. Never learned to swim. Had zero desire to paddle a canoe. No, Mason was happy staying as far from the afternoon water activities as possible. But many, many nights when they'd planned to meet, this was where she'd find him.

Exactly here, she realized now, as she turned to face the water, the view stirring memories inside her brain as if the cells had just come alive. The group of huge maple trees directly across the water, the tippy top of the water tower that was just visible over the tree line to the right, the long dock just a little off center to the left. It was perfect and exact in her memory, and Mason had loved it here. How had she forgotten? The rock cliff and the tree stand were both places they'd met, but here? This was Mason's favorite spot of all. Remembering Jack's words, she turned to study the trees behind her.

It didn't take long to find it, and when she did, her eyes filled with tears.

She walked into the woods, maybe about three trees deep, and there it was, right at eye level. Carved into a thick trunk, the heart stared back at her as if it had been waiting for discovery all this time. The outline of a heart, and inside ME + CC. Mason Evans and Cassidy Clarke.

She reached out and ran her fingers over the carving. It had grayed and weathered and now almost looked like it had grown there with the tree. She had a quick vision of young, gangly Mason standing there with his Swiss Army knife—much like the one he'd given her, but bigger—digging away at the bark, and suddenly a memory hit.

"Hey, you okay?" Frankie's voice was soft, behind her, and a gentle hand lay on her shoulder. "Oh, wow, look at that. Did your friend do that?"

Cassidy nodded. "I'm just remembering meeting him here one time in the middle of the night. We sat talking and it wasn't until a few minutes in that I realized his hand was bleeding. He sort of brushed it off, said he'd grabbed a branch on his way through the woods, but now I'm wondering..."

"If he did it while he carved this."

"Yeah."

"He really cared about you," Frankie whispered, almost to herself.

Cassidy inhaled and let it out slowly. "He did. And I feel like I let him down."

Frankie's hand tightened on her shoulder. "You couldn't have known," she said. And she was right, but it didn't matter. Because Cassidy *should have* known. They stood quietly, just looking, as she ran her fingers in and around the heart, following the line.

"I think this is the spot," she said finally. Turning to look past Frankie and toward the water, she gave a nod. "This is where he'd want to be, I think." She hadn't brought his ashes with her, but she knew without a doubt that she could find this spot again with no problem. She'd bring him here. Soon.

"Good." Frankie stood next to her silently for a moment. Then, "I found a tree, if you're still interested in that."

She squinted for a second before remembering why they'd traipsed through the snow in the freezing cold—which she became suddenly, shiveringly aware of—in the first place. Frankie's eyes held sympathy, and they still had that sparkle, though it had dimmed just a touch. "Yes. A tree. Show me." Giving herself a full-body shake, she shed her anguish, her sorrow, her guilt, at least for now. She'd revisit it later, she knew. Until then, she followed the beautiful woman with the saw through the woods.

❖

"How the hell did you manage to gather the ingredients for eggnog?" Cassidy asked many hours later as she sipped from the clear glass of creamy goodness Frankie had handed her.

"First of all, I'm a chef. You seem to keep forgetting that." Frankie was on her back on the living room floor, head and shoulders under the Christmas tree, sawing off a few small branches that were interfering with the tree stand that had to be older than she was.

"Are you kidding me? After all the excellent food I've had while here? I have not forgotten that. But a chef, to me, doesn't create drink concoctions." She sipped again, and Frankie peeked at her from between branches and noticed the glint in her eyes. The brandy, probs.

"Oh, but we do." She shimmied out, then turned onto her stomach and slid back under. "Okay, hold it straight." When she got the okay from Cassidy, she tightened the screw-in thingies that were meant to keep the tree upright.

"I think that tree stand is older than I am," Cassidy said, echoing Frankie's earlier thought.

"I think you're right." A couple more twists. "There. What do you think? Stand back a bit."

Cassidy backpedaled until she was almost to the fireplace, tipped her head one way, then the other. "I think it's good."

"Thank Christ," Frankie muttered, feeling like a turtle as she slid herself back out and finally stood up and brushed her hands on her thighs. She joined Cassidy across the room and stared. "You know what? This is a pretty perfect tree."

"It really is. Nice choice, you." They stood there for a few more minutes before Cassidy said, "Ready to decorate?"

"Absolutely."

They strung the lights together and added the few decorations Cassidy had bought at Dobbs's, as Kelly Clarkson sang holiday tunes to them from the speaker Cassidy'd set on the table. They worked astonishingly well together, handing the lights to each other around the tree and pointing out bare spots. When that was finished, Cassidy fashioned strings and needles while Frankie got things ready for making an enormous pot of popcorn.

"You're doing it the old-fashioned way, I see," Cassidy said, coming into the kitchen as Frankie swirled oil into a large pot.

"It's the only way to make it, as far as I'm concerned."

"I don't think I've ever done it this way. I wouldn't know how. I am a put-the-bag-in-the-microwave kind of girl."

"Allow me to show you." Frankie took the lid off the pot. "First—oil. You can use any, but I prefer canola oil for this. Not too much. A few swirls. Too much and it'll burn, which means your popcorn will burn. Nobody likes burned popcorn." She replaced the lid. "Then, let it get hot."

She liked having Cassidy in her kitchen, and that was beyond new. Normally, she hated people in her kitchen, in her space, in her way. She preferred to be left alone to do whatever it was she was doing, without watchful eyes or annoying questions or hovering. But Cassidy was different.

Good Lord, Cassidy was different. Instead of irritating her, having Cassidy close almost felt like it energized her. She wanted to show her the things she could do, the things she could make. She wanted to perform for Cassidy.

"Okay, to check if it's hot, you want it to be shimmering. See?" She lifted the lid. When Cassidy shook her head, she went on. "If you can't tell, just flick a sprinkle of water in." She did so, and the oil sizzled. "See?"

This time Cassidy nodded.

"Now, we test a second way." She tossed four kernels into the pan and replaced the lid.

"Not sure that's gonna be enough to string around a tree. Just sayin'."

"Ha. Hilarious." As if on cue, a kernel popped, the other three close behind. "Now, we're ready." The rest of the kernels went in, and it wasn't long before the kitchen was filled with the sounds and smell of popping corn. In a small pot, Frankie was melting some butter, and when she met Cassidy's eyes and raised eyebrows, she said, "Well, we're not gonna string *all* of it, right?"

Fifteen minutes later, they were seated at the dining room table.

They each had two bowls of popcorn, one for stringing and one for eating. Kelly Clarkson had taken a bow and made way for John Legend, his warm molasses voice filling the house. Cassidy hummed along and Frankie took a moment to just watch her. Her dark eyes as they focused on the task, her hands, the long fingers deftly pushing the needle through the popcorn, her full lips, shining because she kept licking them in concentration.

"I've never done this before," she said.

Cassidy seemed surprised. "No?"

"Nope. My mom loves Christmas, but I don't think this is something she ever did as a kid, so it didn't get carried along. I like it, though. It's fun."

"The last foster home I was at, the woman really loved the holidays. It was probably my favorite one. Kerry, her name was. Her husband was a dick, but she was nice. She always had us string popcorn and cranberries." She stopped working and gazed off into the distance. "I think it was twofold for her. One, it was inexpensive. Definitely cheaper than buying ornaments. And two, it kept us busy." She laughed softly through her nose.

"How many of you were there?"

"In that house? Kerry had two of her own kids and three fosters. We moved in and out. When one of us would age out, she'd get another in pretty fast."

"How long were you there?"

Cassidy scrunched up her nose. "A year and a half?"

"When you say her husband was a dick…" She didn't know how to ask what she was asking, but Cassidy caught right on.

"Oh no. No, not at all. He left us all alone. Meaning he wasn't really interested in us at all. We were Kerry's hobby."

"Hobby, huh? Ouch."

Cassidy shrugged. "I had a roof over my head and food to eat, so I was good."

She nodded and left it at that, but part of her ached for young Cassidy. To count a roof and food as all you needed as a kid to be *good* broke her heart a little bit. What about love? What about support and advice and guidance? She'd had all those things in her family, and it was just hard for her to grasp not having even one.

They spent the rest of the afternoon finishing the decorations and putting them on the tree. Later that night, they sat in front of the fire, close together on the couch, all the lights off except the ones outside and the ones on the tree. Instrumental holiday music echoed softly through the house as they sat quietly, Cassidy in Frankie's arms.

"This is awesome," she said, her voice a whisper, and she tightened her grip on Cassidy.

"It is," Cassidy replied. "Thanks for indulging me with the popcorn and cranberries."

"Are you kidding? I loved doing that. In fact, I'm going to make that a holiday tradition from here on out."

"Yeah?" Cassidy turned in her arms to look her in the face.

"Yes." Frankie kissed her. She couldn't not. That's how she felt around Cassidy now. Like she needed to always be touching her, always be kissing her. It was alarmingly unfamiliar territory, and rather than spending her energy analyzing it, she simply acted on it. "From now on, it's popcorn and cranberries on all my trees."

Cassidy nodded her clear approval. "I like that."

They didn't need to sleep on the mattress in front of the fire any longer, but they hadn't yet put it and all the bedding back into Frankie's bedroom. One more night, she thought, not at all unhappy about it. Exhausted from the busy day—and, Frankie realized, probably some residual fatigue from being sick—they decided to turn in early. For the first time since they'd begun having sex, they went to sleep without it, instead snuggling into one another, holding each other, cuddled together. Frankie decided to play a little mental game with herself to see which body parts of hers were touching which body parts of Cassidy's each time she woke up, knowing that it would happen several times, as it always did. But the unexpected happened instead.

Frankie didn't wake up once until morning, when she woke alone in bed, to the sound of Cassidy in the shower.

CHAPTER TWENTY

It was time.

The thought came out of nowhere in the wee hours of the morning. Woke Cassidy out of a sound sleep just as harshly as if it had shaken her awake.

It was time.

Cassidy knew it. She did. She lay there in the early morning hours, blinking, the dark not as thick and heavy as it would've been without the Christmas lights outside. And the tree was still lit. Frankie snored quietly beside her—had she slept all night? She turned, studied Frankie's profile in the dim light. Her straight nose, the thick eyebrows and long lashes casting shadows onto her exquisite cheekbones. God, she was beautiful…and Cassidy had become far too comfortable.

She looked at the ceiling, away from Frankie. She had to start thinking about going home. That's what this was. Her conscience was kicking into high gear, because she clearly hadn't been listening to anything subtle. Jenna was pissed, as were several of her clients, and she understood that. Of course she did. How could she not? This was not like her. She was a workaholic. Always available when her clients needed her. When her employees needed her. Always. She didn't just run off to the mountains for weeks at a time. She wasn't that person.

Except, apparently, she was.

She took a breath. There'd been a reason. Of course. Mason's death had done a number on her, and she hadn't really understood it until that very moment. She'd needed to flee, to get away, to run. And now? Now, she needed to get herself together. She had some calls to make today. She'd been putting people off for too long, and patience was running thin.

Frankie stirred, turned on her side, and nuzzled into Cassidy, threw a leg over hers, draped an arm across her middle, and just like that, all those thoughts flew right out of her head. She didn't want to go back. She wanted to stay right here, this way, wrapped up with this woman, in this place where they were the only two people in the world.

She closed her eyes and let out a long, slow breath.

What the fuck had she been thinking?

She must have managed to drift off for a little while because the next time she opened her eyes, there was a pink tint to the morning light. Not quite dawn, but close. Next to her, Frankie still slept, and for that, she was grateful. The woman never got a decent night's sleep, so this was new.

Carefully untangling herself from Frankie's body, she slid out from under the covers and padded to the bathroom. A hot shower and some clean clothes and she felt a little better. Not a lot, but a little. She stared at her own reflection, studied her own dark eyes, looked deeply into them as if they held some sort of answer, some solution to what she was feeling. The guilt was still there, of course. She was starting to think it was going to live with her forever, and she'd have to find a way to deal with that. But something new had blossomed. Some seed of… what was it? Something she hadn't planned on and certainly wasn't ready for.

But still…

"No." She said it aloud. Right to her own face in the mirror. No, she had to nip it in the bud. Because, seriously, what did she think was going to happen? Was she going to live happily ever after in the middle of the freaking woods with Frankie? Was that what Frankie thought?

Her head had started to ache, a low-key pounding behind her eyes. She sighed and decided to deal with the thing she'd come here to do. Yeah, she'd take care of that first. Put these others issues on a shelf for now.

Plan in place, she found a bottle of Motrin and shook a few tablets into her hand, then downed them with some water. It was gonna be a day. She could tell already.

❖

"Enough of this, Francesca."

Frankie blinked in surprise at the tone of her mother's voice on the phone.

"Enough. Enough of this beating yourself up and walling yourself off and living in the middle of nowhere all alone. And at Christmastime!" Her mother's voice broke, and Frankie braced for the tears, but they didn't come. Instead, her mom pulled herself together, cleared her throat, and said it one more time. "Enough."

"Mom, I'm just…" She paused, and it was her turn to clear her throat. "I don't think I'm ready."

"Honey." Her mom's voice softened this time. "You may never be ready. You know that, right? I mean, do you think the way you feel is just going to go away? That you're going to just wake up one morning and feel all better?" There was no accusation in the words, no blame, no irritation. They were gentle. Calm. "No. What will happen is that you will just find a way to accept it and get on with your life."

Frankie cursed the lump that had formed in her throat, the one that blocked all the words.

"I'm not going to tell you again that it wasn't your fault, that there is no blame, that it was a horrible, terrible accident. Because you know all that." Her mother paused, as if she knew Frankie needed a minute. Then she added, "I want you to come home."

"I know," Frankie said. "I know. I need a little more time." And then, because she needed something positive to tell her, she added, "And I'm not alone. Cassidy's here, remember?"

"Is that the woman you mentioned before? She's still there? Over the holidays?"

Frankie almost laughed at the bewildered tone of her mother's voice, because there was no way she understood spending the holidays without family. It just wasn't done in her mom's world. "She doesn't have any family. She used to come here when she was a foster kid. To the camp. Over the summer."

"*Oh*," her mom said, drawing the word out. "That's so sad. That she doesn't have any family."

"It is." She thought about Cassidy and how she'd left so quickly this morning, stingy with the eye contact, as she shouldered a bag that Frankie assumed had her friend's ashes in it. And then suddenly, inexplicably, she didn't want her to be alone. She just didn't. "Mom,

I gotta run. But I heard you. Okay? I heard you. I'm doing my best. I love you."

They signed off—she got the impression her mom had more to say—and Frankie got herself dressed and headed out into the winter morning.

The cold hit her like a slap. Hello, December. Wow. Even having been on the mountain for as long as she had, the weather could still take her by surprise. It wasn't snowing, so following the tracks Cassidy had made earlier wasn't hard, and Frankie set off, inhaling the fresh air, letting it fill her lungs, freeze them, wake them up. Before she'd come here, she'd had no idea how much she loved the mountains. The woods. Nature itself. She could live out here. Easily. The thought surprised her.

Her brain was a jumble as she walked, different topics vying for front and center. Her family. This place. Her old life. This new one. And Cassidy. Always Cassidy. Where had she come from? And why? Why had she been sent to Frankie? Was there a lesson here? Something else? Something more than that?

She'd slept through the night last night. The whole night. No nightmares. No trouble falling asleep. No trouble staying asleep. She'd woken up feeling refreshed—actually refreshed—for the first time in months. *Months.* And she knew why. Exactly why. It was Cassidy. Cassidy and her calm, warm presence.

What the hell was she supposed to do with that? She honestly didn't know, but did she need to? Did she need to understand it all? Couldn't they just…be?

It took her a good half hour of walking before she reached the pond, close to the spot Jack had pointed out to them, the tree with the initials carved in it. And then she stopped.

Cassidy was there, standing at the base of the tree, a small box in her hands. Frankie wanted to give her privacy, but at the same time, it was hard to watch, hard to witness the sheer sadness, the anguish that was so clearly stamped all over her face. Cassidy's lips were moving and Frankie wondered what she was saying. It took everything she had not to step forward, not to intrude, but something within her told her not to, that this was something Cassidy needed to do. On her own.

She stayed where she was and waited.

❖

"I hope this is the right place for you," Cassidy said quietly. She stood at the base of the tree where Mason had carved their initials in the center of a heart so very many years ago. It was such a sweet thing to have discovered, and it made her both happy and sad. Happy that she'd had somebody who'd loved her enough to immortalize her name. Sad that she'd never been able to be what Mason had deserved—and even sadder that he'd never stopped wishing she had.

"What a sad fucking ending." She hadn't meant to say *that* out loud, but the words were there, the anger was there, sudden and hot. God, Mason made her feel so many different things. How was it possible for one boy to do that? For one man to do that? To make her feel loved and wanted and frustrated and angry and fed up and devastatingly sad all at the same time? Because that was Mason, in a very large nutshell. "Why weren't you more careful? Why?" She felt her anger go from simmer to almost boil as she thought about him. "It was so stupid. Why were you so *stupid*?" And that was all she needed to release the tears that she'd known were on their way since she'd opened her eyes that morning.

But not just tears. Sobs. Full, aching, racking sobs, ones that hurt her ribs and made her feel like she'd never be whole again. Sobs for Mason. For the life he wouldn't have. For the sadness that had filled his heart. For the pain he couldn't assuage. And for her own inability to help him. For her unwillingness to put herself out there any further than she had. For the guilt she felt and the blame she knew she'd likely never completely crawl out from under.

Her legs wouldn't hold her any longer and she sank down until she sat in the snow, the tree's trunk against her back, and she gazed out over the water and didn't try to stop herself from crying. Out here, she could just let it all go. Maybe that's what had led her here in the first place? She cried openly. Not quietly. She let it all out and had no idea how long it had been when things finally started to calm down.

And then there were footsteps crunching through the snow.

And then there was Frankie. And the relief Cassidy felt at her presence was wonderful and awful.

She sat down next to Cassidy in the snow and was quiet for a long moment before asking softly, "You okay?"

A shrug. "Depends on your definition of okay, I guess."

A nod. "Totally get that. I've done exactly this more than once out here. Except sometimes, I actually scream."

Cassidy turned to her, but Frankie was looking out at the water. "Yeah?"

Another nod. "Scream, yell, swear really loudly."

That brought a smile to her lips, the vision of Frankie hurling obscenities into the beautiful, peaceful blue of the sky. Just for a second. And then the sadness descended again like fog falling over her, and she sighed. "I'm just so fucking angry at him. And at myself. I should've been there for him."

She wasn't expecting a response from Frankie. She was more just thinking out loud. But Frankie spoke anyway. "Let me ask you something: Do you think things would've changed for him if you'd been around?"

Another big sigh from her that morphed into a frustrated groan as it came out. "I don't know. Probably not." She knew this. She'd been over it in her head a million times. "But I could've been a better friend. I think that's the bottom line for me. He deserved a better friend than the one I was."

They were quiet as Frankie seemed to analyze her words. They listened to the sounds of nature around them. A snap of a twig here, the rustling of snow and leaves there, and there was something incredibly comforting about just sitting there in the silence with Frankie next to her.

"I wish I could say something to make it better," Frankie finally said, her eyes still straight ahead. "I could sit here and tell you that you did the best you could, and that you can't blame yourself for Mason's accident, and that holding on to your guilt will eat you alive inside. And it would all be true. But I don't think it will make a damn bit of difference to you, to your heart." She looked at her then. "You and I are so very much alike that way."

And instead of being upset, instead of feeling worse, something in Cassidy eased then, loosened its grip. Because the reality was Frankie understood. Frankie got it. And it was the first time in a very, very long time that somebody had. "What do we do?" she asked, and the anguish in her voice was clear even to her. "Do we just…learn to live with it?"

"I've been out here for going on three months now trying to

answer that very question." Frankie gave a snorted laugh that seemed like a mix of humor and sarcasm. "But I'm starting to think that, yeah. That's exactly what we do."

"Yeah…" Another long pause before, "How?"

"No fucking clue."

And they laughed. Both of them. Deep, hearty laughs that felt good. For the first time since her arrival nearly two weeks ago, she felt like she was in exactly the right place doing exactly what she'd come there to do. Slowly, she pushed herself to her feet and picked up the box that now held Mason. Not for the first time, she was amazed by how small it actually was. How six foot three Mason had been reduced to a box not much bigger than the size of a brick.

Frankie stood, too, and took a few steps back, clearly giving her some space.

Cassidy looked out at the water and again could see her teenage self sitting next to teenage Mason, all gangly arms and legs, talking about everything and nothing. Then she looked up at the tree, at her initials and his, tucked so tightly together inside the makeshift heart. A lump formed in her throat, and she didn't even try to swallow it down. She let it be.

"I hope this is the right place for you, Mason," she said quietly. "I know you loved it here. Be at peace, okay?" Then she opened the box and the plastic bag inside and scattered some of the ashes around the tree trunk. Taking the rest, she walked toward the water to the spot she estimated was about where they'd sat all those times and scattered the rest. Then she dropped her arms to her sides, the empty box in one hand, and released it all. The pain. The sadness. The hope that Mason was now someplace warm and happy. She wasn't religious, didn't know what she believed in, but she really hoped for peace for her friend. She let out a long slow breath. "That's enough now. Enough."

And when she turned, there was Frankie, waiting patiently for her to do what she needed to do, not hurrying her, not interrupting. She walked back to the tree where Frankie stood.

"Hungry?" Frankie asked.

"I could eat."

"Well, I just happen to be a chef."

"Oh yeah? Lucky me."

And together, they walked back to the house.

CHAPTER TWENTY-ONE

The board is not happy, Cass. Not at all." Jenna's voice the next morning was more desperate than angry, and Cassidy knew she'd reached the end of her rope. "I've done my best to cover for you, but…"

"But Madame Bird is pitching a fit." Madeline Bird was their top investor. She's the one who gave Scentsibilities an influx of cash when it was desperately needed, the one who explained to Cassidy and Jenna why they needed a board and investors. They'd been so new to corporate business, and she'd happily taken them under her wing, two female business owners. And they were grateful. But Madeline Bird did not suffer fools, and she did not like being disobeyed, and she would not ever understand abandoning your post to grieve your friend because you felt guilty you weren't there for him. She'd never do that. Not the abandon her friend part. The feel guilty part. She was icy and brittle and brilliant and had little patience for such silly emotion, as she'd once called it.

"Yes," Jenna said, seemingly relieved to not have to explain herself. "I'm sorry. I covered for you as long as I could," she said again, "but there's been little blips of talk, and I don't like it, and you really, *really* need to come home now."

The board could remove her. That was the drawback of a board. They could remove her from a place of power in her own company. She covered her eyes with her hand and did her best to keep it together. She needed to fix this. Fast.

"It's okay, Jenna. Really. You've been great, and I so appreciate what you've done. I'm so sorry I put this all on you. I'm headed home ASAP." The words were out before she even thought about them, but they felt right. Something about finally scattering Mason's ashes had freed her from feeling tethered to this place.

At least, tethered by Mason.

Frankie was another story.

"You are? Really?"

"Yeah. I've taken enough time. I've put enough on you."

There was a pause, as if Jenna was taking it in. "You take care of what you needed to there?"

"I did. I think it was right."

"Good. And…the girl?"

A sigh slipped out before she could catch it. "Yeah, that'll be harder." She hadn't given Jenna all that much information about Frankie, but also? Jenna wasn't stupid. In fact, she was incredibly intuitive, and she knew Cassidy better than most people did, and Cassidy was sure she'd probably put a lot of the pieces together.

"You seem to have a great connection there. Any chance of seeing her, down the line?"

Goddamn it, she didn't want to think about all of this. She'd been actively trying not to. She and Frankie lived on opposite coasts. Frankie's family was in New York. Cassidy's business was in San Diego. You couldn't get much more long distance than that. Not to mention, they hadn't even discussed any of it. What they were. What they expected. What they wanted…Although she was pretty sure Frankie would be happy to stay there on the mountain and away from her own reality for the rest of her life.

"I don't know. Probably not."

"Oh. Really? That's too bad." And Jenna really did sound disappointed for her. "Are you sure?"

"No."

And then they were quiet for what felt like a long while.

Finally, Jenna spoke, her voice soft and laced with a sympathy that Cassidy didn't want because it only made her eyes fill with tears. "For what it's worth, I've missed you terribly."

"It's worth a lot, and I've missed you, too, babe."

The mood lightened instantly. "So I can tell the board you're on your way?"

Now that she'd decided, she knew it was the right move. "Yes. I'll find myself a flight as early as I can, hopefully tomorrow. No idea if there will even be one, but I'll get back as soon as I can. I'll keep you posted. Okay?"

"Fantastic. I can't wait to see you."

She hung up and stood there, the phone in her hand, and looked out the window of the bedroom that had gone from being her room to just a bedroom. Because her room had become wherever Frankie was sleeping. Last night, they'd moved to Frankie's bedroom, dragged the mattress back, made the bed, and slept there. They'd made love, and there had been something sweet and almost desperate about it, because they knew. Cassidy was convinced that their bodies understood the end was near for them. Scattering Mason's ashes had shifted something in the air between them. In the air in general. Frankie wasn't going to be surprised when she told her she was leaving.

But it was going to hurt. It was going to hurt both of them.

Desperate was not a good look. On anybody. But Frankie felt it like it was something that had been injected into her blood.

Cassidy was leaving. Of course she was.

She was stir-frying some vegetables and chicken for their dinner, using a big pan that wasn't a wok but was the closest thing in the kitchen. She tossed them in a little oil, added some seasonings, tossed some more. The smell was heavenly, but she barely noticed. Because Cassidy was leaving.

"Can I help?" Cassidy's voice behind her startled her, and she felt her whole body flinch.

A nod toward the cupboard. "Plates." The rice was done and keeping warm in a pot on the stove. It was going to get gluey soon, so she removed the lid and scooped it onto plates Cassidy set down, relieved to see it was still fluffy. Once a chef, always a chef, even while her heart was squeezing in her chest. She scraped the veggies and chicken evenly onto the rice, sprinkled on some salt and pepper, and handed Cassidy a plate. Silently, they carried them to the living room instead of the dining room, because the area near the fireplace had become their space. Frankie took the hammock chair. Cassidy took the chair next to it, which they'd stopped sliding over and just left there instead.

"This is delicious," Cassidy said after a couple bites.

"Thanks."

More silence. Frankie wasn't hungry but made herself eat a few bites.

"So..." Cassidy said.

"You're leaving."

Cassidy's eyes widened in surprise for a second before she pressed her lips together in a thin line and tried to hold Frankie's gaze. Frankie wouldn't let her and returned her focus to her food.

"Yes. I have to. My company needs me."

"You've barely been gone for three weeks," Frankie said with a scoff. "If they're struggling already, they've got bigger problems than you being gone." It was snarky. And kind of mean. And Frankie didn't care. There was an element of something—worry? panic?—bubbling up inside her, a slow simmer that she knew was heading for full boil. She just didn't know how to stop it.

"My business partner says the board is getting antsy." It seemed important to Cassidy that she explain, but Frankie had a hard time listening, to be honest. "We're not a huge company, but we've done well, and at the slightest hint of mismanagement..." Cassidy shrugged, clearly shooting for nonchalant. "They could remove me."

"So you have to go." Snarky. Again. God, what was wrong with her?

"So I have to go. Yes."

She nodded. Once. *Then just go already*, she wanted to shout. And at the same time she wanted to say any number of things that were the opposite: *Please stay. You're the only light I've had in my life in nine months. I'm not sure I'll survive if you leave. I think I'm in love with you...* That last tidbit was a surprise—and it wasn't. Her feelings for Cassidy had grown intense, true, but Jesus, Mary, and Joseph, they'd only known each other for a couple weeks. Feelings of love didn't develop that quickly.

Did they?

All of that went through her head before she said what she did.

"Okay." She picked up her plate and took it into the dining room, a room they hardly ever ate in, and sat down at the table. Her stomach was churning sourly, and her appetite had flown out the window at Cassidy's words, but she pretended. Shoveled food into her mouth and made herself chew it.

"That's it?" Cassidy followed her a minute or two later, plate in hand. "*Okay?*"

She shrugged. "What more do you want me to say?"

Cassidy's dark eyes went comically wide, and she stared. Blinking. Just stared and blinked at her. And then her shoulders dropped, like she was simply giving up. With a heavy sigh, she sat at the opposite end of the table and picked up her fork. "I don't know," she said finally. "I mean, did you think I could just stay here forever?" There was an edge to her voice, similar to the way she'd sounded when she'd first arrived, and Frankie recognized now it was her standing up for herself voice.

"No," she said. *Yes*, she thought. Was that so wrong?

"This is really good," Cassidy said after a long silence, and when Frankie looked up from her plate, Cassidy was smiling and her eyes were shimmering with wetness.

"Thanks."

"I'm gonna miss your cooking."

"I'm gonna miss you." With those words, all the winds of anger went right out of Frankie's sails. She felt her own eyes well up, clenched her jaw to keep herself from crying.

Cassidy wasn't as stoic. She let her tears slide silently down her cheeks as she ate, every now and then glancing up at Frankie and giving her a sad smile.

It seemed to be by unspoken agreement that they wouldn't make love that night. The night before had been hard enough, emotionally, and Frankie didn't think she could do it again without breaking down. Cassidy seemed to feel the same way, so they snuggled together in Frankie's bed instead.

"Are you excited to get back?" she asked on a whisper after they'd settled in. Cassidy's head was tucked up under her chin, her arm thrown across Frankie's middle.

"I mean, there's an element of that, yeah. I'm almost never gone more than a couple days."

"I bet you miss the weather." She gave Cassidy a squeeze.

"Oh my God, you have no idea. I live pretty close to the beach, and I love to walk on it. I'll tell you, walking in the sand is almost as hard as walking in the snow."

"But a lot more pleasant, I bet, given the sun and warmth and silly things like that."

"Little bit." The silence lasted a few moments. Then, "When will you go home, Frankie? I mean, you *will* go home eventually, right? Your poor mom."

It was a subject she actively avoided thinking about, because if she thought about it, she'd have to think about why she was there in the first place. And thinking about the accident was never something that took her to a good place. "Eventually," she said vaguely.

It was Cassidy's turn to squeeze her. "I wish you'd ease up on yourself. What happened was awful and tragic and horrific. But it was an accident, and some day, you're gonna need to let it go. You can't live out the rest of your days as a hermit up here on the mountain. The world deserves to have you be a part of it. A bigger part than doing your impression of Jack." She pushed herself up onto her elbow to look down at her, and Frankie could've sworn she felt Cassidy's eyes look into her soul as she whispered, "I personally think the world is lucky to have somebody like you in it."

And then she was kissing her, and the whole *we should just cuddle tonight* idea vanished into the ether like steam. Cassidy kissed her softly at first, and she shifted her body so she lay fully on Frankie's. Frankie opened her legs to make room for Cassidy's hips, as she'd done multiple times in the past two weeks. They fit together like they were made to, like they'd been built just for that. Frankie slid her hands up the back of Cassidy's shirt, reveling in the indescribable softness of her skin. Seriously, how could one woman be this soft? It was otherworldly. Her hands trailed up to Cassidy's shoulders, and then she thought, to hell with it, and pulled the shirt up and off. And then Cassidy was topless. She pushed herself up to her knees, straddling Frankie, her breasts on display, and Frankie felt a surge of wetness between her legs because sweet baby Jesus, was there anything in the world sexier to look at than a topless Cassidy, straddling her hips, bathed in moonlight?

No. The answer to that question was a resounding no, and Frankie let her eyes feast for a moment before reaching up and cupping both breasts in her hands.

"Cassidy," she whispered, and Cassidy looked down at her, and their eyes locked and held.

"Francesca," Cassidy whispered back, then leaned forward and crushed her mouth to Frankie's.

The rest was a melding. Of mouths. Of bodies. And if anybody asked Frankie, she'd have said of souls as well. She'd never connected to anybody the way she did to Cassidy. Last night, there'd been a strange feeling. A desperation of sorts. But tonight, there was nothing but connection. Melding was absolutely the perfect word. There were times where she had no idea where she ended and Cassidy began. There were times when she had no idea what Cassidy was doing to her, where she was touching her or with what. All she knew was that, in that moment, it was her and Cassidy and their hearts and their souls and that was all that mattered.

The rest could wait.

And it did. For a while. They made love well into the night, stopping only briefly for air or water before they slid back into that blending of bodies. Cassidy had to get on the road early to make her flight, but Frankie didn't care, and Cassidy didn't seem to either. They stayed up, stayed touching and kissing and thrusting and stroking until the sky began to morph from inky black to burgeoning indigo. Frankie fell asleep not long after Cassidy's breathing had gone deep and even as she lay in her arms, but only out of necessity. Her brain was a whirlwind, but her body was wrung out, and her eyes drifted closed while the sky was still deep purple, and the house was silent.

The next morning was harder than Frankie expected it to be, and she got the impression it was the same for Cassidy. Neither of them said much as Cassidy packed her things and hauled her bags down the steps and outside and into the rental.

Frankie approached her with a cup of coffee, and they stood there, side by side in front of the big picture window, and sipped their coffee silently, watching the woods. Frankie had filled the feeders while Cassidy was upstairs, and now the cardinals and chickadees and sparrows were chirping up a storm as they ate, joined by the squirrels and an occasional chipmunk on the ground.

Cassidy leaned against Frankie. Frankie put an arm around her, and if they could've stood like that, just like that, touching and quiet and content for the rest of time, she'd have been perfectly okay with that.

But they couldn't.

She felt Cassidy stir and knew she was about to speak before she even took a breath.

"I should probably get going."

Such a simple statement. How could five words slice her heart open? How was that even possible?

But she didn't say that, didn't ask the question. Instead, she nodded and removed her arm from Cassidy's shoulder. Cassidy turned to face her, then set her mug on the windowsill and did the same with Frankie's. Then she took both Frankie's hands in hers, held them, and looked deep into her eyes. Frankie swore she could feel it inside, touching her heart, her soul. Her eyes welled up before she even thought they might.

"Please take care of yourself, Francesca." Her voice was soft, just above a whisper, and Frankie wondered if it was because she was afraid it would break if she spoke louder. She cleared her throat and gave Frankie's hands a small shake. "Don't make me worry."

She nodded. It was all she could do because she was now afraid *her* voice would break if she spoke.

"I had no idea what to expect when I came here. I wasn't even sure if it was the right place for me to be, but you helped me see that it was. Thank you for that. *You* were unexpected." And before Frankie could respond—which she couldn't because the lump in her throat was baseball sized—she pushed up onto her toes, pulled Frankie's head down, and kissed her. Softly. Sweetly. And when she lowered back down, a small sound left her lips, a combination whimper and cry, and then she turned without another word and left the house.

Frankie stood in the doorway and watched her get into her car, start the engine, plug in her phone. The air was brisk. Cold. She didn't care. She stood there, no coat, hands in the back pockets of her jeans, and watched as the most amazing thing that had happened to her in a very, very long time put her SUV into gear and drove away.

Only then did she let the tears flow and the sob burst from her throat, and she shouted her pain into the air.

It echoed back to her.

CHAPTER TWENTY-TWO

Cassidy didn't even realize she'd been daydreaming until the rap at her open door startled her enough to make her flinch. She glanced up to see Brittany, her admin, standing in her doorway and looking apologetic.

"I'm so sorry. I didn't mean to scare you."

Cassidy waved her off. "No worries. What's up?"

"I just wanted to remind you that you have a call with Kevin Hooper from Target at two, and I emailed you the reports you asked for. And…" She crossed the office to Cassidy's desk and set down a grande-sized cup. "I went to Starbucks on my break and got you a latte. You seem so sad lately—I wanted to do something to cheer you up."

Cassidy felt that goddamn lump clog her throat. Again. The same one that had been showing up on a regular basis for over a week now. She swallowed twice, trying to find her voice, and when she didn't, Brittany frowned.

"I'm sorry. Did I overstep? I overstepped." She waved a hand. "It's none of my business. I'm sorry. I—"

"Brittany." There it was. She did have a voice after all. Now, how about a smile? Or at least a small grin? Could she manage that for this poor girl who was just trying to be kind? She focused on fixing her face and knew she'd found it when Brittany visibly relaxed. "It's okay. Stop worrying." She gestured to the latte. "This was really nice of you. Thank you."

"You're welcome." She backed toward the door and gave her a shrug. "You're just usually so happy and…well, it's hard to see you this down. I hope you feel better soon."

And she was gone.

Thank fucking God because she was worried she might start crying right there as she sat at her desk. It wouldn't be the first time since her return ten days ago. And yeah, the CEO crying in her office was a great morale booster for the office. Stellar. She shook her head, picked up the latte, and took a sip. Vanilla with a pump of caramel. Just the way she liked it. Brittany paid attention. She jotted herself a note to give the girl a raise next quarter.

She had ten more minutes until her call with Target. The old Cassidy would've used that precious time to get one more thing done, to cram in one more call or answer as many emails as possible. The new Cassidy? The one who'd been changed on a mountain in the snow? She preferred to stare out the window. The sun had never made her angry before. Not once. The moment she'd moved to San Diego and had begun to experience its absolutely perfect weather, she'd fallen in love with the sun. Its daily appearance. Its perfect seventy-two-degree temperature. What wasn't to love about that? But now? Now, she longed for snow. And crisp fresh winter air. The crunch under her feet. The crackling of a fireplace. Thick, warm socks—she'd kept the pair Frankie had lent her and wore them every night, despite her apartment being a perfect seventy degrees.

And Frankie.

She worried about Frankie. All the damn time. She'd known she would but didn't expect to at this level, pretty much every minute of every day. She'd texted. She'd waited a few days, not wanting to jump right in, wanting to get herself home and settled and take some time to let her brain decompress from the whirlwind that was late November–early December for her.

Frankie hadn't answered.

If she was being honest with herself, she wasn't all that surprised. Frankie was in a place only she could get herself out of. But she had to *want* out, and Cassidy honestly wasn't sure if she did.

Still.

She missed her.

She picked up her phone and typed out a quick text before she could second-guess herself.

Thinking of you...

Simple. Honest. She hit Send.

"Cassidy?" Brittany's voice broke through her thoughts through the speaker on her office phone. "Kevin Hooper from Target on three." "Okay, thanks." She inhaled deeply. Slowly. Let it out. Then she gave herself a shake, hoping to shove thoughts of Frankie into a corner for now so she could focus on her job. She picked up the phone and forced some cheer into her voice.

"Kevin, hi, how's the weather in Minneapolis today?"

❖

The days were a little duller now.

That's how Frankie looked at things now that Cassidy had gone home. And that was how Frankie needed to force herself to look at things: Cassidy hadn't left. She'd gone home. There was a difference.

Didn't feel like one, though, really.

That first night in bed without her had been brutal. And how was that even fucking possible? It's not like she'd been sharing a bed with Cassidy for years. Or even months. It had been days. She didn't understand what had happened to her. How she could have grown so used to somebody's presence in her life after such a short time? Especially given how isolated she'd made herself, and yes, she knew that right there could be the argument. That she'd isolated herself and when somebody else had come along, she'd clung to them. But she didn't think that was it. No, she *knew* that wasn't it. She was a reasonably intelligent woman, and she was completely aware that she'd started to fall for Cassidy Clarke, and *that* she had no idea what to do with.

Not that it hadn't rattled around in her brain since the second Cassidy had left. Not that she wasn't supremely irritated at her stupid self for not saying something—anything—to Cassidy about it before she'd gotten into her car and driven away. Not that Cassidy wasn't texting her on and off to see how she was doing.

Not that she'd answered.

And why hadn't she? Why was she being rude?

Before she could drive herself even more bananas with those questions, the back door burst open, and Reiko came blowing into the kitchen with the winter wind.

"Hey," she said, unzipping her coat and sliding it off, but leaving her hat on, per usual.

"Hey." Frankie had to stop stirring the hot chocolate she was making and think about what day it was, and when she realized it was indeed a weekend, she tucked away her Why Aren't You in School speech. "What's up?" She automatically got the milk and added more to the pan, along with cocoa and vanilla, so there was enough for both of them.

"Ugh," Reiko said and infused it with the weight of the world as only a twelve-year-old could do. "My mom is such a bitch."

Frankie snapped her head around. "Watch it. I know you two struggle, but she's your mom, and it's not cool that you talk about her like that."

"Why not? She drives me crazy. She thinks she needs to be my mother *and* my father, and it's so…intrusive."

"And have you talked to her about it? Or do you just yell at her?" Frankie kept her voice calm, which was a feat, given how badly she wanted to stick up for Eden.

"Ugh, all she wants to do is talk. Like, can't we just be quiet sometimes? It's why I come up here."

"You come up here to run away from your problems, let's be honest. You can't keep doing that. It's not healthy."

"Isn't that why you're here?"

Frankie blinked.

Well, shit.

She stopped stirring but kept her eyes on the pan. *Seriously, Universe? A twelve-year-old? That's how we're doing this?*

"Yeah, well." Honestly, what could she say? The kid wasn't wrong. In fact, she was much righter than Frankie cared to admit. Like, she was exactly right. And for the first time, Frankie made herself stop and think about that.

Giving herself a shake, she refocused on the hot cocoa and poured it into cups. Then she sat with Reiko in silence for a long moment. They blew on their drinks and sipped in tandem, like they'd been choreographed.

Finally, Frankie cleared her throat. "I want you to do something for me."

Reiko met her eyes, and Frankie was startled to see in them a flash of both a child and a wise adult. It was an interesting glimpse of who

Reiko would be when she was grown. Frankie didn't know why or how she could see that, but she could. Reiko gave a wary nod.

"I want you to cut your mom some slack."

Reiko sighed. Loudly. The child.

"Listen, she lost your dad, too. Right? And she's your mom and she's worried about you. That's what moms do. They worry about their kids. All the time. Forever."

"Does your mom worry about you being up here all by yourself?"

"Endlessly. Yes."

"Do you cut her some slack?"

A good question and far too wise a one for a kid to ask. "Probably not like I should."

"I will if you will." Reiko blinked her big brown eyes at Frankie and waited.

"Deal." Frankie held up her pinkie and Reiko curled hers around it.

Later that day, after Reiko had gone home on the promise that she would give Eden more of a chance than she had been, Frankie's mind went in all different directions. More snow was forecast, so she chopped up more wood and toyed with the idea of dragging her mattress back out into the living room in an attempt to recapture some of the feeling of when Cassidy had been there. She made a big pot of chili, heavy with beans and ground beef, and a pan of cornbread to go with it. The only way to keep from constantly thinking about Cassidy, how much she missed her, and how she really should respond to her texts because she was being fucking rude by not doing so, was to stay busy.

She filled up a plastic bowl with chili, a smaller one with plain burger, wrapped half the pan of cornbread in some foil, and headed out to Jack's place. The walk there, the conversation, the walk back—that would kill much of her day. Tomorrow, she'd start on painting the upstairs rooms Ethan Lustenfeld had asked her to in his last call.

The day was brisk. Overcast and cold. The snow hadn't begun yet, so the path through the woods to Jack's place wasn't as hard to walk as it had been last time. She trudged along, catching a couple deer in the process of searching for food. The sky was a light gray, not heavy with precipitation yet, but Frankie could smell that it was on its way. Something Jack had taught her in her second week there—what the snow smelled like when it was still hanging in the air. Crisp and fresh and wet. She smiled as she walked along.

It didn't occur to her until she could see Jack's cabin that Duke hadn't come barking out to greet her like usual. Maybe they were eating inside. Food always won first place in Duke's list of things he paid attention to, thus the bowl of ground beef she was carrying.

At his front door, she stomped the snow off her boots and knocked. "Jack? It's Frankie. I brought you some dinner."

Silence.

Okay, maybe he was out for a walk or hunting or something. She glanced around, but the only fresh footprints in the snow seemed to be hers. She knocked again. "Jack?"

And that's when she heard it. The soft, low, gentle whine. Duke.

Her heart rate kicked up because she knew something was wrong, and she grabbed the door handle and let herself in.

She'd only been inside a few times. She and Jack tended to have their chats outside among the trees, so Duke could run around. She'd forgotten how very small the place was. Basically, one big square. Jack's bedroom and living room were one and the same, and he lay on his back on the twin bed, unmoving. Duke was curled up next to him, his doggie chin on Jack's chest. Which was not rising and falling.

"Oh my God," she whispered.

It was very clear he was gone, but she checked for a pulse anyway. Nothing. His eyes were slightly open, his lips parted, the pallor of his skin that dull gray that said no blood was flowing beneath it. He was under a blanket, as if he'd been asleep, and she wondered if he'd gone that way. In his sleep. She hoped so. "Oh, Jack."

She stood there for a moment, allowing herself time to get her bearings because, hello? She'd never discovered a dead body before. Poor Duke looked heartbroken as he lay there with his master, and she wondered how long they'd been like this. He would have to come back with her. She pulled out her phone and was unsurprised to see she had zero reception.

She pursed her lips and blew out a slow breath, and then her eyes welled up and she knew she needed to take a minute, that Jack deserved to have somebody mourn him. She let the tears track silently down her cheeks as she glanced around. She paused on a framed photograph she had never noticed on the mantel of his small fireplace. It was clearly a young Jack, clean-shaven and with his arms around two boys that looked much too much like him to not be his sons. Jack had kids? A family? And yet chose to live out here in the wilderness all alone? Where he subsequently died alone?

A wave of panic suddenly washed through Frankie, hot and weird, and it made her feel jumpy. Nervous and jerky. This could be her. She turned back to Jack, dead in his bed, alone, with nothing but a loyal dog to mourn his loss, and holy fucking shit, this could just as easily be her. She and Jack were not so different. Knowing he had family somewhere made that all too clear to her, and she suddenly felt like she was suffocating, like she couldn't get enough air. She looked around in a panic, hurled herself at the door and out into the cold, fresh air where she took a moment to just breathe.

And then out of nowhere, a calm hit. It was the strangest thing. Just an unexpected calm, and she spoke out loud, nobody to hear her but Duke.

"No."

She said it firmly. Loudly enough that the dog raised his head and looked quizzically at her.

"This is not going to be me. It's not." And then it was as if her legs lost the ability to hold her up. She dropped to her knees and a sob ripped from her lungs. "Please, God, don't let this be me." Tears flowed as she rocked forward and backward on her knees, her arms wrapped around herself. "Don't let this be me." She whispered it over and over again. And all she wanted right then? The only thing on the planet she could think of to make her world right again? Was Cassidy. And so she cried some more.

But not for long because just as quickly as it had shown up, the panic was replaced by solid, staunch determination. Hard and strong. She pushed herself to her feet again. No, this would not be her, goddamn it. She would *not* go out like this, alone in the woods with nobody looking out for her. She had a family, goddamn it. She had friends. She had *a life*. Or at least, she had, before the accident. Before she decided to put it all on a shelf and isolated herself out here. She had the power to make changes in her life. She always had. She was the only one who could.

She stroked Duke's big head gently, lovingly. "Come on, buddy. You have to come with me now, okay?" Looking around the small space, she spotted a leash hanging on a nail in the wall. Jack hardly ever leashed Duke except for during hunting season, but she wasn't sure he would come with her, so she clipped the leash to his collar and gently tugged him off the bed. Then she gazed at the still face of the man she knew little about but had liked a lot. "I hope you've let go of your demons and found peace, Jack." Then she pulled the blanket up over his face. "Come on, Duke. Let's go."

Surprisingly, the dog followed her, but slowly and with little of the exuberance she was used to from him. He was mourning and she knew that. She'd help him with that. She knew how.

They retraced her steps, but at a much slower pace. She held her phone out in front of her until she had bars, and then she dialed.

"9-1-1, what's your emergency?"

CHAPTER TWENTY-THREE

Christmas was literally only two days away.

It was a very busy time of year at Scentsibilities. The holiday party had happened the night before. Holiday bonuses were given to all the employees. Vacations and time off were planned, and they shut down production for the week between Christmas and New Year's Day, so lots of stuff got crammed into that last week before Christmas. It was a time of year that Cassidy truly enjoyed, even without any family. She liked to spend time with her friends, be generous to her employees, and basically relax and breathe a bit.

But this year?

This year was different. This year, instead of celebratory and cheerful, she felt empty. Unfinished. Like part of her was missing. Even when she'd been missing Mason the most, she'd never felt like this. Like she was missing a limb. Like there was a hole inside her. A void.

A Frankie-shaped one.

Yeah, she knew that. Of course she did. She wasn't stupid. She had just hoped the feeling would ease up. Die down. Go away.

It had done none of those things. In fact, it had intensified.

Frankie hadn't answered her texts, and that was probably a pretty obvious ticket to the clue bus she should be riding. But she felt like she knew Frankie well enough—*after three weeks? Really?*—to know that she was a person who'd need time. Cassidy arrived at conclusions pretty quickly. She'd always been a quick thinker and a quick analyzer of her own feelings. She didn't think that was Frankie. "I mean, come on, she's been living alone in the wilderness for three months now," she muttered aloud to her empty office.

It was going on seven in the evening on the twenty-third, and she'd been there since before seven that morning. She'd spent the last couple of weeks catching up on the things she'd neglected while in the mountains. Patching up holes and mending relationships with clients. She'd worked hard, stayed in the office late, mostly because when she went home, all she did was reminisce about mountain air and wood fires and deer walking through the snow and hammock chairs and making love in front of the fireplace. If she focused on work, she could keep her mind busy. And if she stayed at work long enough, she would be so tired by the time she got home that she'd fall into bed and sleep almost immediately.

She dreamed about Frankie, but there wasn't much she could do about that.

She heard the squeak of wheels in need of some WD-40 before she saw Harvey, the guy who cleaned the offices at night, push his cleaning cart into view. They'd become used to one another's presence lately, she and Harvey, and he rapped on her doorjamb like he had every night this week.

"You still here, Ms. Clarke? S'late." His skin was dark, his hair white, and the lines in his face made him seem wise, but kind, like everybody's loving grandpa. He'd been with the company for several years, was a fixture there. He'd mentioned several times to her how proud it made him to see a woman of color as the CEO. She liked that.

Cassidy nodded and gave him a smile. "Afraid so."

"It's the holidays, you know." He used a rag to wipe down the windowsill, then tucked it into his pocket and unhooked a dust mop from his cart, swiped it along the floor as he spoke. "You shouldn't be here so late."

"What do you do for the holidays, Harvey?" she asked him, suddenly wanting to know, then propped her chin in her hand. "You got family?"

"I do." Harvey nodded but didn't look up and didn't stop mopping. "Four kids, three grandkids. They all come over. My wife cooks up a storm." He smiled as he put his mop back. "My favorite time of year. I love having them all under the same roof again." He walked toward her desk, and she handed him her wastebasket. "You?"

"I don't have any family," she said, "but there is a person that I think I really have grown to care about."

"Yeah? That's good. Lotta people don't ever get that."

She nodded, her thoughts swirling.

"You gonna be with that person for Christmas?"

A shrug. "No, I don't think so."

"You should. Make it happen."

"You think?"

"You kidding? Ma'am, it's Christmas and life is damn short. Take it from a man who's survived two heart attacks and colon cancer. If not now, then when?"

"Yeah, maybe…" She left the sentence unfinished.

"No maybes about it. Trust me." He put a clean bag into her wastebasket and handed it back to her. Then he gave her a smile and a nod, wished her a Merry Christmas, and headed down the hall to the next office.

She sat there for a long while after that, her mind a swirl of thoughts and ideas and emotions and confusion and longing and…

If not now, then when?

Then she blew out a breath. There really was only one thing to do. She grabbed her phone and made a call.

"Hey, Cass." Jenna's voice was cheerful, and the background noise made it pretty clear she was in a bar or a restaurant. "Everything okay?"

"I have to go back." Cassidy blurted it without preamble. Without hesitation.

"What? Go back where?" There was a shuffling sound. "Hang on, I can hardly hear you. Lemme get someplace quiet." A few seconds passed, and the background noise faded. "Okay, I'm in the ladies' room. Go back where? What are you talking about?"

"I think I love her." The words even surprised Cassidy when they came out of her mouth.

"*What?*"

"It makes total sense now. God, no wonder I've felt so weird lately."

"This is the mountain chick we're talking about, I assume."

"Frankie. Yes."

Jenna's voice grew stern. "Cassidy. Are you sure? I mean, you've known her for what? Two weeks? Three? Has she even returned your texts?"

She'd told Jenna about texting Frankie and how Frankie hadn't responded. But Cassidy knew her well. Better than she even thought she did. And she knew Frankie would need time to absorb before she reached out. She just *knew*. "Not yet. But she will."

"Why don't you wait until she does?"

It was a valid question, but Harvey's words echoed through her brain once more, and at the same time, Mason's face materialized in her mind, as if to punctuate what Harvey had said. "Life is short, Jen. If not now, then when?"

Jenna was quiet for a few seconds, and Cassidy could picture her making her thinking face, the little divot between her eyebrows creasing deeply, as it always did when she was trying to solve something. "I'm standing here against the sinks in the bathroom of Corey's and trying to come up with a good answer to that. But honestly? I've never known you to be this…distracted. By anyone or anything."

She opened her mouth to respond, but no words came to her, so she waited until Jenna spoke again.

"And that tells me that there's something there." Her voice went soft, and then she blew out a long, slow breath. "Okay. Go. Why not? Things at work are winding down for the holiday. I can cover you."

"Seriously? You'd do that? Again?"

"Is this something you need to do?"

She answered without hesitation. "Absolutely."

"Then go. I've got you."

"Jenna, I don't know what to say."

"You're my bestie, Cass. I want you to be happy. Just, do me a favor?"

"Anything."

"Don't be gone for weeks on end, okay?"

"I promise." There was a beat before she added, "Hey, Jenna? Thank you. I love you, you know."

"I love you, too, even when you're a giant pain in my ass. I hope you can get a flight this late."

"Me, too. Merry Christmas, Jen."

"Back atcha, Cassidy. Go get the girl, okay?"

❖

There was no way to get directly to the Adirondacks from San Diego. Not at this time of year. Not at such a last-minute date. Cassidy snagged the last seat on a Christmas Eve flight into Chicago O'Hare, then on to Buffalo, then to the tiny Saranac Lake airport. It was going to take her some time, but she'd get there. Eventually. Hopefully, before Christmas was over.

The plane jerked as the wheels touched down, and she put her hand on the seat in front of her to brace. They taxied, parked at the gate, and then came the sardine-can crowding of everybody trying to get off the plane at once. She rolled her eyes at the guy who cut her off in the aisle so he could get off the plane a full three seconds before she did, but after several minutes, she was off the walkway and into the airport itself.

She hated O'Hare. It was always overcrowded and far too huge. But she'd been through it dozens of times during her travels to see clients, so she knew it well. She had time to kill before her connection—the board said it was still on time, which was a miracle in itself, frankly—and looked for a bar with an empty seat where she could grab a drink and maybe a late lunch.

As she walked through the airport, passing other gates, she started typing out a text to Jenna to let her know where she was. She'd promised Jenna—and herself—that she'd stay in better touch so that Jenna didn't get overwhelmed by unforeseen issues covering her work. She sent the text, hauled her computer backpack up farther on her shoulder, and glanced to her left.

Holy shit.

She stopped so abruptly that the guy behind her ran smack into her back, apologized, and went around her. She became a rock in the stream, the flow of busy, hurried travelers moving around her as she stood still. And stared.

At Frankie.

Frankie, who was dressed in jeans and black ankle boots and a white V-neck and a black coat.

Frankie, whose hair was pulled back into a low ponytail.

Frankie, who had apparently just gotten off a flight and was walking quickly through the gate area straight toward Cassidy, but looking down at the phone in her hand. When she glanced up, their eyes met and she stopped dead in her tracks, garnering her a dirty look from the woman behind her, who went around with a muttered, "Jeez, lady."

"Cassidy?" she said, bewilderment clear in her voice. And then Cassidy was in her arms, hugging her, and kissing her face. She couldn't stop herself and they stood there in the middle of the terminal like a tree growing in the midst of a rushing river, forcing people to walk around them. She didn't care about the dirty looks, the sighs of annoyance. Did. Not. Care.

Because *Frankie*.

"What are you doing here?" Cassidy asked, a mix of thrilled and bewildered. What in the world was happening?

"I'm"—Frankie glanced down at her feet—"on my way to San Diego." She looked up. "You?"

"On my way back to Shelton, New York. Seems I miss my mountain. And everybody on it."

"Your mountain, huh?"

"Yeah."

"Well. I think your mountain misses you. So does everybody on it. Including me." Frankie cleared her throat. "Especially me."

The annoyed looks and muttered comments were increasing as the two of them stood in the middle of the walkway, so Cassidy took Frankie's arm and tugged her toward a nearby bar. "I think we should talk. Drink?"

"Yes, please. Possibly several."

They found a small table for two in a far corner of the woefully unoriginal airport-themed bar and restaurant called Flight Plan. They each had a carry-on, and Cassidy had her backpack, and they piled them all next to the table, then sat. And stared. All Cassidy wanted to do was stare at Frankie's beautiful face. Her dark eyes. Her curls, pulled back, yes, but a few were staging a daring escape and dangled near her cheeks.

For her part, Frankie stared back, her eyes intense, a ghost of a smile on her face.

"I mean," Cassidy finally said, "what the actual fuck, right?" Frankie barked a laugh. "Who'd have predicted this?"

"Did you text me? Tell me you were coming?" Frankie asked.

Cassidy cleared her throat and gave her a look. "So you could ignore it like the rest of my texts? No, I didn't."

Frankie had the good sense to blush and look sheepish. "Yeah, I'm sorry about that. I…"

The waitress interrupted them to take their orders. A beer for Frankie, a glass of cabernet for Cassidy.

"Jack died." Frankie said it so matter-of-factly that Cassidy thought she'd heard her wrong.

"I'm…What?"

"Yeah. I went to check on him last week and found him dead in his bed. A heart attack in his sleep, they said."

"Oh my God. Frankie." She reached across the table and closed her hand over Frankie's forearm. "That's awful. I'm so sorry. He was nice. I liked him. Are you okay?" Seriously, what more did the Universe expect this poor woman to deal with?

The waitress delivered their drinks. Frankie picked up her beer. "To Jack?"

"He was a good guy. To Jack."

They touched their glasses together and sipped in silence. Wow. This was not at all what Cassidy had expected. None of it. Not running into Frankie. Not sitting at O'Hare having drinks with her, both of them miles from home. Not hearing about Jack's death. No, she hadn't known him well at all, but what she did know, she liked. And he'd helped find the perfect spot for Mason's ashes, so she felt like she owed him a debt of gratitude. Then she gasped as something occurred to her.

"Oh God, what about Duke?"

Frankie smiled. "He's with Reiko and Eden right now, but he's going to be staying with me from now on."

Well, that was perfect, and she said so. "I think that'll be good for you both."

"Yeah."

Conversation seemed to stall then, but Cassidy could tell that Frankie had something on her mind. She'd learned her signals, and right now, she was gazing off toward the terminal, seemingly watching people flow by. But Cassidy suspected she was actually gathering her thoughts. She sipped her wine and waited.

"Jack is why I'm here," Frankie finally said. "Well, not here, sitting in O'Hare. But on my way to you."

"Explain."

Frankie set her beer down and slowly turned the glass in both hands, seemingly collecting her thoughts. "I don't know why Jack was the way he was. Living in the woods alone. I know there was a reason. Something he did or was a part of? But I know from Eden that he exiled himself there years ago. Even working at the camp was a form of exile for him. Away from his old life. After the camp closed, he just stayed."

Cassidy nodded and thought of the comparison between Frankie and Jack, how alike they were, but she said nothing. Didn't want to interrupt Frankie's flow.

"We were kind of alike," Frankie said, as if reading Cassidy's mind.

Cassidy nodded again.

"When I found him, he was all alone with poor Duke lying with him. And he had a photograph on a shelf that..." She cleared her throat and Cassidy saw there were unshed tears in her eyes. "I think they were his kids, and I wondered if they even knew where he was, if they'd even care that he died, and God, Cassidy, I don't want to be that. I don't want to be him. I don't want to die all alone because I couldn't get past one particular moment in my life." The tears spilled over and tracked silently down her cheeks. Her dark eyes were wide, fixed on Cassidy, and Cassidy's heart squeezed in her chest. Frankie reached across the table and took her hand. "And the first person I wanted to say that to was you."

She hadn't expected this. Not any of it. But all she could do was smile. Big. She squeezed Frankie's hand in her own. "I'm so glad. I'm so glad you were going to fly clear across the damn country to tell me that when you could've just called."

"It was really nice of you to meet me halfway," Frankie said with a grin, and then they both were laughing. Once that died down, Cassidy looked into Frankie's eyes.

"My turn for confession. I realized some things, too."

"Yeah? Tell me."

"I learned that work isn't everything. I mean, it's a lot, given I built my company from the ground up."

"I mean, duh," Frankie said with a nod.

"But it's not everything." She brought her other hand to the table so that Frankie's hand was in both of hers. She studied it, Frankie's hand. How it was strong, but also pretty. Her long fingers and neatly filed nails. A flash of those hands on her body, what they were able to do to her, sent a wave of heat through her. "I've never had much in the way of family, and I have only a handful of friends that I trust with my heart." She took a beat to collect her thoughts, feeling like she was kind of all over the place here. "When you didn't return my texts, I tried to shrug it off."

"I'm sorry about that," Frankie began, but Cassidy squeezed her hands and shook her head.

"No. No, you don't have to be sorry. I think we were both trying to make sense of those weeks we spent together. What they meant. Why they felt the way they did. At least, that's what I was doing."

Frankie nodded. "Same."

"Here's what I know—I have never felt with anybody in my entire life the way I feel when I'm with you. And I've been on my own long enough to know that's kind of a big deal."

More nodding from Frankie. "I feel the same way."

"Yeah?"

"Yeah."

"Then what do we do about it?"

There was a moment then, where they held eye contact. Just looked at each other, and Cassidy would've sworn in that moment that she could see into Frankie's very soul, see everything within her, and there was so much good. So much love. It brought tears to her eyes. Frankie squeezed her hands, then reached out and brushed the wetness from her cheek with a thumb.

Frankie glanced at her phone sitting on the table, then very quietly, she spoke. "I don't know about you, but I've missed my connection. What if we just stayed here for a while. Get a hotel room that has room service. Just *be* together. It's Christmas Eve."

She'd forgotten momentarily that it was. The restaurant had windows that looked out onto the tarmac. Fat snowflakes were floating to the ground. Combined with the holiday decorations in the dining area and the carols on the PA, how could she have possibly forgotten? So different than San Diego, but also so very apropos.

"I think that sounds perfect."

CHAPTER TWENTY-FOUR

The Holiday Inn was the only hotel with a room left. Appropriate, Frankie thought, since it was a holiday and all. They took the shuttle, checked in, and were led to the only suite left. Seventh floor. End of the hall. Perfect.

Of course, they could've put the two of them in the housekeeping closet and Frankie would've been totally fine with that. Because she was with Cassidy and there was nowhere in the world she'd rather be.

They'd taken a quick zip across a couple streets to an open 7-Eleven and grabbed beer, soda, and a bunch of snacks, since the clerk at the hotel had informed them there'd be no room service as the kitchen staff had been sent home for the holiday. Neither of them had checked luggage, so they'd be good for a few days.

She'd called her mother to tell her, and her mother's tone was… different this time. Relieved, Frankie thought. Relieved she was off the mountain. Relieved she wasn't alone. Not thrilled she wasn't coming home for the holiday, but still, relieved.

Man, she was going to owe her mother some serious one-on-one time when she got through this.

When she got through this?

Huh.

That was the first time she'd actually entertained the idea that she would. That she would get through this. Well, wasn't that interesting?

"What are you thinking?" Cassidy asked, pulling her out of her head and into the present.

Frankie threw the drapes open so they could see the snow. "I'm thinking how absolutely perfect this is." She turned to look at Cassidy.

"I need you to know that there is nowhere in the world I'd rather be right now. Not on the mountain. Not with my family. Not alone. Right here with you. That's the perfect spot for me." She was actually a little surprised by the vehemence in her own words, but fuck it. She meant them, and it was about time she said them.

She saw Cassidy swallow, and in the next second, she had crossed the room and was in her arms. Their lips met in a flurry of kisses, as if they'd been waiting for hours just for that. Frankie took Cassidy's face in her hands and pulled back, laughing at the sudden onslaught. And then they were looking into each other's eyes, and Frankie felt her own face grow as serious as Cassidy's as she watched. And then Cassidy whispered words that wormed straight into her heart and made themselves a home there.

"I love you, Francesca."

"I love you, too, Cassidy." It wasn't even a question. There was no hesitation. Frankie didn't care that she'd only known the woman for a handful of days. She knew. *She knew.* Cassidy had come into her life for a reason, and Frankie never wanted her to leave. She pulled her close, held her tightly, never wanted to let go, but finally did. "How did we get here?" she asked, honestly wondering as she held her arms out to her sides. "I mean, do you believe in fate? Or that everything happens for a reason? Or that you learn something from everybody who crosses through your life? Any of that hokey bullshit? Because I never did. But now, I wonder."

Cassidy unscrewed the cap from a bottle of soda and took a swig, then shook her head. "I don't know. I don't care. All I'm sure of is that I'm supposed to be here. Tonight. With you."

Their gazes held, and Frankie felt a warmth from within that she hadn't felt in weeks. No, months. Possibly ever. She didn't know how any of this had happened, but she felt jolted. Knocked out of her rut. Freaking *finally.*

They spent Christmas Eve cuddled on the bed surrounded by bags of potato chips and Cheetos and Doritos and Rice Krispies Treats for when they needed sugar instead of salt. They drank beer and watched *A Christmas Story* more than once, and it was perfect. And then they spent the wee hours naked and writhing and professing their newfound love out loud, over and over. Cassidy's breathing became deep and even somewhere around two in the morning, and Frankie held her and watched the snow falling outside before following her into sleep, her last thought being nothing but how content she felt.

They slept in until around eight when the sun streamed through their window, and Frankie opened her eyes to find Cassidy propped up on an elbow looking down at her.

"If you weren't so beautiful, I might find this a little creepy," she said with a grin.

"You don't sleep that often, so I like to witness it when you do." Cassidy ran a fingertip down her arm.

"I sleep when I'm with you."

"How come?"

She knew the answer to this now. "Because I feel safe with you."

"You are safe with me. I promise." They shared a soft kiss, and when Cassidy pulled back, it was clear she had something on her mind.

"What?"

"I was thinking about something."

"Uh-oh." That earned her a playful slap.

"It's a little off-the-wall…"

Frankie pushed herself up so she was sitting with her back against the headboard, the covers up over her breasts. "I can handle off-the-wall. Tell me."

Cassidy shuffled her position so she was sitting, too, but cross-legged and facing Frankie. "Didn't you say that Ethan Lustenfeld was looking to sell the camp?"

Frankie nodded. "Yeah, that's what he told me. That's the whole reason he hired me, to keep the place from falling apart until he could unload it."

Cassidy nodded slowly, and Frankie could practically hear the wheels in her head cranking. Finally, very slowly, she said, "I said it before, but don't you think it would make a really great bed-and-breakfast?"

Frankie blinked at her.

"Like, not the cabins. Obvi. But there are, what, three rooms upstairs and three downstairs? With some remodeling, adding of bathrooms, revamping the downstairs and getting some more modern furniture, updating the kitchen. Can't you see it? A mountain getaway? People could hike. See the fall foliage. Cross-country ski. Snowshoe. Canoe in the summer. You could do all the cooking. It would be like having your own restaurant, but with way less pressure. I could run the business side of things…" Cassidy's voice drifted off, but her eyes were sparkling. Full of ideas.

"What about your current business?"

A shrug. "I could be bicoastal. We'd have off-seasons. I could fly back and forth when I needed to." She looked into Frankie's eyes. "I mean, I haven't ironed it all out, but it's been niggling at me for a while now." She studied her. "You're not sold."

And Frankie barked a laugh. Because not sold was the farthest thing from the truth. "I have actually had the exact same idea. Exact same. More than once."

"No."

"Oh yes."

They sat there for what felt like a very long time, just staring at each other. Frankie's brain was a whirlwind of possibility, and she could tell by Cassidy's wide eyes that hers was the same.

"We could do this," Cassidy said.

A nod. "We could. I know we could." And nothing had ever been truer. Frankie didn't understand it, the certainty. The lack of worry or concern. Again, she just knew. She reached across the space between them and grasped Cassidy's chin in her hands, made her look in her eyes before she spoke. When she had her full attention, she said, very firmly, "I love you, Cassidy. I hope you know that. I hope you get that."

Cassidy's face softened, and her smile blossomed, and she did. She did get it. Frankie could see it on her face. She understood that those three words were not words Frankie spoke lightly. Or often. In fact, aside from her family, she'd only said them to one other person in her life, and that hadn't worked out. So this was a big deal. But somehow, Cassidy knew that, knew her.

"I do know it. I do get it. And I love you back."

EPILOGUE

Twenty-one months later

"Here they come!" Cassidy's voice was a squeal, high-pitched like a little girl's, and she bounced up and down, clapping her hands together in excitement. Duke couldn't help but be infected by her jubilation, and he bounced around to celebrate with her, little huffs that weren't quite barks puffing from his doggie lips as if he was working hard to stay quiet.

Frankie rolled her eyes as she entered the living room from the kitchen but smiled at her girlfriend's giddiness. Cassidy's level of excitement was super cute, but she herself was much more of an internal excitement kind of girl. She was thrilled this was happening— their very first guests were pulling up the driveway, if the crunching of new gravel was any indication—but she was also super nervous. The butterflies she'd woken up with in her stomach had become flying saucers as the morning progressed, banging around in her stomach like they were trying to escape. More than once, she'd half expected a reappearance of the toast she'd had for breakfast, but so far, nothing, thank goodness.

Cassidy opened the front door to await their guests. She was dressed in dark jeans, a yellow T-shirt, and a dark green windbreaker with their new Camp Lost and Found logo embroidered on it in yellow. Their slogan was *Lose yourself...and find yourself again*, and they'd been working their butts off for more than a year and a half in preparation for this day. She stood on the new wraparound front porch, Duke seated at her side, a bright yellow bandanna around his furry neck.

She glanced around and felt herself puff up with pride. The whole place had been remodeled, but the basic bones stayed the same, including the fireplace, which she'd stoke up later, as the evenings in September could come with a chill. The huge dining room table had been refinished, new chairs purchased, and all guests were welcome to have dinner together if they didn't want to go into town. A plate of fresh blueberry muffins she'd made that morning was placed neatly in the center, flanked by two vases of wildflowers Cassidy had picked yesterday.

At the base of the stairs, they'd added a front desk, a place to check in, get information on Shelton and nearby towns, sign up to borrow snowshoes or skis in the winter or a canoe in the summer, for guests who didn't bring their own. Their logo was the silhouettes of three deer in yellow on a green background, and a wood carving of it that Luthor had made for them was mounted to the face of the front desk. She had her meals planned out for the next four days, the fridge was stocked, and each room had an ice bucket and a bottle of champagne to welcome its occupants. It was their opening weekend, and they were booked.

Booked solid.

Holy crap, they were actually doing this.

Her hands started to shake with nerves, and she quickly turned on her heel and hightailed it back to the kitchen for a moment. Couldn't have guests seeing her being a nervous wreck. She heard car doors slam and muffled voices, and she braced herself with both hands against the sink.

Just breathe, she thought. *You got this.*

And she did. She wasn't worried—she was just nervous. She gave herself a moment and did the breathing exercises her therapist had taught her—yep, that was something Cassidy had talked her into, and she was right. Therapy had done wonders on her guilt-ridden brain and her broken heart. She blew out a breath and stood up straight. Better. With one nod to no one, she headed back out to the front.

And stopped dead in her tracks.

"Frankie, I'd like you to meet our very first guests here at Camp Lost and Found," Cassidy said, her smile so wide it was almost laughable. "Mr. and Mrs. Sisto from Newburgh."

And then she was enveloped in her mother's arms, and then her father's were around both of them, and they were all crying amid the cacophony of *oh my God*s and *how did you pull this off*s and *this place looks incredible*s.

When they finally separated into three human beings again, her eyes found Cassidy's, which were also wet. Frankie's heart swelled, and her face must've asked the question because Cassidy just shrugged and said, "It was only right that they should be the first ones to see all your hard work."

And before anything more was said, Reiko came through the front door, hauling two suitcases. She wore a yellow T-shirt like Cassidy's and looked to her as she said, "The Evergreen Room, right?" At Cassidy's nod, Reiko said to Frankie's parents, "Allow me to show you to your room."

Frankie's mom made an I'm-impressed face, stroked Frankie's cheek with her palm, and then her parents followed Reiko up the stairs. She was fourteen now, and strong and funny and one of Frankie's favorite people in the world. She worked for them on weekends and occasional evenings when they needed an extra set of hands. She was thankful for the break from Eden. Eden was thankful for the break from Reiko. Teenagers, man. Frankie shook her head with a smile, then wrapped her arms around Cassidy from behind.

"How the hell did you pull of booking my parents without telling me?" she asked in Cassidy's ear.

Cassidy turned and her arms came up around her neck. "You, my love, are often in your own little kitchen world back there. I could be having belly-dancing lessons out here and you'd never notice." She kissed her softly.

"*That* I would notice. You're amazing," Frankie said, looking into her eyes. "You know that?"

"I know *we* are amazing. Yes." The sound of more crunching gravel could be heard, and Cassidy gave her one last peck. Then her eyes got wide again. "More guests!" She turned to the door. "Come on, Duke. Time to be a greeter."

Reiko came bounding down the stairs, her eyes bright. "Your dad tipped me ten bucks," she stage-whispered, and Frankie smiled and shook her head. Reiko followed Cassidy and Duke outside just as Cassidy could be heard saying, "Welcome to Camp Lost and Found. We're so glad you made it."

She turned and headed into her kitchen. That's right. It was *her* kitchen now, and when it had come to the remodel, she'd had free rein. "I don't know a thing about restaurant kitchens," Cassidy had said. "This is all you, babe. Do what you want." There had been a generous budget, and she'd been careful not to get things she didn't expressly need. After all, the most people she'd ever be cooking for at once was twelve. But she'd upgraded the appliances and splurged a little on a nice set of heavy deep green stoneware dishes, something rustic to go with the ambiance. She had her own knives and a lot of utensils, and she'd had things moved around and arranged in a way that worked best for her methods. And now? It was her kitchen in her business and by tomorrow morning, she'd have twelve strangers—well, ten strangers and her parents—to dazzle with her cooking.

She was a chef in her own kitchen.

She was in love so deeply, it made her heart ache with joy.

And she was okay. Better than okay. She still had the nightmares on occasion, but not nearly as often. She slept better. Not great, but better, and when Cassidy was in bed next to her, she felt safe and loved and even toyed with forgiving herself.

Something she was working on in therapy.

Cassidy flew to San Diego every few weeks to pop in on her company, meet face-to-face with clients, and generally spend time with her employees, so they knew she hadn't abandoned them. But she always came back to Frankie. Always.

It seemed fitting that they'd ended up in exactly the place they'd started.

The swinging door she'd added to the kitchen pushed in, and her mother entered, a big smile on her face, and a bouquet of daisies in her hands.

She looked around, her eyes wide as she took in the space. "This is beautiful," she breathed. "And I want you to show it all to me, every detail. But first"—she held up the flowers—"I want you to take me to the garden. I want to do that, first thing."

Frankie nodded once and grabbed her jacket as they headed out the back door.

The day was gorgeous. Crisp and sunny. Fall came faster in the mountains than it did back home, but she was used to it by now.

"What's going to happen with the cabins?" her mother asked as they walked past them and into the woods.

"We haven't decided yet. We're toying with keeping a couple of them. Fixing them up for people who might want more of an actual camping experience than a pampered in a B and B one. Still working on that."

Her mother nodded and then became quiet as they walked. It didn't take long before they reached a clearing.

Frankie'd asked Ethan Lustenfeld if they could tear down Jack's dilapidated shack and make the space into a garden where people could come and sit. Think. Dream. He'd agreed with no argument and had even paid for it to be done. Now, there were flowering bushes and a stone path that wove around in circles, a couple benches for sitting and ruminating or just watching nature. A few birdhouses had been mounted. There was a small wooden sign posted in the center that said: *Welcome to the Gratitude Garden. Thank you, Jack.*

Frankie watched as her mother went to the very center of the garden, right to the sign, and squatted down. She laid the flowers at the base of the sign and said quietly, "Thank you, Mr. Healey, for giving me my daughter back. I hope you're at peace now."

Frankie's eyes filled with tears. She'd told her mother all about finding Jack and how it had spurred her to stop living her life in isolation. She owed him so much, and her mother knew that. She stayed where she was, let her mother do her thing, and when she returned to Frankie, they both laughed at the tears they'd each shed.

"I wish I could've thanked him in person," her mother said, tucking a strand of honey-blond hair behind her ear. Then she looked around, picked a bench, and sat. "This is beautiful. You designed it?"

Frankie nodded and joined her on the bench. "I've learned a lot about gratitude in therapy, and I thought it would be nice to have a place where people can come and sit and think about it, about being grateful for what they have instead of sad about what they don't." She could feel her mom's eyes on her, and she turned to meet the gaze.

"Do you know how proud I am of you?" her mother asked quietly. And Frankie nodded. Because she did.

❖

Cassidy was exhausted but couldn't remember a time when she'd been happier. True, the bed reflected in the mirror where she was checking her hair looked awfully inviting right about now, but if she crawled into it, she be asleep in seconds, and her work wasn't quite done yet. She and Frankie had been going nonstop for days in preparation for this very first opening weekend, and now it was here and almost everybody had checked in—two couples were scheduled to show up in the morning—and the eight guests who were there were all joining them for dinner.

How was it possible that she could fall in love in less than three weeks and it had lasted nearly two years now? It didn't seem feasible, especially to somebody logical and practical like herself. Yet, here she was, during opening weekend of the bed-and-breakfast business she was now running with the woman she loved. And she did—she loved Frankie more than she ever thought possible. It was a little mind-blowing. And a lot awesome.

The smell of roast chicken had been wafting through the house for the past forty-five minutes, and Cassidy knew Frankie was in her glory in the kitchen right then. She quickly got herself together, reglossed her lips, and headed out to the dining room to help set up for dinner.

Less than an hour later, eight guests—including Frankie's parents—were seated around the large rectangular table. Chicken and potatoes and green beans and salad all had been placed on the table, ready for a family-style meal. Frankie had wanted the first meal to be more homey than fancy, just to welcome everybody. Tomorrow's menu was much more ambitious and would give her a chance to really show off her culinary skills. But now? The whole house smelled like a home, and it put a lump solidly in Cassidy's throat.

Frankie was seated at one end of the table, and Cassidy poured champagne for everyone, then took her spot at the other end, raising her glass.

"I'd like to propose a toast," she said, then waited for quiet to descend. "Normally, the hosts wouldn't be sitting here with the guests. This is your weekend, your getaway, and we wouldn't intrude. But being that this is our first ever dinner for guests here at Camp Lost and Found, we hope you don't mind our participation." She smiled at the group: Frankie's parents, Janet and Keith from Massachusetts, David and Brandon from New York City, Zoe and Morgan from Northwood, New York. A nicely rounded group of nice people, all their eyes on her. "This place is a dream that neither Frankie nor I knew we had within us. I didn't grow up wanting to run a B and B. I have my own business. Frankie is a trained chef. When we met here almost two years ago, neither of us had any designs on this camp. We were here for very different reasons." She met Frankie's eyes across the table, and everything within her settled and calmed. That's what Frankie did for her, and it was something she'd never gotten from anybody else in her life. "I came here to deal with grief. Frankie was here to handle guilt. And somehow, the Universe saw fit to push us together, no matter how much we resisted."

"You didn't resist that much," Frankie chimed in, earning a chuckle from the guests.

"How could I?" Cassidy countered. "Look at you." She waited a beat while Frankie grinned and blushed and everybody saw it. Then she went on. "But there was something about this place. About the house, about the woods, about the pond, about the very atmosphere that hangs in the air here. I had never felt so at home, and I think I can speak for Frankie and say she felt the same. And it wasn't until I left and went back home to San Diego that I realized—home for me is actually here. With Frankie. With all of you. This camp was one of the few places I felt safe as a kid, and that hasn't changed, except now? It is home." She raised her glass. "So please join me in toasting Camp Lost and Found. Our motto is *Lose yourself...and find yourself again* because that's exactly what happened to both of us. We hope you love this place as much as we do and come back to visit us often. To the very first weekend of Camp Lost and Found!"

Glasses clinked, and *hear, hear*s went around the table, and then it was time to eat. The guests dug in and began chatting with each other across the table, talking about jobs and hometowns and pets and kids. It was exactly perfect, and again, Cassidy thought about how very happy she was, happier than she ever expected to be. When she glanced toward the other end of the table, Frankie was looking at her, that beautiful smile on her face. She mouthed "I love you," to her and Frankie mouthed it back.

She had come to Camp Lost and Found with the intention of

finding herself again, but she found so much more than she ever expected.

She found herself.

She found home.

She found love.

What could be more perfect than that?

About the Author

Georgia Beers lives in Upstate New York and has written more than thirty novels of sapphic romance. In her off-hours, she can usually be found searching for a scary movie, sipping a good Pinot, or trying to keep up with little big man Archie, her mix of many tiny dogs. Find out more at georgiabeers.com.

Books Available From Bold Strokes Books

A Haven for the Wanderer by Jenny Frame. When Griffin Harris comes to Rosebrook village, the love she finds with Bronte de Lacey creates a safe haven and she finally finds her place in the world. But will she run again when their love is tested? (978-1-63679-291-0)

A Spark in the Air by Dena Blake. Internet executive Crystal Tucker is sure Wi-Fi could really help small-town residents, even if it means putting an internet café out of business, but her instant attraction to the owner's daughter, Janie Elliott, makes moving ahead with her plans complicated. (978-1-63679-293-4)

Between Takes by CJ Birch. Simone Lavoie is convinced her new job as an intimacy coordinator will give her a fresh perspective. Instead, problems on set and her growing attraction to actress Evelyn Harper only add to her worries. (978-1-63679-309-2)

Camp Lost and Found by Georgia Beers. Nobody knows better than Cassidy and Frankie that life doesn't always give you what you want. But sometimes, if you're lucky, life gives you exactly what you need. (978-1-63679-263-7)

Fire, Water, and Rock by Alaina Erdell. As Jess and Clare reveal more about themselves, and their hot summer fling tips over into true love, they must confront their pasts before they can contemplate a future together. (978-1-63679-274-3)

Lines of Love by Brey Willows. When even the Muse of Love doesn't believe in forever, we're all in trouble. (978-1-63555-458-8)

Only This Summer by Radclyffe. A fling with Lily promises to be exactly what Chase is looking for—short-term, hot as a forest fire, and one Chase can extinguish whenever she wants. After all, it's only one summer. (978-1-63679-390-0)

Picture-Perfect Christmas by Charlotte Greene. Two former rivals compete to capture the essence of their small mountain town at Christmas, all the while fighting old and new feelings. (978-1-63679-311-5)

Playing Love's Refrain by Lesley Davis. Drew Dawes had shied away from the world of music until Wren Banderas gave her a reason to play their love's refrain. (978-1-63679-286-6)

Profile by Jackie D. The scales of justice are weighted against FBI agents Cassidy Wolf and Alex Derby. Loyalty and love may be the only advantage they have. (978-1-63679-282-8)

Almost Perfect by Tagan Shepard. A shared love of queer TV brings Olivia and Riley together, but can they keep their real-life love as picture perfect as their on-screen counterparts? (978-1-63679-322-1)

The Amaranthine Law by Gun Brooke. Tristan Kelly is being hunted for who she is and her incomprehensible past, and despite her overwhelming feelings for Olivia Bryce, she has to reject her to keep her safe. (978-1-63679-235-4)

Craving Cassie by Skye Rowan. Siobhan Carney and Cassie Townsend share an instant attraction, but are they brave enough to give up everything they have ever known to be together? (978-1-63679-062-6)

Drifting by Lyn Hemphill. When Tess jumps into the ocean after Jet, she thinks she's saving her life. Of course, she can't possibly know Jet is actually a mermaid desperate to fix her mistake before she causes her clan's demise. (978-1-63679-242-2)

Enigma by Suzie Clarke. Polly has taken an oath to protect and serve her country, but when the spy she's tasked with hunting becomes the love of her life, will she be the one to betray her country? (978-1-63555-999-6)

Finding Fault by Annie McDonald. Can environmental activist Dr. Evie O'Halloran and government investigator Merritt Shepherd set aside their conflicting ideas about saving the planet and risk their hearts enough to save their love? (978-1-63679-257-6)

The Forever Factor by Melissa Brayden. When Bethany and Reid confront their past, they give new meaning to letting go, forgiveness, and a future worth fighting for. (978-1-63679-357-3)

The Frenemy Zone by Yolanda Wallace. Ollie Smith-Nakamura thinks relocating from San Francisco to her dad's rural hometown is the worst idea in the world, but after she meets her new classmate Ariel Hall, she might have a change of heart. (978-1-63679-249-1)

Hot Keys by R.E. Ward. In 1920s New York City, Betty May Dewitt and her best friend, Jack Norval, are determined to make their Tin Pan Alley dreams come true and discover they will have to fight—not only for their hearts and dreams, but for their lives. (978-1-63679-259-0)

Securing Ava by Anne Shade. Private investigator Paige Richards takes a case to locate and bring back runaway heiress Ava Prescott. But ignoring her attraction may prove impossible when their hearts and lives are at stake. (978-1-63679-297-2)

A Cutting Deceit by Cathy Dunnell. Undercover cop Athena takes a job at Valeria's hair salon to gather evidence to prove her husband's connections to organized crime. What starts as a tentative friendship quickly turns into a dangerous affair. (978-1-63679-208-8)

As Seen on TV! by CF Frizzell. Despite their objections, TV hosts Ronnie Sharp, a laid-back chef, and paranormal investigator Peyton Stanford have to work together. The public is watching. But joining forces is risky, contemptuous, unnerving, provocative—and ridiculously perfect. (978-1-63679-272-9)

Blood Memory by Sandra Barret. Can vampire Jade Murphy protect her friend from a human stalker and keep her dates with the gorgeous Beth Jenssen without revealing her secrets? (978-1-63679-307-8)

Foolproof by Leigh Hays. For Martine Roberts and Elliot Tillman, friends with benefits isn't a foolproof way to hide from the truth at the heart of an affair. (978-1-63679-184-5)

Glass and Stone by Renee Roman. Jordan must accept that she can't control everything that happens in life, and that includes her wayward heart. (978-1-63679-162-3)

Hard Pressed by Aurora Rey. When rivals Mira Lavigne and Dylan Miller are tapped to co-chair Finger Lakes Cider Week, competition gives way to compromise. But will their sexual chemistry lead to love? (978-1-63679-210-1)